characters and judicious use of Scottish dialect add to the story's appeal." —*Publishers Weekly* on *Deadly Editions*

"Filled with literary references that will tickle bibliophiles."
—*Kirkus Reviews* on *Deadly Editions*

"Vivid descriptions of Edinburgh enhance the well-crafted plot. Cozy fans will look forward to the further adventures of smart and intuitive Delaney."
—*Publishers Weekly* on *The Stolen Letter*

"The history Delaney uncovers . . . is fascinating and nicely woven into the tale." —*Booklist* on *The Stolen Letter*

"Shelton stocks her tale with appealing characters and intriguing Nessie lore. Cozy fans will be rewarded."
—*Publishers Weekly* on *The Loch Ness Papers*

"A complex plot . . . and an enchanting Scottish setting combine to create a clever entry in a capital series."
—*Richmond Times-Dispatch* on
Lost Books and Old Bones

"A complicated mystery with plenty of historically based characters and whose ending provides more than one kind of surprise." —*Kirkus Reviews* on *Lost Books and Old Bones*

"This spotlessly clean, fun-filled read takes plenty of twists and turns on the way to the satisfying ending."
—*Publishers Weekly* on *The Cracked Spine*

"Shelton's breezy cozy series may interest readers who enjoy Sheila Connolly's 'County Cork' mysteries."

—*Library Journal*

"Move over, Claire Fraser; American bibliophile Delaney Nichols is about to take Scotland . . . by storm!"

—Ellery Adams

"Full of wit and whims . . . delightful characters . . . fantastic!"

—Jenn McKinlay

"A sleuth who'll delight book lovers."   —*Kirkus Reviews*

"Endearing characters, and prose that immediately transports readers to enchanting Edinburgh . . . and leaves them eager for a return trip."   —Lucy Arlington

"For book lovers, mystery seekers, and anyone who enjoys a determined new heroine. Sure to be a winning series."

—Erika Chase

"[For] readers who appreciate bookseller sleuths such as Marianne Macdonald's Dido Hoare or Joan Hess's Claire Malloy . . . The feisty Delaney is an appealing protagonist and the secondary characters are charming as well."

—*Library Journal*

"Shelton's lovely depictions of Edinburgh, its denizens, and its bookshops will enchant lovers of cozies with a Scottish setting."   —*Publishers Weekly*

BY PAIGE SHELTON

FATEFUL WORDS

A SCOTTISH BOOKSHOP MYSTERY

Paige Shelton

St. Martin's Paperbacks

For my grandmother Ruth, who, long ago now,

always found me the best thrift-store treasures.

Miss you. Love you.

Published in the United States by St. Martin's Paperbacks, an imprint of St. Martin's Publishing Group.

FATEFUL WORDS

For information, address St. Martin's Publishing Group, 120 Broadway, New York, NY 10271.

www.stmartins.com

Library of Congress Catalog Card Number: 2022049102

ISBN: 978-1-250-78955-6

Our books may be purchased in bulk for promotional, educational, or business use. Please contact your local bookseller or the Macmillan Corporate and Premium Sales Department at 1-800-221-7945, ext. 5442, or by email at MacmillanSpecialMarkets @macmillan.com.

Printed in the United States of America

Minotaur hardcover edition published 2023
St. Martin's Paperbacks edition / February 2024

10   9   8   7   6   5   4   3   2   1

CHAPTER ONE

I hoisted the velvet-lined box onto the table.

"Delaney?" the man behind the table asked, his blue eyes peering at me over round wire-rimmed glasses perched at the end of his nose.

"I am." I smiled and extended a hand. "You must be Michael."

"Guilty." He smiled too as we shook over the table.

The gray hair that circled his head tufted out around his ears. I didn't think he was a full five feet tall, and even with just a couple of words, I could tell his Scottish accent was strong. But I'd been in Scotland long enough not to have to strain too hard to understand—if he spoke slowly enough.

"Thank you for taking the time to talk to me today. This place is busy."

"Aye, it usually is on Saturdays, but I've a few moments."

"If a customer stops by, I'll step back."

Michael nodded. "Much appreciated."

I'd come to meet Michael at a place I would have called an antiques mall back in Kansas. My grandmother had loved shopping at them. She'd also loved her weekly Goodwill trips, adventures I'd joined her on willingly because I'd always come out a winner, finding a new toy or doll that had barely been used but was sure to thrive under my love.

The Scotland Antiques Center was a large old warehouse fitted with tables and stalls that displayed so many different wares that my head swam as I'd made my way toward Michael's stall. My boss and the owner of the bookshop where I worked, Edwin, told me he wouldn't allow himself to visit the center because he wasn't immune from thinking there was yet another sort of collection he might need to begin, and his good sense told him that he'd begun enough already.

I agreed with him. I was still busy going through the vast amount of collections he'd accumulated over the years. It would be nice to catch up before adding something else.

In fact, it was one of these collections that had brought me to the center—well, technically, Michael had been the draw. When I'd researched local experts on the type of items I was working to organize and catalogue, his name had come up time and time again.

"Michael Norway, Local Spectacle and Monocle Expert," his website and Facebook page had said. Judging by the pieces over his display tables, I knew I'd found the right person.

"What can I do for you, lass?" he asked.

I put my hand on the top of the box. "I work at The Cracked Spine in Grassmarket. It's a bookshop, but the owner of the shop, Edwin MacAlister—"

Michael laughed. "Och, lass, I've heard of him. All of us in the trade have. We all knew about his very own warehouse long before it was made public knowledge."

I smiled. "You're probably good at keeping secrets then."

"Aye."

The collection I'd brought with me today, along with all the others I'd been tasked to organize, had been housed in Edwin's warehouse—mine too, according to him—a modernized and temperature-controlled room at the back of the bookshop's building, a place where Edwin had once spent most of his time. Now it was my space, and where I spent most of mine.

It had been a secret for a long time, but sometimes secrets were too dangerous to keep, so though it wasn't publicized, no one denied its existence any longer.

"If you know about the warehouse," I continued, "you know about Edwin's collections."

"I've heard many stories, aye." He looked at the box and then back up at me. "I'm guessing this is one I might be able to help you with."

"I hope so." I opened the box.

Inside it were so many pairs of old glasses and monocles that it had taken me two days to catalogue them all. I'd struggled to understand the value—though I was pretty sure none of them were worth much anyway—so I'd sought out Michael.

"Ah." He smiled. "Aye, this is my bailiwick. Are you looking for someone to purchase them?"

"No—not yet, at least. I'd like to hire you to appraise them, though. Edwin's . . . not much for making money off his collections, but it is my job to create a full catalogue with as much accurate information as possible."

Michael's eyebrows rose. "Gracious, that's a big job, I'm sure."

I laughed. "Job security."

"I suppose so." He put his hands on his hips. "Would you like me to look through them now?"

"Oh. I didn't think that would be a reasonable request." I grabbed a folder from my shoulder bag and opened it. "I've numbered each item, created a spreadsheet. I could leave all of this with you and come back . . . well, whenever you let me know you're done."

Michael took the folder and looked over the contents. "Aye. You are an organized one. Do you hire out?"

I smiled. "Well, I'm too busy right now, but if this job ever ends, I'll let you know."

"Aye." Michael bit his bottom lip as he did a slow once-over through the box. "I would be happy to do this for you and for Mr. MacAlister. It might take me a week. I'll give you a ring."

"Wonderful. Thank you!"

"And I won't charge you a thing."

"Oh, no, that's not fair. Please, it's only right that you're paid for your services. It's not my money, it's Edwin's. He approves of these types of transactions."

Michael's eyebrows came together as he frowned at me. "Well, we'll talk about it when you pick them up. For now, though, I have something for you."

"Oh, that's not—"

"No, this is how I do things." He turned and reached toward a tree display of monocles hanging from chains. He brought it over to the table in between us and studied it a long moment.

I wanted to finish my sentence and tell him it wasn't necessary to give me anything, but I got the distinct impression that would have been terribly rude, so I waited and watched.

He pondered the tree for a long moment, tapping his fingers on his lips and glancing up at me a few times as I smiled awkwardly.

Finally, he reached into the chains and worked to pull a specific one up and over all the others. "Aye, this is the one." He held it toward me and demonstrated how the tarnished cover could be swung to display the glass monocle. It was old, but, like all the ones I'd researched, probably not valuable. "This is the one that calls out to me. You must have it."

"Goodness, that's lovely," I said.

"Here, lean forward."

I did as he asked, and he hung it around my neck. "That is perfect."

The chain was long enough that I could easily grab and look at the pendant. I held it and swung the cover, then held the monocle up to my eye. Closing the other eye, I peered through. I was a few years away from needing reading glasses, but when I did, this would be a very cool way to have at least part of a pair with me.

As I pulled the glass away again, I noticed something on the back of the tarnished cover.

"I think there's an engraving here," I said.

"Maybe. I think I've noticed that before. Can you read what it says?" Michael adjusted the glasses he wore, and we both looked.

Because of the tarnish, it wasn't easy to decipher it at first, but the words came clear only a moment later.

I gasped and looked at Michael after he read the engraving aloud. "Did you know I was coming today?"

"Well, you said you'd be stopping by soon when you rang me. Why?"

"I mean, is this on purpose?"

"I don't know what you're saying, lass." He seemed genuinely confused.

"My husband's name is Tom. This says, 'With love, Tom.'"

"Aye?" Michael smiled.

"Yes."

"Braw! It's pure chance, lass, but I've always been good at matching things with the right people. It's a gift."

"I'd say." I studied his face, looking for something that gave him away, uncovered his trick, but I couldn't find anything.

He did say he was good at keeping secrets, though.

"I would like to pay you for this." I reached into my bag for my wallet.

"Oh, no, lass, that would take away the magic."

"Magic?"

"Aye. You dinnae believe in magic?"

"Well . . ." I put the wallet back in my bag.

I'd come here to hire him, and he'd given me a gift I couldn't have imagined ever receiving. I didn't quite know how to respond. Finally, something came to me.

"Thank you, Michael. I will cherish it."

"Aye? Well, you've made an old man's day, then."

"It's mutual. Thank you again."

"You're welcome." He grabbed the box I'd brought in and put it on a table at the back of the stall. He turned to me. "I'll ring you as soon as I have this done."

It was a polite dismissal, but I was still too stunned to move. Nevertheless, Michael gave me one more smile, then turned his attention to an approaching customer.

I mouthed "Thank you again" at him before I turned to

leave, making my way down aisles much more crowded with customers than they'd been when I'd come inside just moments ago.

I passed stalls with any number of things that might have interested me if I hadn't had to get to work. Paintings, old appliances, jewelry, furniture, even things from the world I currently worked in—books and manuscripts. I smiled extra at those stall workers just in case they recognized me from the bookshop.

That had become a new thing—being recognized because of where I worked. It was my red hair, my American accent, and the fact that I worked for Edwin, who was a local celebrity of sorts. He'd done great things with his money, and that in itself had garnered him plenty of attention. He'd also been involved in some shady dealings, some of which had been uncovered in the local press. Most recently, Brigid McBride, a local reporter and onetime girlfriend to my husband, had done a weeklong feature headlined "Edwin MacAlister, the Man and His Mysteries," and we'd all gotten even more attention.

It had been a complimentary piece, but Brigid hadn't shied away from uncovering some of the mysteries, including a guessed dollar amount regarding Edwin's true wealth.

The number had been stunning. I'd known he had lots of money, but it was lots more than lots if Brigid had been correct. I hadn't asked anyone—Edwin or my other coworkers, Rosie and Hamlet—if they could or would confirm. I hadn't wanted to know. It was none of my business, and though I'd never struggled too much to pay my bills, even my overactive imagination didn't know what to do with that much money, making it downright overwhelming to even think about.

Though the article wasn't the only reason people recognized me, the picture with all of us at the bookshop had certainly caused more people to send double takes my direction.

Today, though, the stall workers were busy giving their customers all their attention, and I left the building without anyone sending me a familiar wave and smile.

I turned my face up to the sun as I stepped outside. Though it wasn't warm, the early June day was filled with blue skies and a bright sun. It would cloud up and rain soon enough.

I stepped to the side of the front doors, out of the way of the foot traffic, and looked at the pendant again. In the light, I could see the engraving even more clearly. It said exactly what Michael and I had thought it said. I knew I would cherish it forever simply because it bore Tom's name, but I had to figure out a way to pay for it.

A ruckus across the street pulled my attention that direction. Police officers were escorting a couple kids out of another warehouse, though the front of this one was overgrown with shrubbery, the building painted with graffiti. It had been an old natural gas manufacturing facility, according to the dilapidated sign out front. I'd seen it as I'd made my way into the antiques center and thought it seemed fascinating. I'd thought about exploring it, but it seemed clear that the police wouldn't approve.

I turned away from the brouhaha and hurried toward a bus stop, passing another interesting building as I went. It was yet another warehouse, but this one's front garden was groomed, and the sign that announced the business inside was almost brand-new—it appeared that it was a restaurant of sorts, something that included whisky tasting and sampling.

My brother, Wyatt, had been in town in January. If I'd known about this place back then, I'd have made sure he had a chance to visit it. As I boarded the bus, I filed it away for future adventures.

I'd planned to spend the rest of the day in Edwin's—well, my—warehouse, the one in the back of the bookshop, maybe working on a new collection, though I hadn't determined which one yet. As the bus pulled to a stop near the bookshop, I disembarked with a pep in my step and a smile up toward Tom's pub. I couldn't wait to show him the monocle, but that would have to wait. It was time to get to work.

But, as I'd come to experience a few times now, life in Scotland often surprised with a change of even the most solid of plans.

CHAPTER TWO

"Oh, thank goodness ye're here, lass," Rosie said as she looked up from her desk.

Hector, the cutest miniature Yorkie in all the world, came my direction, a notable concern in his trot and expression. I reached down and picked him up on my way to the desk.

It was covered in folders, some open, exposing the papers inside.

"Rosie, are you okay? What's going on?" I scratched behind Hector's ears.

Rosie's hair was never pulled back into her signature bun perfectly, but there was a wildness to the flyaways, as well as to her eyes, that I hadn't seen before.

She took a deep breath and let it out, her shoulders slumping. A long moment later she looked up at me again. She seemed to have found some composure.

"Lass, Edwin has been called away."

"Okay."

"The tour begins today."

"Oh!"

I'd all but forgotten. I never concerned myself with Edwin's yearly Edinburgh literature tours. They were his thing, the one thing he hadn't delegated to someone else since he'd stepped back from his duties at the bookshop.

"Oh, no," I said, ominously this time. "Called away? Where?"

Rosie shook her head. "Not important at this time, but he can't lead the tour now."

"Are you . . ." I put Hector down.

That didn't make sense. It was a walking tour, and though Rosie was still mobile enough, she couldn't walk long distances comfortably. She and Edwin were in their seventies, but Edwin's mobility hadn't diminished much at all.

That left Hamlet and me.

"Where's Hamlet?" I said, hope filling the question.

Rosie shook her head again. "With Edwin."

"I don't understand—where did they go?"

"I'll explain later, but for now, it appears you'll be leading the tour, lass."

"No. No, no. I don't have . . . I don't know . . . I'm not even Scottish!" It was a strange thing to say; I'd probably gone there out of pure desperation.

Rosie fanned her hands above all the files. "These will fill in all the blanks."

"The blanks? There's nothing *but* blanks!"

I was a team player, always willing to do whatever was asked of me, but this expectation wasn't something I could comprehend.

These tours were the stuff of legend, literally. They were always small groups, and Edwin believed in giving each member as much personal attention as he could. There was no way a bunch of files could prepare me to give a tour that would do it proper justice. I knew I should have joined previous years' tours, but I'd always been busy. If I did do this, it was sure to be a disaster.

I looked down at Hector sitting at my feet. He seemed to send me some encouragement. All I wanted was for someone else to do this—even the dog would be better. Wouldn't he?

I looked at Rosie, the panic I'd seen coming from her now making its way through my system.

"Oh, Rosie," I said.

"I'm sorry, lass, but it's the only option."

"Okay," I said, sounding pathetic. I cleared my throat. "Okay, well, I guess I'd better start studying."

"Aye, lass. Aye." Rosie pushed back from her desk and gave me the chair.

I did the only thing left to do—got to work.

"Welcome!" Rosie said to the group of four, all of them with wide, eager eyes. "Welcome to The Cracked Spine."

They each either nodded appreciatively or said "Thank you." I heard English, but one "Danke" was in there too.

I stood next to Rosie as she held Hector, and I smiled at our visitors. I tried my best to look natural.

"Come join us in the back," Rosie said. "We've some coffee to warm yer bones and some sweets to fill yer stomachs."

Rosie and Hector led the way. I let the others go before me, smiling at each of them as they passed by. From the files, I'd memorized their names, but they didn't know me yet.

We were all about to be introduced, and they were probably

about to be mightily disappointed. Who wouldn't be? They'd expected Edwin here to greet them and then host them on a beloved tour they'd had to be invited to in order to join. No one but Edwin had ever led the tours; substitutions hadn't been part of the deal.

Every year, he chose four "winners" he would escort around Edinburgh, certainly with panache and in ways that I was sure only Edwin could pull off. The attendees were chosen based upon letters they sent him. He had a knack for putting well-suited groups together—in fact, there had been two weddings as the result of the tours, though matchmaking had never been part of the plan.

But that was the rub—it wasn't just a tour. I could have googled some information on and handled a simple tour just fine. No, Edwin didn't do things on any sort of normal scale. His guests were treated to a week or so of immersion into parts of the city of Edinburgh and some of its contributions to literature and film. There was too much to be comprehensive, but Edwin loved books and movies, and he loved Edinburgh. He would take his favorites from each of those loves and create a memorable journey for his guests—and they were always his guests. He paid for everything.

He was so good at it—maybe one of the best from the accolades I'd heard—and he'd done it for decades.

Once the four were seated around the back table, Rosie offered them a tray of cookies. She'd run to the bakery next door to grab the treats and then gather coffee and tea from the kitchenette on the other side of the bookshop, the side where the warehouse was located. I called it "the dark side" simply because it was darker over there—until you were inside the warehouse, at least.

After everyone took a moment to sample the refreshments, Rosie and I stood at one end of the table.

"We are so glad to have ye here," Rosie continued her cheery greetings. "I do need to tell ye, though, that there's been a wee change of plans . . ."

She had their attention.

"This is Delaney Nichols, and she will be yer guide for the next few days." Rosie smiled. She held Hector in one arm and gestured toward me with the other.

You could see the wave of disquiet move over and through the four of them. En masse, they seemed to slow their chewing, and those who'd been holding mugs set them back on the table.

"For the whole tour or just part of it?" Meera Murphy asked.

I'd learned that she was from Dublin, that she was in her late thirties, and that she'd just begun studying at the university. She was lovely, with big blue eyes and jet-black hair.

Rosie had finally told me that Edwin and Hamlet had gone to London, but not why. Her tight-lipped frowns had my imagination conjuring the worst—that he was ill, needing to see doctors found only in London, and that Hamlet was there to assist him with whatever else he might require.

Rosie hadn't denied the idea, but she hadn't confirmed it either.

"Aye, lass, the whole thing," Rosie said to Meera.

I sensed Rosie brace herself. We'd talked through all of

it—at least as much as we could over the last three hours. This wasn't going to be good news to the tour group, but we could get through it. We needed to get the objections out in the air first off, attempt to calm the waters, and go from there. As much as they would dislike the reality, attempting to obscure it would be even worse.

"But . . ." Meera continued. She looked at me. "I mean, you seem like a lovely woman, but, well, we signed up for Edwin MacAlister."

"Yes," I said. "It is with deepest apologies that he cannot be here, but I am thrilled to be the one guiding the tour in his place. It's an honor."

I tried very hard not to make the words sound forced, but I was sure they did.

"Where is Edwin?" Kevin Moore asked. She—yes, she—was somewhere in her seventies and had come from the place Edwin had gone, London. Her deep British accent was almost as difficult for me to understand as some of my Scots-speaking friends had been when I'd first moved to Scotland. Her letter to Edwin had been about a time when she was a child and was able to gift a book to the queen. From that moment on, she'd been smitten with all books, everywhere. She had her own bookshop in London, where she'd worked almost every day for fifty years. She'd let her daughter run the shop while she was gone but had been hesitant to leave—and was only doing so for something as magnificent as one of Edwin's tours.

"He's had some business call him away—that's the best I am able to share," Rosie said. "He's deeply sorry and wants you all to know that he would never miss this unless it was completely unavoidable. Also, he said you could all return next year, on him again, when he's sure to be back."

That offer did two things—it seemed to lighten the air, which had become heavy with regret, maybe even close to anger, but it also filled it with some doubt: what would *guarantee* that he'd be here next year? The unknowns were frustrating for everyone.

"I have corresponded with Edwin for many years. I was very much hoping to meet him in person. However, I will attempt not to ruffle the waters. Or feathers, whichever," Gunter said.

From Berlin, Gunter had kept up a relationship with Edwin via letter and email for almost thirty years. Gunter dealt in old documents in Germany. He and Edwin had lots in common, though Gunter's English had been rough until about ten years ago. He told Edwin he wanted to attend one of the tours one day, and had worked on his language skills in part for that purpose. Rosie thought he'd probably be the most disappointed of all of them. I was grateful that he tried to hide it.

"Thank you, Gunter," Rosie said.

We all turned toward the one person we had yet to hear from. Luka King was from Australia. His dark eyes matched his dark skin, and his closely shorn hair made him appear almost completely bald. He was in his early forties, and had been the wild card of the group, or at least that's what Edwin had written in his notes about him in the files.

Via social media, Luka had come upon someone talking about Edwin's tours. On a whim, he'd sent Edwin an email, telling him that if Edwin, via one of the tours, could turn

Luka into a reader, Luka would donate a large sum of money to Edwin's favorite charity.

The email from Luka had gone on to say that reading fiction was a waste of time and there were so many better things people could do with themselves. Life, to Luka, was about work. He'd been in construction since he was a teenager, and now he owned a few construction companies. He'd written to Edwin thinking that Edwin wouldn't reply. In fact, he'd later apologized to Edwin for the email, saying he hadn't meant to be snarky, and he wished he hadn't written it in the first place. What business was it of his if people wasted time reading?

Edwin wasn't one to back down from any sort of challenge, though. Rosie had told me that there was just something about Luka's email that touched Edwin's heart. He knew he needed to get Luka on a tour. If anyone could make someone fall in love with literature, it was Edwin.

However, I wasn't a qualified replacement for the task of transforming Luka. I wasn't even close. Sure, I loved books as much as Edwin and my coworkers did; we all cherished the fact that we got to work in a bookshop. But there was something about Edwin that was so distinctly him, no one would ever be able to duplicate that part of his personality that could spread the love of books like it was free candy. People ate it up. I'd seen it plenty of times.

I told myself that I would have to be happy with showing Luka the sights. He would not be transformed like he'd thought he might be, but I knew he'd enjoy Edinburgh.

Everyone enjoyed Edinburgh, and that's the main thing I had going for me—a city that on its own could charm pretty much anyone. I'd make sure Luka had as good of a time as I could show a stranger who didn't like to read.

Luka finally realized that everyone was looking at him, waiting. His eyebrows rose, as if he was genuinely surprised that we were curious to hear what he had to say. I hoped Luka wasn't about to ruin everyone else's seemingly positive outlooks.

"Well," he began, and I could hear his Aussie accent just with that one word. "I would say that I feel a little bit of what the others have mentioned, but there's one more thing I'd like to add."

The pause went from dramatic, to pregnant, to a bit overdone, but he did continue.

"This bookshop might be one of the most beautiful places I've ever seen."

Rosie and I smiled at each other, and I realized I had that going for me too. This bookshop, this place was made with magic, probably the same kind Michael had spoken about just that morning. And it wasn't only because of Edwin. Rosie had also made this the kind of place where people wanted to be, and if you were here long enough, well, shoot, you might as well pick up a book and give it a go.

We might have a shot with Luka after all.

"Besides, I've come too far not to try. Edinburgh! I've never been, and I'm happy to be here." Luka smiled at Rosie.

"So glad to hear it," Rosie said. "Could we show you around the bookshop, then?"

No one had finished their refreshments, but they all stood. It wasn't a big store, but it was full of every sort of thing anyone would enjoy reading.

Rosie and I showed them where we shelved things. Yes, Jane Austen was in the As, but she was also in the part of the shop that held the classics. We carried books from contemporary writers, too, but they were on different shelves. Every time we filled the Ian Rankin or Val McDermid sections, they would empty quickly, with a few customers inquiring about them almost every day.

In fact, I'd spotted Mr. Rankin about town a time or two and had smiled and almost waved at him like I knew him. I guess I kind of did, but he certainly didn't know me, even if my picture had been in the paper recently.

Once everyone understood the layout of the shop, they asked about the door at the top of the stairs, up where an alcove with other filled bookshelves was located.

We explained that it led to the building next door, attached to this one, but that that side had never gotten the attention this one had.

Rosie gathered a stack of books from her desk and met everyone at the back table again. No one seemed to mind revisiting the treats or topping off the teas and coffees to warm themselves up. Today was just the welcome day, a day to catch up on rest from the travel. The jet lag was very real. The tour was set to begin tomorrow. I was grateful I'd have more time to study and prepare.

"Here's a gift for all of ye for this afternoon and tonight. Inside each book is a voucher for a dinner at the takeaway restaurant across the market. Enjoy relaxing and reading. If ye're not weary, it's not too cold outside for a walkabout. Also inside each book is a wee map. It's there to tell ye how to get up to the Royal Mile. We'll be giving ye more maps as the tour continues, but tonight is for eating, reading, and relaxing if ye're so inclined."

"*The Prime of Miss Jean Brodie*," Meera said as she took her copy of the book from Rosie. "I've heard of it but never read it."

"Aye," Rosie said. "Please understand that though Edwin has a fondness for all books, some of the stories you'll hear about on the tour are dated, and many things have changed for the better since they've been written. As it happens, discussions about stories always take place amongst the group, but the reason we're mentioning any book is simply because of our fair city's inclusion in it. In this one, in fact, ye'll see mentioned our verra own Grassmarket." She nodded toward the front window. "That's where ye are, in Grassmarket."

"Is the inn we're staying at part of Grassmarket?" Luka asked. "It's called the Green Inn, and it's just the other side of this square, up the curving road."

"Aye, that's West Bow, or Victoria Street; that's the way ye take up to the Royal Mile, and, aye, the Green Inn is a part of Grassmarket," Rosie said.

"And across there is the most adorable pub," Kevin added.

"And tonight, drinks are on the owner. His name is Tom, and all you have to do is tell him you're with The Cracked Spine group and he'll take care of you," I said.

"Now, that's more like it," Luka said with a playful smile. "Sure, I'll take a free book and all, but a drink will do the trick even better. Thank you, Edwin!"

"That part is Delaney's doing," Rosie said quickly. "Tom is her husband."

"Lovely," Kevin said. "I used to be married to a pub owner a long time ago. Gracious, we had a good time, but he certainly had a wandering eye. I found someone better eventually and freed that pub owner to let his eye wander all he wanted."

I winked at Rosie. I wouldn't share with them that I'd been warned plenty about Tom's previous wandering eye. It seemed to have landed firmly on me and I had no concerns.

Rosie winked back. None of my friends and family thought Tom was anything but fiercely loyal to me and our marriage.

"Will you be joining us this evening, Rosie, Delaney?" Gunter asked.

If Edwin were here, he'd join them, and somehow manage to spend a little of the evening with each of them, making them all feel like the most important person he'd ever met. I would try, but I wasn't sure I could pull it off as well. Still, though, I'd been ready for the question.

"I'd love to grab dinner at the takeaway, and then I'll be in the pub. And, if anyone wants a partner up to the Royal Mile, I'm happy to join in."

"Dinner and drinks sound perfect," Kevin said as she stood. "As for me, I think I'll retire to my room for a bit, maybe catch a nap. Should we plan on dinner at a specific time?" She looked around.

"I say dinner at six, then the pub afterwards," Meera said. She smiled at Kevin. "I'm a little tired from the travel too, and we probably had the shortest trips of anyone. I'll walk up to the hotel with you."

Gunter joined them, but Luka stayed behind. Once everyone else was gone, I sat at the table across from him as Rosie and Hector greeted a customer.

"Everything okay?" I asked him.

"Everything is fine," he said.

But I could tell it wasn't. "Luka, I know this isn't ideal, but it was unavoidable. I'm so sorry. We're all so sorry. Edwin would never miss out on a tour unless there was absolutely no other option."

"I appreciate that."

"Thank you. What else is bothering you?"

"I've seen the movie." Luka held up the book we'd given him.

"I have too. Isn't Maggie Smith wonderful?"

"She is." Luka nodded. "But now I know what happens. If we discuss it, I can cheat because I've seen the movie."

"Oh. Well, cheat all you want, if you promise me one thing."

"Okay."

"Read one chapter. Just one."

Luka sent me a side-eye. "It's that good of a book?"

I laughed. "Actually, I have a few problems with the book—it was written when misogyny was considered . . . I don't know, attractive."

"Yikes."

"Right. But the thing about the book, the story, is the surprises. The characters you think are going to come out on top, don't, and others do. It's something not many books can get away with anymore. And the author is a beloved Scot."

Luka thought a moment. "Okay, well, I already know the surprises from the movie."

"Not with the same nuance, Luka. If you read the book, you'll see what I mean. When a writer can do that seamlessly, it's . . . amazing."

Luka smiled and nodded.

I continued, "That's not what we're really here for anyway.

Edwin told me that the tour groups ultimately end up talking about the books, the stories, et cetera. But this is mostly about the locations. This is about Edinburgh, and I think you're going to love it. I know you've challenged Edwin to make you enjoy reading. I'm not sure I have the same flair he does for such things, but I do love books."

"I think I'm going to love Edinburgh. Reading? Well, I don't know."

"There are no non-readers, Luka, just people who haven't found the right books yet. What do you like to do with the small amount of free time you have?"

"Surf," Luka answered quickly.

"Do you like to watch sports? Are you into politics at all?"

Luka fell into thought again before he spoke. "I'm just a regular bloke, Delaney. I suspect I'm pretty simple, but I do like movies where they blow things up." He held up the book again. "I saw this at my sister's house one holiday. I would never have chosen to watch it."

"And you haven't read any Clancy?"

"Who?"

"Tom Clancy?"

"No, but I've seen some of the films, I'm sure. Sounds familiar."

"Hang on." I stood and made my way to the shelf with Clancy. I picked out one of the books that hadn't been made into a movie and brought it back to Luka. "Try this one. It's not set in Scotland, but we won't tell the others." I winked.

Luka reached for his back pocket. "How much?"

"This one's on the house."

"No—"

"Edwin would insist."

"Thank you, Delaney." Luka stood and cradled the two books. "See you at dinner?"

"I look forward to it."

I watched him leave, making his way toward the hotel cat-ercornered from Tom's pub. I sighed. It was either going to be a long week or the fastest of my life.

I just hoped I could manage it all well enough.

CHAPTER THREE

I closed the door and then waved one more time at Rosie and Hector through the front window. The warmth of the inside lights was appealing as a chill nipped at my nose. Rosie would go home soon, but she had paperwork to catch up on before she could relax and unwind. She'd been amazing today, and I knew she was tired. Somehow, she'd prepped me for my tour duties as well as taken care of customers.

I'd asked if she wanted to join us for dinner and drinks. With a strained expression, she'd said she would if she could be of help. I'd told her that Tom and I could take care of everyone just fine. She'd seemed relieved.

Rosie hadn't ever been all that involved in the tours either. Sure, she'd helped with setting up blocks of hotel rooms, but after a number of years, that task was accomplished quickly with a phone call to the Green Inn manager, and Edwin had even done that most of the time.

Edwin had immersed himself in knowing and understanding the groups he'd invited. I'd asked Rosie how much preparation he did, but she wasn't sure. She was aware that the tour locations themselves were second nature to him by now, but she didn't think he ever did the tours the same way twice. He would let the group's personality guide the journey.

I wasn't going to do that. I had a plan, and I was going to stick to it.

As I stepped away from the bookshop, I paused and took in the sights. Though it was dark outside, Grassmarket was busy, bustling. Summer was fast approaching, but even in early June, there were few truly warm days.

It still wasn't raining, though.

Lit by old-fashioned streetlamps, the market's square was a place for all sorts of gatherings, day or night: street performers, farmers' markets, parades. I'd seen so many things over the last couple of years that almost nothing surprised me.

I made my way up toward the pub, smiling at other shop employees I'd come to know or at least recognize over time. They smiled and waved back, some of them calling out "Hey, Delaney!" as I went. This place across the sea from where I'd been born had become home in almost every way.

I still missed my parents and brother, but Tom and I were going to Kansas to see them next month. We were both looking forward to it, though I always smiled when I thought of my husband, perhaps in his kilt, standing amid a Kansas wheat field, looking both stunning and misplaced.

He'd be perfect, no matter what.

It wasn't quite six yet. I wanted to grab a moment to check in with the hotel manager and talk to Tom before the evening unfolded. When I'd called him, Tom had worked to hide his surprise at the turn of events—and then to hide his concern over Edwin.

Rosie still wasn't telling what was going on, and my imagination only continued to conjure the worst. I'd texted both Edwin and Hamlet, but neither of them had answered yet. I was trying not to be irritated on top of concerned, but it wasn't easy.

I glanced in the pub's window as I passed by, spotting Tom and his employee Rodger serving drinks and chatting with a few customers. I crossed the street and grabbed the inn's door handle, making my way into the small, modernly outfitted lobby.

With five stories and stairways that seemed to go this way and that, there was a wonderful variety of room offerings—anything from a setup with three twin beds to a suite with a seating area and one king-sized bed. The tour group members were always each given their own room, of course.

As I stepped toward the front desk, I heard voices coming from an office set back and behind the counter.

"You can't ask me to do that!" a female voice seethed.

I'd lifted my hand to ring the bell on the front counter, but pulled it back. My curiosity got the best of me, and I wanted to hear what was said next.

"I can ask you to do anything. I'm the boss," a male voice said.

I quickly decided it was time to put a stop to whatever all that was. I lifted my hand again and rang the bell.

After a moment of shuffling noises, two people emerged from the office. I recognized the manager from spotting him around Grassmarket or visiting with Edwin. I thought his name was Geoff.

"Hi, I'm Delaney Nichols, part of Edwin's tour group."

The man's cheeks were red as he smoothed back a swath of dark hair that had fallen into his eyes. He was probably in his forties but had a round face that made him seem younger. The woman, who was probably in her twenties, was darker skinned, with a heart-shaped face and long dark hair pulled back into the smoothest ponytail I'd ever seen. She was quite stunning.

I tried not to look back and forth between them as if I was questioning what might have been going on, but they both still seemed perturbed—their eyes in squints, mouths in frowns. However, I guessed that what I'd heard was probably something as simple as a boss asking a worker to do something she didn't think was in her job description.

"I'm Geoff," the man said. "This is Carmel."

"Nice to meet you," I said.

Geoff bit his bottom lip and took a deep breath as if to steel himself. "Ms. Nichols, there was . . . I need to let you know that there was an issue with Edwin's card. I've been trying to reach him."

Carmel nodded. "Yes, and we were to kick out your guests if this wasn't paid by tomorrow morning," Carmel said as if she'd intended to land a blow. She crossed her arms in front of herself and frowned smugly at Geoff.

Geoff gave her a distinctly angry glare before he turned back to me, his cheeks even redder now. "Well . . ."

"Edwin was called away, but I work with him at the bookshop."

"Aye. I've seen you." Geoff smiled now, working hard to transition into something friendly.

I was surprised by the news, but this was something I could handle. I swung my bag off my shoulder and grabbed my wallet. "I can take care of this." I didn't mind paying. Edwin would reimburse me. I *was* bothered by everything else, though. What was going on with Edwin? I worked to keep my cool. "Here you go." I handed my card over the counter.

Geoff nodded. "Thank you. Edwin's always told me the tours were his thing only, that no one else at the bookshop was really involved. I wasn't sure, but I also knew he was good for it."

I smiled, remembering what Carmel had just said about the deadline. "At least until tomorrow?"

Geoff blanched. Of course Geoff hadn't wanted that part shared. Carmel had done it for a reason I could only guess she was either fed up with him or just liked to cause trouble. I couldn't possibly know which, and I didn't really need to know.

"No, no. We would always know Edwin was good for the money," Geoff was quick to repeat.

I nodded. I didn't allow myself much more than a moment's conjuring of a scene in which the four people Edwin had invited to Edinburgh were thrown out of the inn, their luggage behind them.

The brief picture angered me. I shook it away. It hadn't happened. No need to spend any more time dwelling on it.

We were all silent a moment as my credit card was processed. I held my breath, hoping that whatever had tripped up Edwin's wasn't contagious to mine.

Geoff looked up at me with an even more natural smile a moment later and handed me the card. "Thank you."

Again, I worked to hide what I was really feeling, which was now relief.

"Well, thank you. I know Edwin has been fond of this inn for years. I suspect that tradition will continue," I said, though I added a tiny bit of doubt to the tone, just because I could.

"We always appreciate him—you *all,* actually," Geoff said.

I decided it was time to change the subject. "So, everyone appears to be settled in?"

Geoff looked at Carmel, who nodded.

"One of the men asked for new bedding," she said.

I nodded. "Why new bedding?"

"Ours had just been washed and it smelled too strongly of soap. He—his name is Gunter, I believe—said the scents were giving him a headache and would we mind rewashing with something with no scent. It was no problem. We do get asked that every now and then. I'm just telling you in case he mentions something. He seemed satisfied with the new sheets I brought up, but just let us know if he needs anything else."

I sensed she was genuine. I'd already decided not to like Geoff, though I knew that might not be fair. In fact, Edwin was always complimentary of him.

Everybody knew what she was called, but nobody anywhere knew her name.

I was startled by the sudden voice in my head. The character, Beloved, from Toni Morrison's book of the same name, was speaking to me. My bookish voices, tricks of my intuition, came to me every now and then. Lots of times I couldn't figure out what they were trying to say, but this one was pretty easy. Things might not be what they seem.

I didn't know what had been going on with these two, what had caused the spiteful tone I'd overheard, why Edwin's card hadn't worked. Carmel wasn't hurt and didn't seem bothered. Her body language now bespoke nothing but comfort and confidence. Maybe Geoff was short on money and had been depending upon Edwin's payment to catch up on some bills. Maybe it was all just the way they worked together.

Okay, step back, Delaney, I told myself.

"Thank you. We all appreciate all you do," I said.

They smiled. We all smiled, and I left a moment later, back to worrying about my boss and wondering what in the world was going on.

"That is odd, but I suppose it can happen to anyone. Even Edwin," Tom said doubtfully.

"Exactly, but it's so . . . unexpected, unusual." I grabbed a pretzel from a bowl he'd set out in front of me.

Dinner was less than an hour away, but I'd forgotten about all the other meals of the day. I hadn't eaten anything, even a bakery treat that morning, and the pretzels had reminded me I was famished.

Tom stepped closer to where I was seated, at the side of the bar, and grabbed his phone from his pocket. He took advantage of a small lull in business to make a call. I watched and listened as he left a message.

"Hamlet, Tom here. I know Delaney has tried to call you and Edwin, but we're very concerned. Just a quick update would be helpful. Thanks." He ended the call and looked at me. "I know you've got it handled, but I thought one more person jumping in might prompt someone to give you a ring."

"Thanks." I took a deep breath and let it out. No matter what, I couldn't let the tour group see any of my unease. "I think it will be fun. I wish I'd gone along on a previous tour."

Tom smiled. "Delaney, you are nothing if not fun. You'll be fine. I'm happy to come along at any moment. Rodger said he'd be available for the next few days."

I perked up. "Really?"

"Aye."

"That's great news. Maybe you could join me tomorrow. It's the first day. We've got Greyfriars Bobby and places along The Royal Mile."

Tom looked toward his friend and longtime employee. "Rodg, care if I take tomorrow off?"

"Not a bit, boss. I was just waiting for you to ask." Rodger smiled at me.

"Thank you," I said.

"Anytime, Mrs."

Technically, I was "Ms." and I'd kept my last name, but Rodger never meant it as anything more than a friendly nickname.

"What's that?" Tom asked as he reached for the pendant.

"I forgot! I didn't even tell Rosie about it. Look."

I told them the story of my time at the antiques center, which now felt like a hundred years ago.

"That's amazing," Tom said as he held it toward the light to read the engraving.

"I know. I love it."

"That's spectacular," Rodger added.

Tom let go of the pendant, and I slid off the stool. "Well, we'll be over after dinner. You'll get to meet everyone."

"We'll be here." Tom smiled, and winked at me.

Tom would definitely be an asset. The tour members would love him, and he knew Edinburgh almost as well as his father Artair and Edwin did, though Tom was less likely to bring up the city's history as often as the older men were inclined to do.

I hurried over the market square and crossed the street to head to the restaurant. I wasn't in a hurry as much as I just wanted to warm up a bit.

It was a fish and chips takeaway, and one of my favorite places to eat in all of Edinburgh. The lobby was tiny, but there were a couple stools inside and two long benches out front for diners to sit and enjoy their food if it wasn't too unpleasant outside.

It seemed like an indoor eating night, but we were going to be cramped.

"It'll be fine," I muttered to myself.

They were all there already, waiting for me in the small space.

"There she is!" Hugo, the cook and restaurant owner, said.

"Am I late?" I asked.

"No," Meera said. "We're early. We all rested a little and then walked up to the Royal Mile."

"Well, I passed on the walk," Kevin said, "but joined in when they got back."

"That's great! Did you enjoy the Royal Mile?"

Everyone seemed to have enjoyed it just fine.

We ordered and then managed to gather in a comfortable

circle to the side of the front door. Our dinners were served in paper boats, which we could all hold in our hands or on our laps as we ate our fish and chips.

"Tell us about your name and your bookstore," Meera said to Kevin.

Kevin's eyes lit. "Ah, yes, my name. I bet you all think it's because my parents wanted a boy?"

We all nodded.

"That's not it at all. My mother—long gone now, of course—had a couple miscarriages before she had me. She spent one night praying to St. Kevin, telling the saint she would name a child after him if she could keep one." Kevin shrugged. "And here I am."

"I love that," Meera said.

We all nodded and made noises of agreement.

Kevin continued, "Anyway. The bookstore. It's a small place, not as lovely as The Cracked Spine but every bit as magical, if I say so myself. Not far from Buckingham Palace. There are so many books inside it that it's difficult to walk around." Kevin paused. "But I know where every single one of them is located. My daughter rang today asking about some titles, and I directed her right to them."

"I would love to see it," I said. Everyone else made more noises of agreement.

"You're always invited."

"What's it called?" Meera asked.

Kevin smiled. "Kevin's Books."

"That seems perfect," Gunter said.

"Gunter," Kevin began, "you're in the rare book and manuscript market in Germany, correct?"

"Yes."

"What's the most wonderful thing you've ever found, or maybe just worked with?" Kevin asked.

Gunter fell into thought as he chewed. Once he'd swallowed, he said, "You can imagine the intrigue brought by almost anything Egyptian. I was once presented with the opportunity to purchase some rare papyri—Egyptian writings on papyrus. The man who brought it to me was a stranger, though, and I knew something was wrong. I called the authorities right away. For an afternoon it was very exciting—the police, officials from Germany's artifact department were all in my apartment. Ultimately, the man who attempted to sell to me was arrested, though I don't know what happened to him or how he managed to steal the papyri in the first place. I did find out that it was over four thousand years old, though, and contained a diary of sorts of a man who worked on the Great Pyramid."

"Goodness, you could have made a fortune!" Meera said.

"How much could you have made off it, mate?" Luka asked. We all wanted to know.

"In theory it was priceless, but in practice, probably nothing." Gunter shook his head again. "I simply would have been the one arrested, and it would have eventually ended up with the authorities anyway."

We all fell silent a moment, probably each of us pondering such a find.

"Was it written with hieroglyphics?" Kevin asked.

"Yes. It was amazing," Gunter said. "I was so flustered by the whole thing, I didn't even snap a picture of it. The authorities took it away quickly and didn't feel the need to report back to me what they ultimately did with it."

Kevin turned to Luka. "I've never been to Australia, but I've always wanted to go. Is it wonderful?"

Luka nodded. "It's home. I grew up in the Outback until I was about ten, which was an experience in itself, but I've lived in Sydney most of my life. It's a wonderful city, and very different than Edinburgh." He looked at me. "No haggis there, but some interesting food. Will we have haggis?"

I tried not to wrinkle my nose. "Not my favorite, but I've eaten more haggis since moving to Edinburgh than I ever thought I would, which might be saying something. You'll have plenty of opportunities to try it."

"I'm game," Meera said. "I've never had it either, though I've been to Scotland a time or two."

"Edinburgh?" Luka asked.

"No, Glasgow."

"I'd like to see that city too, but I couldn't schedule enough time to extend the visit," Luka added.

"Where are you from, Delaney?" Gunter asked.

"America. Kansas."

"Did you attend university there?" Kevin asked.

"I went to the University of Kansas. It's in Lawrence. Before moving here, that's as far as I'd gone from home, which wasn't very far."

"Really?" Kevin said. "What made you move to Edinburgh?"

"I was laid off from my job, and then I saw an advertisement."

"Oh? Tell us all about it," Kevin prompted.

It wasn't just Kevin who was curious—everyone else was looking at me with equal interest. So I told them about the ad that mentioned a desk that had seen the likes of kings and queens, and how working in an old bookshop in Edinburgh had seemed as much a fantasy to me as Dorothy's adventure in Oz. They knew all about that one, of course.

"Are you a Scottish citizen now?" Luka asked.

"I married a Scot, so I get to be both."

"The pub owner?" Kevin said, suspicion lining her tone.

I smiled at her. "Yes, that's the one. You'll meet him soon. He's right across the way." I nodded that direction.

"We look forward to it," Gunter said.

"And there's beer?" Meera asked.

"Yes, there's beer and other things too."

"Well, I could use a good, cold beer. How about the rest of you?" Meera said.

The noises were all in the affirmative. We ate, somehow avoiding feeling too crowded. We finished our dinners fairly quickly and all decided it was time to give Hugo his lobby back.

We made a line and deposited our paper boats into the rubbish bin by the front door as we left the restaurant, Hugo sending us good wishes and telling us we could come back anytime we wanted.

CHAPTER FOUR

As a group, we made our way toward the pub. The dinner conversation had been easy, and it felt like friendships were beginning to form. I'd once heard Edwin comment about the one-week length of the tour. He'd said it was just enough time to see the good things and keep the bad things well-hidden.

"Delancy." Meera touched my arm as the others filed inside. "Forgive me. I'm going to run up to the Royal Mile. There's something I need to purchase there."

"Oh, sure." I squelched the desire to ask her what she needed to buy so urgently. She'd just been talking about wanting a beer. "We can stop by any shop over the next few days if you'd like to join us tonight."

She shook her head. "I'm beat and need to get this done. Share my apologies, okay? I don't want to be a downer."

"Of course. See you tomorrow?"

"Tomorrow." She nodded.

I watched her hurry off and then disappear around the

corner. There was nothing wrong with what she was doing, but it seemed somehow out of place.

I stood in front of the pub a good long moment, shaking off the sense that something wasn't quite right. Then I spotted movement at the corner of my eye, so I turned toward the inn.

Someone had exited its front doors and was running toward the takeaway restaurant, the direction we'd just come from. The person was dressed all in black, including a ski mask hat that covered his face. At least I thought it was a him, and he was taller than average.

"What's . . ." I muttered. Still from across the street, I turned my attention back toward the inn just as Carmel came through the door.

She was unstable on her feet, seemed to sway some, and was that blood on her head?

I took off toward her, crossing the market and the street quickly.

"Carmel, are you okay?" I said as I reached for her arm.

"Took . . . hit . . . oh," she said before she went down.

I managed to catch her before she fell, hard. I noticed someone on her other side. Gunter. I didn't see him come back out of the pub, but I was glad he was there. We looked at each other and then eased Carmel to the ground, resting her head on my lap. I reached for my phone and dialed 999 but was immediately placed on hold.

"Grab Tom. My husband," I said to Gunter as I nodded toward the pub.

He hadn't said a word, but his wide eyes were filled with concern as he stood from the crouch and then hurried into the pub. When 999 finally answered, I told them to send help.

They kept me on the line as a crowd began to gather around Carmel and me.

She was still breathing, but I didn't know the extent of her injuries. It occurred to me that I hadn't watched where the figure in black had run. I peered that way now, but there were too many people in the way.

"Delaney?" Tom said as he crouched next to me. He put his finger to Carmel's neck and then looked at me. "Strong pulse."

"Good."

"What happened? Are you all right?"

"I'm fine."

I was just about to tell him what I'd seen when a scream cut through everything else. It seemed to be coming from around the corner and partway up Victoria Street, the direction Meera had gone.

Tom and I looked at each other, but neither of us moved as everyone else who'd begun to gather around was now pulled that direction.

Thoughts were racing through my mind so quickly that I couldn't quite keep up. Somewhere in there, it occurred to me that if someone was screaming, they probably needed help. I just hoped that whoever tried to help them wasn't running into more danger.

A moment later, more screams filled the air.

Tom looked at me, a question in his eyes.

"Yes," I said. "Go see what's going on."

A moment later, it was just me and Carmel on the sidewalk in the market. I could see some of the back of the crowd trailing around the building, but I'd lost track of everyone from the tour. They were probably over there too.

I looked down toward the other end of the market, at the bookshop's windows, darkened except for a meek glow from a night-light Rosie had taken to plugging in at night. She and Hector had gone home.

The commotion unraveling on Victoria Street wasn't getting any quieter, and I kept talking nonsense to Carmel to try to rouse her.

Relief spread through me when a police car and an ambulance pulled to a quick stop in front of us. Quickly, EMTs and officers rushed our direction. Tom had returned, and he grabbed the attention of one of them.

"This woman needs medical attention, but there's more going on over there," he said as he pointed up Victoria.

"What's going on?" an officer asked as an EMT crouched to look at Carmel.

Tom took a quick but deep breath. "It appears someone has jumped off . . . the roof."

"What?" I asked.

But Tom was giving his attention to the emergency people only.

"Here, we've got her," one of the EMTs said to me.

I looked at the woman, whose competent eyes looked hard back at me. Gently, I removed myself from under Carmel's head and stood up.

Another EMT put his hand on my arm. "Are you okay?"

"Yes, I'm fine."

I'd lost Tom again, and figured he must have gone back to the crowd. Had I heard right? Had someone jumped off the building?

I was in such a hurry to see what was going on that I stumbled.

"Hey," Tom said as he reappeared and grabbed my arm.

"Tom! What's—"

He pulled me close, and we stepped back from the crowd. I couldn't tell if it was my heart beating so fast or his, but I could feel the booming. Maybe it was both of us.

He held on tight as he said, "Aye, someone jumped off the roof of the inn, it appears. I can't be sure, but I think it's the manager, Geoff."

I pulled back and looked up at him. He wasn't one to joke about such things, but I had to be sure. No, he wasn't kidding.

The events of the last few moments slogged through my mind. Meera walking away, the man running, the blood on Carmel's head. And then I remembered the others. "I need to gather the tour group, make sure they're okay."

Tom nodded. "Let's get them into the pub."

In demanding, no-nonsense tones, the police asked the crowd to disperse. You could feel the shock rippling through the cold night air. I didn't want to see the body on the road, but I was pretty sure I could recognize those who had—they had the tautest frowns and glassiest eyes. The strange curiosity of people who just couldn't look away.

It didn't take long for Tom and me to round up everyone but Meera from the tour and get them inside the pub. I texted her. She said she had neither heard nor seen the commotion, that she was still up on the Royal Mile but would stop by the pub when she headed back to the inn. She must have been moving quickly to miss it all.

Tom locked the pub's door and turned off the neon OPEN sign. Though you could tell he was rattled too, Rodger set out shots of tequila on the bar, just in case. Luka and Gunter partook, but Kevin and I just wanted glasses of water.

We all sat in tall chairs in a semicircle.

"Is everyone okay?" I asked. "Is anyone here hurt?"

Kevin, Luka, and Gunter looked at each other and shook their heads, rumbles of "no"s filling the air in the pub.

It wasn't a big space, had never even seemed roomy to me, but tonight more than ever before I was glad for the close walls, the sense of safety they offered, even if we all knew that safety was never guaranteed.

I hadn't forgotten to tell an officer what I'd seen, the man running away from the hotel. The officer had taken my quick statement, my name, my phone number, and then sent me on my way as he hurried to help the other first responders.

"What happened?" Gunter asked. "I mean . . . what in the world happened?"

Right. I knew what he was asking. What events could possibly have taken place to cause the hotel manager to jump from the roof?

I shook my head and looked at Gunter. "The police will figure it out, but I saw a man in black running from the inn. Did you see him too?"

"I didn't." He shook his head. "I stepped out of the pub to see where you and Meera had gone. I saw you running across the way. I followed. Where *did* Meera go?"

"She told me she wanted to run up to the Royal Mile to buy something. I texted with her. She's fine, and said she would stop by here later." I nodded toward my phone, which I'd set on the bar.

"Did you tell the police about the man in black?" Kevin asked me.

I nodded. "Yes, but I will follow up with them tomorrow. I wish I'd noticed where he ran." I looked around. "Did anyone else see anything suspicious?"

"No, nothing" seemed to be everyone's answer. They'd all seen the body, though, and that was rough on everyone.

I sighed. "I'm so sorry for all of this."

"Oh, Delaney, it's not your fault the hotel manager jumped from his building," Kevin said, her British accent stronger even as her voice seemed to pitch higher.

I forced a sad smile. "Well, I hope not, at least."

"Maybe he didn't jump. Maybe he was pushed," Kevin said. She took a sip of water, but then reached toward the bar for one of the shots and downed it quickly, nodding with satisfaction as she set the empty glass down.

Surprisingly, a murderous scenario hadn't even crossed my mind. I was sure it would have eventually, but there were so many other things my brain was trying to work through first.

"Good point," Luka said to Kevin. He looked at Tom, "Are you Delaney's husband?"

"Yes," I interjected. "This is Tom and Rodger. And this is Gunter, Kevin, and Luka."

"Tom," Kevin said before any further greetings could be made, "did you know the hotel manager?"

"Aye. I did know him, but only a wee bit. He was a friendly customer here in the pub whenever he stopped by, and he always had a kind word, but I'm afraid that's all I can tell you."

"How long have you known him?" Kevin asked.

Tom hesitated, and the rest of us looked at Kevin. Her tone sounded far more official than I would expect from a bookshop owner from London. She noticed the attention.

"Oh goodness, I'm just insanely curious. Apologies."

I knew the feeling.

"It's fine," Tom said. "Well, I guess he's been the manager for at least ten years, but I'm not sure I can tell you more than that. He was married to a lovely woman whom I met only a couple of times, but they divorced a few years ago. I'm embarrassed to say that I can't remember her name. He was remarried to someone I don't think I've met. I've heard her name, though." He looked at Rodger. "Tillie?"

Rodger nodded.

I asked, "Did anyone here notice anything strange over there?"

Gunter rubbed his chin and frowned. "I asked for clean sheets."

"Were your sheets dirty?" Kevin asked.

"No, it wasn't that. Detergent smells can bother me. The sheets were freshly cleaned, but they were scented too strongly."

"I know what you mean," Luka added. "I noticed the same thing, but I thought the smell would mellow by bedtime. Did you get new sheets?"

"I did," Gunter continued. "The young woman . . . who was injured out there, came up to the room and changed the bed herself. I offered to assist, but she wouldn't let me. I left the room so I wasn't in her way, but as I was returning I heard her talking on her phone. The door wasn't shut, but I don't think she would have wanted me, or anyone, to hear her conversation. She was telling someone that she refused to do whatever it was they were asking, and wasn't it against the law to even ask, wasn't it immoral?

"I stopped outside the door to listen, not because I wanted to know what she was saying. I just didn't want to interrupt, and for her to know I'd heard. She ended the call, and I went back into the room a few moments later. She seemed fine."

I didn't share with the others what I'd overheard when I'd visited the lobby before dinner. I would tell Tom later.

"That could be anything," Luka said.

"Yes, it could," Kevin agreed.

Gunter looked at Tom and Rodger. "Do either of you know the girl who was hurt?"

"No," Tom said. "I don't even think I've seen her in the pub, though I'm not sure I got a good look."

Rodger wasn't quite so quick to answer.

"Rodger?" I asked.

"I know Carmel."

"Okay?" I said.

Rodger nodded. "We've been on a couple dates."

"Nothing wrong with that, mate," Luka said.

"Oh, I know, but . . . well, she . . . I don't know how to say this without sounding awful."

"Tell us," Kevin demanded.

Tom blinked at her.

"Oh, I'm so sorry. I'm also way too blunt sometimes. I'm just curious is all, probably too curious for my own good." She looked at Rodger. "If you want to, I know we'd like to hear what you have to say."

None of us could stop ourselves from a tiny release of

laughter, even if it was more to loosen the tension the night's events had caused than that anything was funny.

"Aye," Rodger said. "Aye. It was my impression that Carmel didn't see things the way I did, maybe the way most people do. I got busy in the pub one night and missed her calls. Thirty-seven of them."

"Oh," Gunter said. "That's not a good sign, calling that many times."

Rodger shrugged. "I didn't think so, particularly since she was right next door and could have peeked her head in to see how busy we were, or just have left one message, or two." He looked at Tom. "She's been in, but not when you have." He turned back to the group again. "I wasn't ignoring her; I'm not that type. But she certainly had me second-guessing myself. Our few dates never turned into anything serious. I was up front with her, though, telling her I wasn't going to be a good match for her."

Luka laughed. "No, mate, if you'd been up front with her, you would have told her she'd gone off like a frog in a sock and you were moving on."

"What's that mean?" Rodger asked.

"She was crazy," Luka clarified.

"I can't imagine ever doing something like that," Rodger said.

No, I could never imagine Rodger saying something like that either. But Luka did have a point, even if I didn't want us to dwell on it. Sometimes you did have to be a little blunt in order for someone to get the message.

"You might need to talk to the police," Kevin said to Rodger. "It wouldn't hurt. Who knows what in the world happened over there tonight, but I imagine the police would take any information you wanted to share with them."

"You think so?" Rodger asked.

Kevin nodded. "I do."

"Want me to call Inspector Winters tomorrow morning?" I offered.

Rodger shrugged. "I suppose. I don't know if it matters."

"I don't either, but I'll tell him what you said, see if he wants to talk to you more. How's that?"

"That'd work," Rodger said.

I shared with the others that Inspector Winters was a local inspector whom Tom, my coworkers, and I had befriended over the last couple of years. He was a good guy, an excellent officer of the law, and a loyal friend. Rodger knew him too, though not as well as the rest of us.

Luka worked to suppress a yawn, shrugging and smiling sheepishly as we all noticed.

"We're all weary," Gunter said.

"Right." I stood from the stool. "Do you want to move hotels? I mean, they might not let you stay there anyway, but would you prefer to move even if they do?"

No one wanted to change locations. They all just wanted to go to the rooms they'd already gotten settled in.

"Let Tom and me run over there and see what's going on."

We were greeted by an officer at the door of the lobby and told him about the guests waiting next door. He said that everyone was welcome to return, that the only crime scenes now were on the roof and on Victoria Street; the police would have a presence in those places for the rest of the night. I re-texted Meera, who said she was still out shopping and that she'd see me in the morning. Then Tom and I headed back to the pub.

The guests were happy to hear they could return to their rooms. Any adrenaline left over from the evening's events had dissipated and left us all feeling limp and eyelid-heavy. Well, everyone but Meera, who seemed to have enough energy to shop. I looked up toward Victoria Street. I couldn't see much because of a crime scene van blocking the view. It was Saturday night in Edinburgh, so maybe she was just off enjoying herself. She was a grown-up; she had every right.

After Tom and I said good night to Gunter, Kevin, and Luka, and as we stood outside the inn a moment, I couldn't imagine wanting anything more than my bed.

"I can't say this isn't strange, just leaving them here," I said as we peered up at the building, some windows ablaze with light, some dark.

"You offered to move them," Tom said.

"I did." I looked at my handsome husband and was even more grateful for his being in my life than I'd been a few moments earlier.

"Thanks for everything," I said.

He looked at me and again pulled me close. "No need to thank me."

I didn't know what the next day would bring. Would the tour go on as planned? Would we hear from Edwin? Was Carmel okay? Would we understand what had happened to Geoff?

For that night, though, I had to let go of wanting answers in favor of some much-needed rest. Tom and I headed for our blue house by the sea, the perfect place for getting exactly that.

CHAPTER FIVE

"It's all over the news," I said as I looked at my phone. I wasn't someone who liked to grab her phone first thing in the morning, but today was different.

"I'm not surprised." Tom sat up. "Any answers?"

I read quickly. "Yes. The body was definitely Geoff—his last name is Larson."

"I'm sorry to hear that, but it wouldn't be good news no matter who it was. Jumped or pushed?"

"Unclear at this time. There's no mention here of Carmel or her status, or of any solid suspicions. It just says that the police are investigating. That's it."

"I bet you know someone who would give you more information." Tom ran his fingers through his messy bedhead hair.

It was one of those things he did in the mornings that I'd come to look forward to. I couldn't help but smile at him. "I did tell Rodger I'd let Inspector Winters know that he and Carmel dated briefly and that she might have been a little over the top."

"And maybe ask the good inspector if he knows anything else?"

Tom wasn't kidding around. His tone was serious.

"You're curious too," I said. "More than usual."

"Aye. I knew the man a wee bit, and I'd really like to know what happened. This is all very close to home."

"Is there something about Geoff that you didn't share with everyone else last night?"

"Not really, at least not anything they needed to know. Between you and me, I'd heard that he was almost fired a while ago, but he got his act together. Maybe the police should know that, but not the tour group."

"Oh. Do you know why his job was in jeopardy?"

"I don't." Tom frowned. "Geoff mentioned it almost in passing when we were walking through Grassmarket one day, but we didn't discuss it any deeper than that."

"Huh. I wonder what was up."

"We might find out eventually. What is the schedule for the day, lass?" Tom asked. "I can do whatever you need done."

I sighed. Even though I'd slept, my brain had still been mulling over what we *should* do. This all seemed like a good reason to cancel the tour and put it off until next year, when, hopefully, Edwin would be back anyway. But he would want me to leave that up to the participants. I'd texted them already, and they'd all said they hoped to continue. My concern for Edwin had also been reignited.

"Well, the plan is to meet outside the hotel at ten and then begin the tour. I don't know if that's how it will go down, but that's what I know so far. I'd like to have some time with

Rosie in the bookshop and see if she'll tell me what's going on with Edwin."

"That would give me some time to help Rodger get the pub put together for the day."

"I guess we should get to it then."

We were ready quickly, each of us taking a piece of toast along with us as we hopped in Tom's car and headed to Grassmarket.

I texted the group again, inquiring if they'd been able to grab breakfast at the nearby bagel shop, for which they had more vouchers. They all assured me they'd managed to eat. Before we got out of the car, I showed Tom the return texts, and we determined that a lot could be learned about a person just from one small text.

KEVIN: "All is well, love."
GUNTER: "I had a bagel." And then another text.
"Thank you."
LUKA: "I'm a black-coffee-for-breakfast guy. Theirs was acceptable."
MEERA: "It was open."

We parted ways as we exited the small area where Tom had parked his car for years. I went down to the bookshop, and he went up to the pub.

Rosie was already helping a customer in the bookshop as Hector trotted to the door to greet me. I lifted him to my cheek for our usual morning hello and held him as I made my way to the back table.

There was no sign of Hamlet or Edwin. I checked the normal spots. The place where Hamlet always set a coffee cup was vacant. The hook by the front door where he put his coat was starkly barren. If Edwin was there, he would have folded his coat over one of the back chairs, but there was nothing there either.

When the customer left, three books in tow, Rosie joined us at the table.

"Lass, what in the name of Mary, Queen of Scots, happened in the market last night?"

I told her what I knew and what I'd seen, Hector jumping up to her lap when he must have sensed we were discussing unpleasant things.

"Do ye ken aboot the lass wobbling out of the hotel? Is she okay?" she asked.

"I don't. I haven't heard anything."

"My goodness." Rosie worried at the beads of a colorful necklace she'd donned that morning. "Are ye going to call Winters?"

"I am."

"Good. Please share the details."

Now everyone wanted me to call Inspector Winters and then share. Most of the time, they encouraged me to be careful and mind my own business.

"Rosie, please can you tell me what's going on with Edwin?" I asked. "I'm so worried."

She looked at me and frowned. "I cannae tell ye yet, lass. I wish I could. There's no need to worry, though. He's not sick."

"Then what is it? Can you give me anything general?"

"It's a business thing."

"But he had to leave so abruptly, and he loves the tour."

"Och, he had no choice but to go, but he's healthy as a horse and isnae that all that matters?"

I nodded as I debated telling her the next part. I didn't want her to think I was prying, but she had been involved in Edwin's finances for years—"done his books," as she always said.

"Rosie, Edwin's card was declined up at the hotel."

"It was?"

"Yes. I took care of it, and that was fine, but it was declined."

Silently, she seemed to work through a series of thoughts. A few moments later she tucked Hector under her arm, stood, and hurried to her front desk. I followed.

Once there, she handed Hector over to me. With him now tucked under my arm, I watched as Rosie reached into her sweater pocket and pulled out her very full key ring. Expertly, she twirled it to the key for the desk drawer. Another moment later, she'd removed a gigantic and ancient accordion folder she used for Edwin's accounting.

With confidence, she reached into one of the folder's pockets and pulled out what I thought were statements.

She sat at the desk and started looking through the papers. I wanted to take a closer look myself, but not because I wondered about any money matters. I wondered if the secret to Edwin and Hamlet's trip to London was right there in front of me. But even I couldn't bring myself to be that nosy.

"There it is!" she exclaimed as her finger pointed at something on one specific line. "There it is!"

"There what is?"

"Lass, I need to make a call. You'll stay over here while I run over to the other side."

It took her only a few moments to put the accordion file back into the drawer and lock it again. The keys disappeared back into her sweater pocket and, clutching the papers she'd gathered, she hurried toward the stairs.

Her knees usually didn't like the journey back and forth over the stairs, but today she seemed not to notice much. At the top of this side's landing, she turned and looked down at me.

"Of course, ye'll be reimbursed, lass. I'll take care of it today, but first I need to do this." She held up the stack of papers as if it were a trophy.

"Thanks. Okay. Let me know what I can do."

She disappeared through the doorway a moment later. I thought she shut it a little too firmly.

I frowned at Hector. "What's going on?"

He panted at me as if to say, "Well, at least it's not Edwin's health."

"That is a great point. Shall we call Inspector Winters?"

Hector thought that was a grand idea.

Inspector Winters answered my call on the first ring, not surprised to hear I'd been near the events of last night. He told me he'd be right over to the bookshop to talk about it.

He was there ten minutes later. Rosie had returned from the dark side, and she seemed less burdened, though still not willing to share anything more.

Inspector Winters answered my first question, "Aye, it is suspected that someone else might have been on the roof with

Mr. Larson. However, there is no conclusive evidence that he was pushed. But it's something we're looking at."

"And Carmel. Do you have an update on her condition?" I asked.

He nodded. "She's unconscious—a subdural hematoma. They're keeping her in a medically induced coma to see if the swelling goes down on its own."

"Oh no. What's her prognosis?"

"She's young, and that's a good thing," he said as if he were trying to convince himself, too.

"She wasn't able to tell the police what happened to her?"

"Not yet."

"Did anyone else at the hotel see anything?"

"No. There was no staff there that we have been made aware of but for Carmel and Larson."

"No security cameras in the lobby?"

"None."

"When will we all learn?" I asked.

Edwin had installed cameras in the close—the alleyway—next to the bookshop but none in the store yet. He said he couldn't bring himself to put them inside. He didn't want people "spied upon" as they browsed the books.

However, the camera in the close had helped solve a crime recently, and that had prompted Edwin to rethink the indoor cameras—but just briefly, and none had been installed yet.

"I don't know." Inspector Winters leaned his arms on the table. "Your name is in the report. That's why I wasn't surprised when you called this morning. You saw someone running away from the hotel?"

"I did. I'm glad that got included. I talked to the officer

briefly but I barely remembered to do it, there was so much going on. It's all kind of foggy now."

"To the best of your ability, tell me what you saw."

I replayed the moments. I even closed my eyes to see if I could conjure up anything else that might help. I had nothing. Mostly, I remembered seeing Carmel swaying as she tried to walk.

"Okay." Inspector Winters made a couple notes.

"Did anyone else see what I saw?"

"Nothing mentioned in the report. Sometimes people come forward later, but I haven't received any updates regarding further statements."

"Do you know anything about Geoff Larson?" I asked. "Why what happened might have happened?"

"Not much, yet. I'm an official investigator on this one, though, so I might not be able to tell you as much as I sometimes can." He smiled, though not happily. No one was happy about this turn of events.

"Tom told me this morning that Geoff mentioned his job might have been in trouble a while ago. They were walking through Grassmarket. I think it was a casual conversation."

Inspector Winters made a new note. "I hadn't heard about anything like that. That's good to know. I might call Tom for more details."

"He'd be happy to talk to you, though I don't think there are any more details."

Inspector Winters nodded.

"I overheard something at the hotel, and so did one of the tour group, Gunter," I said.

Inspector Winters readied his pen again. "I'm listening."

I told him what we'd heard, how it seemed Carmel might have been being asked to do something she didn't want to do.

"Honestly," I said, "I felt like sticking up for her, but that's without knowing anything. Maybe the jobs she was asked to do were no big deal. Neither Gunter nor I got any more than what we overheard."

"I'll see what more I can find out."

"And," I said, "there's a little more." I really didn't want to tell him this part, but it might be important.

"Tom's longtime employee Rodger and Carmel dated. Briefly, and not seriously. I . . . uh, well, the best I can tell you is one evening she sent him thirty-seven messages. I know Rodger well enough to know he's a good guy. I think she was a bit much for him, but there are always two sides . . "

"I see. I should probably talk to Rodger, though his where-abouts are well accounted for, I'm sure. He won't be under suspicion. I'll make sure he knows."

"He'll be at the pub all day today, and this evening too."

"I'll stop by."

"What about Geoff's family? How . . . I mean, do they know?"

"His wife knows. I talked to her this morning, briefly. She's a wreck, of course. He has a son from his first marriage. Max. Tillie, Geoff's wife, said she told Max the news, but I haven't seen or talked to him."

"Is there anything I can do?"

"No, Geoff and Tillie were only married last year. She said she'd probably head back to Ireland, where the rest of her family is living."

"I hadn't heard she was from Ireland." I nodded. "Glad she has family."

But the words felt empty. The shock was still raw.

"Aye."

I heard the bell above the front door jingle, and Rosie greeting whoever had come inside.

A moment later, she peered around the half-wall that separated the back table from the rest of the store.

"Lass, ye've someone here to see you. It's Luka."

I walked Inspector Winters to the door and found Luka still standing there, his coat on, his expression serious. I introduced them, and Inspector Winters asked him if he'd seen anything suspicious at the inn. Luka, slightly surprised to be talking to a police official, said he'd seen nothing. Inspector Winters left with assurances that he'd be in touch with us all again.

Once he was gone, I turned to Luka.

"Everything okay?"

"No, lass, everything is far from okay. Can we have a chat?"

"Sure."

Rosie and I exchanged worried glances behind Luka as he made his way to the table. He sat, pulled the Clancy book out of his pocket, and slammed it on the table.

"How dare you," he said.

"Uh-oh." I sat across from him.

Hector jumped onto my lap and then put his paws on the table, staring down the man from Australia who seemed to be angry at one of his people.

It was only when Luka cracked a small smile that I could breathe easy again.

CHAPTER SIX

"I think Hector and I would like to know what's on your mind," I said.

Luka sat back in the chair and crossed his arms. "This book."

"Yes?"

He shook his head and then gave me his full attention. "I was up all night reading it."

A few things ran through my mind, "Ha!" and "Told you so!" were two of them, but I didn't say anything. I just smiled bigger at the new reader across the table.

"It was so good! You know, I've never been captivated by a book in my entire life. The action, the intrigue, one page after another. You were right—maybe everyone can be a reader."

"Yes, I was." I couldn't resist.

Luka laughed. "Well, I just wanted to thank you and buy another book. I'll definitely be donating to Edwin's cause." He paused. "He's coming back, right?"

Ah, there was the real reason Luka had come to talk

to me. I hoped he'd truly read and enjoyed the book, but his main mission had been to check on Edwin. "He'll be back. Again, we're all so sorry he had to leave so abruptly."

"Delaney, I'm not trying to disregard what happened at the inn last night. Perhaps part of the reason I was awake was the horrible turn of events, but it was a good book. However, I would like to know where Edwin went," Luka said, as if he had a right to know. "I'm concerned about him too."

He was a business owner, a successful one. He was probably very used to getting whatever he wanted, used to being in command. I didn't like his new tone, but since I understood where he was coming from—because I got to peruse the file Edwin had put together about him—I didn't take it personally. I realized this was probably how he got things done. Besides, I didn't know the details of Edwin's departure either; a part of me wanted to have such a tone with Rosie, even though I never would.

I sighed. It was no one's business, but Edwin *had* invited them all to the tour. He'd been the one to make it such a big deal over the years.

"I know where he went, but not why. He wouldn't have gone if it weren't imperative," I said. "And, though I wouldn't be at liberty to tell you more anyway, I actually don't know any more than that."

"He's not . . . sick, is he?"

I shook my head. "I've been assured that he isn't, and he really did say that you would all be invited back next year for a do-over with him."

"Well, that's generous, but I just want to make sure he's okay."

I cocked my head at Luka. "Did you know Edwin before you emailed him about not being a reader?"

"I did not, but ever since then I've wanted to apologize to him in person." He paused. "That's really what this is about, Delaney. I wasn't as kind as I should have been, as kind as Edwin was to me. I feel I owe it to him, and I don't like not taking care of such things. Maybe it's selfish of me to want to get that off my chest, but that's just the way it is, I suppose."

I nodded. "I understand. Okay, well, I don't think Edwin thinks that's necessary, and I can promise you, if you'd offended him—and he doesn't offend easily—he wouldn't have invited you. However, you'll get your chance to talk to him at some point."

I hoped I was right.

"Good." He paused again, but only a moment. "Now, where can I get another book?"

I walked him over to the Clancy section. Then I excused myself to let him shop. I told him I needed to run over to "my office" before the tour began.

If he had any questions, he was in good hands with Rosie, and since he hadn't kept up the surly attitude, Hector was giving him a chance now too.

I hurried over to the warehouse to gather the items I'd put together for the tour. I hoped I could handle this. I knew I wasn't Edwin, but that was just going to have to do. One thing at a time.

Once I was inside the warehouse, I felt both satisfaction at how far it had come as well as anxiety that I should be working inside it today. It was in good shape; the shelves were mostly organized. I had things to do, though, and they were going to be ignored for now. I was glad I wasn't on a deadline. I hadn't heard back from Michael Norway, but I hadn't expected to so soon.

I wore the pendant again today. I rubbed my finger over it and wondered how it had only been just yesterday that he'd given it to me. So much had happened.

When I'd first arrived in Scotland, the warehouse shelves had been crammed with all sorts of items, disorganized and a total mess. I'd found collections of things such as old-fashioned mousetraps, Egyptian artifacts (though nothing like Gunter had spoken about last night), bejeweled jewelry boxes, and tapestries. There was still too much in the room to make an accurate count yet, but at least it was all better organized.

It was the one room of the two sides of the bookshop that was climate-controlled, with light streaming in from windows high on the wall and overhead fixtures that illuminated but somehow didn't add any glare when I was working or studying intricacies and details.

I loved this room, and looked forward to being back inside it for a good string of days. I gathered my notes, shutting the ornate red door behind me, and then put the big blue skeleton key into the lock, turning it three times to the left.

By the time I made it back over, Luka had left with two books, according to Rosie. She wished me good luck as I stepped out into the beautiful day—only a little cold, with some good sunshine—and hurried up to meet the group, who'd gathered outside the pub with Tom.

Almost everyone was there.

"Anyone know where Meera went?" I asked.

All police presence was gone, though there were a few

lookie-loos walking by, snapping pictures and muttering about the man who'd been killed last night, pushed off the roof. That hadn't been determined per my conversation with Inspector Winters less than an hour earlier, but I didn't correct anyone.

"She wanted to run back up to the Royal Mile," Gunter offered, though there was a question or doubt or something lining his tone.

"Okay."

I'd told everyone that's what she'd done the night before, too. As we'd gathered in the pub and everyone asked about her, I told them she'd headed up there before the commotion. It had been so immediately before the tragedy that the timing still bothered me, but I hadn't shared that with anyone except Tom.

He stood next to me. "Want me to try to track her down?"

"I'll text her."

But before I could grab my phone, she came through the front door of the hotel. She looked bothered and harried as she joined us. She frowned at me and said, "Sorry about that."

If she'd gone up to the Royal Mile, I hoped she'd accomplished her task, but I'd check with her later.

"Good to see you. You okay?"

"I'm fine, thanks."

I looked around. "Is everyone else okay?"

"Absolutely."

"Yes, Delaney. It was rough last night, and I'm sorry for the loss of life, but we need to get on with things. Nothing is guaranteed," Kevin said. "We are here for a tour. Let's tour."

I nodded. "All right, we're off."

More nods and smiles greeted me, except from Meera, whose attention seemed to be on something on the ground near her feet. I hoped she really was okay. Tom and I shared a quick look. He'd noticed it too. We'd both try to check on her. I remembered that she and Tom hadn't met yet.

"Meera, this is my husband, Tom. He'll be joining us today."

"Pleasure," she said with a quick smile.

"Nice to meet you." Tom made a move as if he was going to offer his hand for a shake, but Meera crossed her arms in front of herself as if making it clear that she didn't want to do such a thing. Smoothly, Tom turned his attention back to me and smiled.

"This way!" I said, and then I turned and led us back across the street, past the restaurant where we'd eaten the night before. That friendly gathering, just like my time with Michael at the antiques center, seemed like ages ago.

Once we were moving up Candlemaker Row and there didn't seem to be too much foot traffic heading our direction, I turned around and spoke to the group as I walked backward. "Did anyone read any of *The Prime of Miss Jean Brodie* last night?"

Even with everything that had happened, Luka had fit in a whole book, though it wasn't the one we'd given everyone.

"I've read it before," Kevin offered. "A few times back in the day, in fact. I was too tired to try it again."

"Seen the movie?" Luka asked everyone.

"I have," Gunter said. "I still think Maggie Smith is beautiful."

"Do you all remember when Miss Brodie showed her students Greyfriars Bobby?"

"I don't, in fact," Kevin said.

No one else offered anything, so I spoke.

"Kind of a trick question. It's not in the book, but it's in the movie," I said. "Edwin always likes to start the tours with a look at the statue and the sharing of the story of the dog's adventures. He likes to point out how different literature can be from the films based on them, and how, even if you do see the movies, you should"—I looked pointedly at Luka—"at least consider reading the books too."

Luka smiled and sent me a conceding nod.

"Oh, that's so true," Kevin added.

We stopped in front of the pub named for the statue.

I nodded toward it. "This is a great pub, and—no surprise—they love dogs. We won't stop inside today, but if you have any free time and you're hungry, I love their buttermilk chicken pie. Okay, this way."

We dodged some traffic and made our way across the street to the peninsula that was at the junction of two roads and held the statue of the black Skye Terrier sitting atop a fountain.

"It was made with two drinking troughs," I pointed out, "one of them ground level. It hasn't run with water since 1957, though."

"The dog visited its owner's grave for years, is that correct?" Gunter asked.

"Yes, Edwin tells me the story has probably been exaggerated for dramatic effect over the years, but it begins with Jock, a poor shepherd who moves to Edinburgh in search of work. It doesn't go well, and he falls into a life of poverty. Lonely, old, and ill, his only companion is Bobby"—I nodded at the statue—"who belonged to a farmer Jock had worked for. When the farmer wanted Bobby back, Bobby refused to go, wanted to stay with Jock. After Jock died, Bobby was still loyal to him, visiting his grave every day for fourteen years." I smiled. "Or so they say."

"What really happened?" Meera seemed to have reengaged with the group.

"Well, I'm not sure anyone knows exactly, but even if it's based on only a little truth, it's a good story, right?"

"Absolutely." Meera nodded.

I had realized something. No, I wasn't Edwin, not even close, but I had my own experience and impressions of this amazing city. I saw it through a visitor's eyes, close to the perspective of my tour companions. Sure, Edwin might have had more flair, but I knew the stories, and I could share them in my own way, maybe by remembering the awe I felt learning them all for the first time.

"When I first moved here, I was overwhelmed," I said. "There is so much history everywhere—so many wonderful things to see. It's no surprise, I'm sure, but I absolutely love a good story. I couldn't take in everything around me fast enough."

"Well, you *are* from Kansas," Luka said, with a smile and a wink.

He was joking, but I nodded. "There's something to that. I hadn't been out of the state, other than to Kansas City, Missouri. I don't know how that happened, but it did. My parents were always too busy with their farm to travel anywhere. My only real escape was through reading. The move here opened my eyes about so many things. So many more stories, so much history."

"You love it, don't you, dear?" Kevin smiled.

"I do." I shared a quick look with Tom.

"Do you still love Kansas?" Luka asked.

"Oh, yes. My parents are still there, and I can't wait to visit them later this summer." I paused. "I'll bet Edinburgh is nothing like Australia."

"No." He shook his head. "I'm no less struck than you were by the beauty, though. I'm not sure I feel history the way you do, but I appreciate what you're saying."

I thought about my bookish voices. They were silent at the moment. My sense of history was part of that intuition, probably. I felt it—sometimes with a heaviness in my limbs, other times just with goose bumps.

"I think some people are more . . . I wish I could think of the English of what I want to say," Gunter said. "In German it's something like *etwas AuBerirdisches spuren.*"

"Maybe she's in tune with something that not everyone is?" Luka said.

"That sounds about right," Gunter said.

I laughed, and Tom and I shared another look. He said, "Aye, that sounds about right."

"Tom," Meera said, "if Edwin were here, what would he add about this statue?"

"Oh, I don't know." Tom rubbed his chin. "I'm sure he could tell you a story or two about something that might have happened to him here near the statue, or maybe a similar experience. He probably has a tale about a dog he once had. I wish I knew."

"Would they be real stories, or would he make them up?" Luka asked, though his tone was friendly.

And again, just like that, I was back to feeling sorry for this group. They'd wanted Edwin. They should have had him, not me. Though Tom did cut a dashing figure, he wasn't Edwin either.

Tom shrugged. "Probably a wee bit of both."

"All right." I consulted my notes. "We're going to catch a bus here and head back up to the Royal Mile." I looked at Meera. "There are some specific things we'll be looking at, but did you want to stop somewhere for something?"

"What?" she said. "Oh, no, I'm good. Thank you, though."

We boarded a bus and exited at the top of the Royal Mile, near the castle grounds entrance. The castle wasn't on the schedule today, wasn't on any of the days' schedules, but there would be time here and there if they wanted to explore on their own.

"It's not really a quick look-and-go," I said, nodding at the structure most associated with Edinburgh. "You'll have some free time if you want to take a tour, though."

"Edwin warned us that many of the 'regular' sights wouldn't be on the tour," Gunter said. "We understand."

"Great. All right, walk this way. In fact, we will begin with a rather popular sight." I gestured with my arm.

There was so, so much. I didn't know how Edwin did it, but Rosie had coached me, reinforcing the fact that Edwin's tours were never really the same each time, that he improvised a lot. The main objective was that the group enjoyed what they were seeing, what they were learning about, and each other.

As we headed down the Royal Mile, I also did a quick point-and-go toward the Writers' Museum.

"You could spend all day in there," I said. "The museum honors the lives of Robert Burns, Sir Walter Scott, and Robert Louis Stevenson. But we have a lot of ground to cover, so that's also something you could do on your own. However, speaking of Sir Walter, follow me again."

We passed many shops, but Meera didn't seem to indicate any interest in going inside any of them. We saw government buildings, restaurants, pubs. At Bank Street, I pointed and told them we'd be visiting a very special pub down there at some point. Finally, we stopped in front of the sort of grand church building that I knew Americans expected to see anytime they visited Europe. This one was one of the more spectacular, or at least it was in my opinion.

We glanced up at the tall front facing, the ornate window frames.

"St. Giles' Cathedral," I said.

"Medieval," Kevin added.

"Yes, but this isn't the original building. This one was built from the fourteenth century to the sixteenth. The original building was small, Romanesque. Some parts of that one remain and have been preserved."

"It's seen many things," Gunter said. "I've read about it."

"Like what?" Luka asked.

I looked at Gunter, who nodded for me to continue. "It was originally a Catholic parish. John Knox was the minister after the Scottish Reformation, moving from Catholic to Protestant. It's seen multiple congregations as well as been used for secular reasons—as a meeting place for the Scottish parliament, even as a prison. As happens throughout history, battles were fought for the beliefs that could be shared inside. Its role in the Covenanters' rebellion led to it being called the Mother of Presbyterianism."

"It's stunning," Kevin said.

"Absolutely," Luka added.

Again, I felt Tom next to me. I looked at him, and he smiled. This was off to a good start and he knew it. I wasn't sure I would really need him along, but I hoped he stayed.

Gunter turned to me. "What literature does this have to do with?"

"Ah. Well, there's a slight twist." I pointed to the area behind the church.

"There was once a group of tenement buildings there called the Luckenbooths. They're mentioned in Sir Walter Scott's well-known *The Heart of Midlothian*. Along with a few sketches, Scott's description is one of the best we have. I won't quote much from books, but I am going to read this to you. It's maybe more descriptive than even some old photographs might have been. Oh, he also talks about the Tolbooth prison, a building that still stands." I pointed toward it. "Punctuation wasn't as important then, so bear with me. I'll quote directly."

I had their full attention.

I cleared my throat and read: "Called the Luckenbooths, which, for some inconceivable reason, our ancestors had jammed into the midst of the principal street of the town, leaving for passage a narrow street on the north, and on the south, into which the prison opens, a narrow crooked lane, winding betwixt the high and sombre walls of the Tolbooth and the adjacent houses on the one side, and the buttresses and projections of the old Cathedral upon the other. To give some gaiety to this sombre passage [well known by the name of the Krames], a number of little booths, or shops, after the fashion of cobblers' stalls, are plastered, as it were, against the Gothic projections and abutments, so that it seemed as if the traders had occupied with nests, bearing the same proportion to the building, every buttress and coign of vantage, as the martlet did in Macbeth's Castle. Of later years these booths have degenerated into mere toy-shops, where the little loiterers chiefly interested in such wares are tempted to linger, enchanted by the rich display of hobby-horses, babies [meaning dolls], and Dutch toys, arranged in artful and gay confusion; yet half-scared by the cross looks of the withered pantaloon or spectacled old lady, by whom these tempting stores are watched and superintended. But, in the times we write of, the hosiers, the glovers, the hatters, the mercers, the milliners and all who dealt in the miscellaneous wares now termed haberdashers' goods, were to be found in the narrow alley."

I looked up from the page I was reading from and took a deep breath. I still had their attention, which I thought a very good thing.

"Oh, my goodness," Kevin said a long moment later.

Tom nudged me lightly with his shoulder and smiled again.

"What?" I said to the group.

"That was lovely," Kevin said.

"I can see it all," Meera added.

I laughed. "I didn't write the words, but, yes, Scott was pretty good at his craft."

"But you read them perfectly," Gunter said.

"You sure did," Luka added.

Tom nodded. "Aye, lass, ye did."

Everyone spent another long moment just looking at where the long-ago buildings had once been.

I gave them all time as my eyes wandered to the church, the kirk, the cathedral.

I cleared my throat. "While we're here, want to take a look inside?"

After another few beats, they all turned to me and nodded. I thought I saw Kevin dab a tear from her eye, and I realized that she must be just as moved by history as I was. Edwin would enjoy this group.

Gunter led us all through the church's front doors. The magnificent high blue ceiling and bordering stained glass windows were what most people talked about after visiting St. Giles. Eyes automatically went upward, and "Wow" or similar proclamations were always uttered.

"The first incarnation of the church was not nearly as impressive," I said. "It was burned down in 1385 by Richard the Second's troops."

"Oh, yes, England and Scotland have long been at each other," Kevin interjected. "Terribly bloody."

I nodded. "That is true." I looked up again, toward some pillars on the high walls. "I know parts have been preserved, but it's said that those pillars might be from the original church, might be some of the last remnants of that time period."

"This is amazing," Luka said.

"Yes, but one more thing you should see before lunch. Follow me," I said.

We moved to the southeast corner of the church building.

"This is Thistle Chapel. It's only thirty-seven feet by eighteen. It was built in the neo-Gothic style to commemorate the holders of the Most Ancient and Most Noble Order of the Thistle, Scotland's foremost Order of Chivalry, which was introduced by James the Seventh in 1687. To me, all of that sounds like a fairy tale, but it's real. This was one of the first stories I loved here in Scotland."

"So interesting," Kevin said.

For a few minutes, the group took in the small, ornate chapel. A rumble filled the silence.

"That's my stomach." Luka laughed.

"Anyone hungry?" I laughed too.

Everyone answered quickly in the affirmative. It was already time for lunch.

CHAPTER SEVEN

Once we were back outside, I faced the group again. "There are a lot of options for lunch, but there's a place I came across just yesterday that samples whisky. I looked them up, and they also have sandwiches and other lunch food. I know we don't want to drink too much, but do you all want to try some Scottish whisky? It's only a short bus ride away, and it's in an old industrial area that might be interesting."

"Can't we do that at Tom's pub?" Kevin asked.

"Aye," he said. "But this place has many more varieties to choose from. It's quite an experience, and since we won't be venturing out to the countryside distilleries, you might be interested."

A consensus was reached quickly, and we boarded another bus.

As we disembarked, I noticed both Meera and Luka looking at the building across the street, the old natural gas processing facility that I'd noticed the day before. Its two-story white stone façade was in bad shape, the windows boarded up, everything else crumbling under layers of graffiti. When I'd first seen it, police officers were escorting some kids away from it. Today, I noticed a chain-link fence around the perimeter, though it was in terrible shape itself and didn't seem particularly useful for keeping trespassers out.

As I joined Luka and Meera, she said, "The sign said it's a part of the old gasworks buildings."

"It's mysterious," Luka added.

"Nature has taken it over," Gunter said as he came up next to me.

It had. The property was being claimed by earth, weeds, vines, and general overgrowth.

"I love old stuff like that." Meera looked at me. "Any chance we could explore?"

I pointed at one of the very obvious signs telling us to keep away. "Probably not."

"We could pretend we didn't see the signs," Meera suggested.

I shook my head and decided to blame my boss instead of just telling her no. "Edwin would have my hide."

"A shame." Meera looked longingly at the structure.

I thought it was an impressive sight, but I had no desire to explore today, like I had yesterday.

Kevin gently took Meera's arm. "Let's get inside. Lunch and whisky are waiting."

The two women and Luka headed to the door as Tom led the way, but I had the sense that Gunter wanted me to stay back with him. I did, knowing that Tom would take care of everyone's orders and make sure no one started their lunch in too boozy a fashion, whatever that took.

"Everything okay?" I asked Gunter.

"It is. Thank you. I'm . . . a little worried about Meera."

"Why?"

"Last night you mentioned she'd gone up to the Royal Mile to shop."

"Yes, right before all the . . . commotion."

Gunter nodded. "I know—she's an adult, and we don't have curfews or anything like that. But I don't think she returned until this morning. I saw her coming in, and so did Luka; we were both in the lobby. I mentioned to Luka that maybe Meera ran back up to the Royal Mile, but I have no idea what went on. Again, she's an adult and if she wants to stay out all night, that's her business, I suppose. It's just . . . I just thought you should know."

Leave it to Gunter to take on the role of the "dad" of the group. It was a twenty-four-hour city, or at least many parts of it were, and it had been a Saturday night. It might not have been the smartest or the safest move, but some people wouldn't be able to resist.

"Thank you, Gunter. I appreciate you letting me know."

"You're welcome." He put his hand on his stomach. "And now, I'm starving."

"Let's eat."

The restaurant was set up cafeteria style—not like your typical lunchroom, but more like a historical hotel lobby that had been transformed, with wood and brass fixtures.

The whisky samples were tiny, offering tastes of many different varieties. I didn't know which one to choose. Most everyone chose four samples, which would equate to one full shot, but I just chose one with a smoky flavor, and the small amount of liquid was more than enough to please my taste buds.

The varieties infused with seaweed, brine, and apple were the group's favorites, but, surprisingly, it was the simple ham and cheese sandwiches that got the most attention.

Though the food was more like something out of my grandmother's kitchen than Scottish fare, the sandwich spread that the restaurant used was a mix of mayonnaise, mustard, and spices I could only credit as tasting like Worcestershire, and it was delicious.

The booze sampling was kept to a minimum. No one behaved as if they'd had too much to drink, which I was grateful for.

The conversation was sporadic, since everyone was hungry and focused on their food, but it was friendly, and mostly about books: what everyone had read recently and what they were looking forward to reading. Even Luka joined in, making everyone laugh at his change of heart.

The group asked Tom about growing up in Edinburgh. He regaled them with stories about his strict parents and all their rules, which, as a teenager, he spent way too much time trying to break. He talked about the time he and a friend had tried to sneak into the castle. A security guard caught them before they made it through the front gates. The guard was friendly and explained how the boys should make better choices. He also told Tom he knew very well who his father was and if he saw Tom ever attempt to step out of line again, Artair would hear about it. For a reason Tom couldn't quite pinpoint, that moment set him more on a straight and narrow than he'd ever been.

"So, it's a small town?" Luka asked.

"Not really. It's more that some families have been in Edinburgh for so many generations that it's almost like a small town. Everyone knows someone who might also know someone in your family. It was difficult to get away with anything."

"I would have struggled," Luka said with a smile. "Fortunately, the Outback wasn't like that."

"Out in the wilds?" Meera asked him.

"Yes, very much so."

"But you moved to the city and became sophisticated," Gunter said, seeming to wonder if he was using the correct words.

"Against my will, back then at least."

A few moments later, we each grabbed our own dishes and took our time making our way to the counter, where we dropped them off and thanked everyone.

En masse, we stepped outside. I was glad it wasn't too cold, even though clouds had started to roll in. I realized that Meera wasn't with us. I suspected she'd run to the loo.

A few minutes later, I peeked my head back inside to see if she was waiting in the lobby. She wasn't there either. I debated checking on her in the bathroom and ultimately decided that it was better to check than to wonder—what if she'd become ill?

I opened the hallway bathroom door and called inside. "Meera?"

There was no answer, even after I said her name a couple more times. Back in the lobby I asked the receptionist if she'd seen a young woman with dark hair and a red sweater head any direction.

"Aye, she went outside, right before the rest of you."

I thanked her and rejoined the others. My eyes scanned the group. No Meera. I looked all around but saw no sign of her. There were no trees or shrubbery to hide someone—the front yard of the place was outfitted with only a small lawn.

I lifted my eyebrows at Tom, who caught my concern and stepped away from the group to join me.

"Meera left the building before we did," I said.

He scanned the property. "She must be around here somewhere then."

"What's going on?" Kevin asked as she joined us.

I really didn't know what else to tell her. "We need to find Meera."

Though there wasn't much to search, we all, in turn, scanned the areas on each side of the building, looked around inside, and then regrouped near the front door.

"Oh!" Luka said as he broke away and hurried toward the street.

We all followed, and when traffic subsided we crossed.

"Look." Luka pointed toward the front door of the abandoned gasworks building.

Like the rest of the building, the door had been enveloped in vines and greenery, but coming out of winter, most of the foliage was brown and crumbly. It appeared that someone had torn away some of the vines and managed to open the door—a door that now seemed to be hanging from only one hinge. I had no idea when that had happened—but I guessed it was at least a day ago. Still, though, Meera and Luka had been interested in the building.

"She didn't . . . ," I said.

"I bet she did," Luka responded.

Not only were there clear NO TRESPASSING signs, but other signs that also meant the same thing were posted here and there: KEEP OUT! NOT SAFE! NO ENTRANCE!

I put my hands up around my mouth. "Meera!"

We were all silent as we waited and hoped for a response, but none came.

The fence gate was holding on by the barest of equipment. Stepping on it was easier than trying to open it. I did exactly that.

"Hang on, lass—let me go." Tom grabbed my arm gently.

"We'll go together." I turned to the others. "You all stay right here."

I had an urge to tell them to call 999, but that seemed like going overboard, at least until we searched a little longer. We might find her right inside. I could admonish her a little and we'd be on our way.

However, it wasn't easy even getting to the doorway to peer inside. The growth had really taken over, though I saw breaks in it that people—maybe including Meera—could use to step their way in.

I held on to Tom's hand as I took a giant step and then found myself right inside the front door.

"Meera!" My voice echoed and sounded tinny at the same time.

"Meera!" Tom jumped over and was right next to me.

It was shadowy and vast inside. I'd been in plenty of small buildings in Edinburgh, but I'd rarely experienced a warehouse like this one.

Though light streamed in here and there through windows, it had to work its way through the boards and dirt that covered them.

Dust motes danced throughout, and a thick layer of grime covered an old desk that tilted as if it had lost a foot. As on the outside, graffiti had been painted throughout. Other furniture and even wall art remained inside, filthy though it all was.

"It's like they just shut the lights off and left one day," I said.

We'd come into a reception area, where four desks remained. A pot of fake flowers was upended on the floor, covered in gunk so thick you couldn't tell the original colors.

"Look." Tom pointed at some footprints that could have belonged to our rogue tour group member.

I figured this was the case, because they were from one pair of shoes, not two like what might have been left by the teenagers I'd witnessed the day before.

I grabbed my phone and switched on the flashlight app. "Come on, Meera! It's not safe in here. You're putting us all in jeopardy."

I shrugged at Tom, hopefully conveying that if it would get her attention, I was happy to use guilt.

I aimed the light along the footprints. It was no surprise that they led out of the room and toward an open doorway.

"Let me check it out," Tom said.

"We'll go together," I said again.

We trailed the footprints and then stopped at the door. It was impossible to take in everything inside the enormous space at once. Old and dirty machinery and equipment were everywhere, some of it seemingly where it might have belonged, other parts strewn. I had no idea what everything did, but the setup was impressive.

Along with more colorful graffiti, we could see food wrappers and improvised bedding, but it appeared not to have been slept on for a while. I thought I saw scurrying shadows that might have belonged to rodents, but I didn't want to dwell on that.

"We're not going in there," I said.

"Meera!" Tom yelled.

There was no answer.

There was no other option by then: I felt like we had no choice but to call for help. We were fairly certain that Meera had gone into the building, and though there was no indication that she was hurt, she might be trapped somewhere.

We turned around and went back outside with hopeful wide eyes, but we were only greeted by the others' curiosity. No Meera.

I grabbed my phone to call 999 but changed my mind at the last second and called Inspector Winters instead.

That was what Edwin would have done.

CHAPTER EIGHT

Inspector Winters didn't arrive by himself—he brought four other officers. The five of them donned hard hats and heavy canvas-like overalls, then went inside to explore after talking briefly to the rest of us.

I put the discombobulated members of the tour group on a bus back to Grassmarket with maps that would get them to other places not on the main tour to explore during the afternoon. They all promised to let the police and me know if they came upon Meera, but I decided they didn't need to hang around while the police searched. Inspector Winters agreed.

Tom stayed with me, and we leaned against one of the police cars and waited outside the building. I kept looking at my phone, but it was eerily quiet. No Meera, no Edwin, no Hamlet. No one. Not even Rosie called to ask how things were going.

We weren't even one hundred percent sure that Meera had gone into the old gasworks building, just that she'd disappeared and wasn't answering her phone. It was all very strange.

The longest half an hour or so later, the officers emerged, dusting themselves off. Inspector Winters shook his head as he made his way toward Tom and me.

"No sign of her, or anyone else," he said. "We managed to search pretty much the whole building, including the most dangerous areas where she might have fallen through a break in the floor. Nothing.

"We did track footprints toward one of the back doors, but it was impossible to know if they were the same prints as in the front of the building. There's a gap back there that allows wind. The dust is less pristine."

"So she might have walked through and just left?" I asked.

"It's a possibility," Inspector Winters said. "I am confident that she's not inside."

I didn't know what to think. It was only day two, the official first day of the touring, and so far the tour group had had to witness someone either leap from or be pushed off a building and one of their members disappearing! We were not headed toward five-star reviews.

"Should I report her missing?" I asked Inspector Winters. "I mean, file something official?"

"Aye. Let's do that." He reached under the overalls and into his shirt pocket to gather his ever-present notebook.

"What's her full name, lass?" he asked.

"Meera Murphy—that's all that was in the file. She's from Dublin."

"All right. Can you give me more information? Her phone number, address back home, any family you might know of?"

"I have more details back at the bookshop, but right now I can give you her phone number." I looked at my phone.

Once Inspector Winters had the number, I said, "That's all I've got on me. I looked at the files before they all got here yesterday, but I don't remember anything standing out about her. Should we head back to the shop?"

"Aye. I'll meet you there. I'm going to stop by the restaurant across the street and ask if they have any security cameras out front that might have caught Meera's movements."

"Good idea."

Inspector Winters asked one of the other officers to take us back to the bookshop. We were there in record time, the two officers sitting up front in the car and silent the whole way.

Tom and I were silent too, and he held my hand tightly.

I wanted to break down a little, maybe cry, but that was the last thing that anyone needed. I had to keep my head about me—it would be the best way to find Meera anyway.

The officers dropped us off with frowning nods.

As we stood outside of the bookshop and watched them drive away, Tom said, "She's an adult and she left on her own. She's been behaving oddly anyway. This is on her, love, not you."

I nodded as tears filled my eyes. "I know, but I still feel responsible."

"You did nothing wrong, lass. She got away because she wanted to get away. We were all there together. No one was slacking on the job, least of all you. Are you supposed to follow everyone to the loo?"

"No, I suppose not." I sniffed and wiped the tears away. "Thanks, Tom."

"My pleasure. Now, let's get in there and search her file. We'll find her, or Inspector Winters will. She's fine."

I'd never experienced Tom being angry at me. Our relationship was mellow, without drama, which was exactly the way I wanted to live my life. Tom did too. But I saw and heard his anger now. He was angry at Meera—much more so than concerned about her.

I realized I had somehow forgotten to tell the police that Gunter thought Meera might have been out all night. I'd fill Inspector Winters in when he met us at the bookshop.

Rosie and Hector were right inside. Her quick smile transformed when she noticed the expressions on our faces, as well as the fact that the tour members weren't with us.

"Oh, no, what's wrong?"

She listened with rapt attention as I gave her a rundown.

"Oh, lass, I'm so sorry," she said as she handed Hector to me. She knew I needed him more than anyone else at that moment.

As he snuggled into the crook of my arm, I said, "I need Edwin, Rosie. And I need the file on Meera. Okay?"

She bit her bottom lip and then nodded. "I'll grab the file and try to reach Edwin. This is most definitely an emergency."

"Yes, it is."

At the back table, Tom and I, with Hector in attendance, opened the file and learned about Meera Murphy from Dublin.

I'd glanced over it quickly the day before when Rosie had told me about my surprise assignment, but I hadn't really digested much about Meera, about any of them.

Now, I was reading it closely, and kicking myself for not

having done a thorough job the first time around. Some things definitely stood out this time around.

"This really doesn't sound like the Meera we got to know over the last twenty-four hours or so, does it?" I said to Tom. "First of all, this Meera sounds younger. I was under the impression that the woman we knew was in her late thirties. This says Meera is probably around thirty."

"And this person sounds shy and bookish," Tom said. "Meera might be bookish, but that's not the part of her we saw. She's secretive, but I'm not sure I would say shy."

I sat back in the chair. Sure, we hadn't known her long, but it was long enough to question some discrepancies.

I said, "She has an agenda. Something is going on with her."

Inspector Winters came into the bookshop and joined us at the table. Rosie was on the dark side, talking to Edwin, I hoped.

Without comment, Winters took the file and slid it in front of him as he sat down. His intensity was ramped up.

Tom and I shared a look but remained silent while he perused the folder.

A minute later, he sighed and sat back in the chair, falling into thought as if he might have forgotten we were there.

"Inspector Winters?" I prompted.

He blinked and then looked at us as if he was surprised we were in the room. I felt an apology rise up my throat, but then I remembered I was where I was supposed to be.

"Something's up," he said.

"Okay?"

"I stopped by the inn."

"Okay?" I said again.

"Meera Murphy never checked in. In fact, she canceled her reservation yesterday morning. She wasn't feeling well. You received no such message?"

"No, I thought . . . maybe she called Edwin . . . but who . . . what's going on?"

"I'd like to know."

We heard Rosie come through the door at the top of the stairs.

"In the back," I called.

A moment later, she came around and held her phone toward me. "It's Edwin."

I reached for the phone so quickly that I almost lost it in the handoff.

"Edwin? Are you okay?"

CHAPTER NINE

"I'm fine, lass. Fine." He sounded tired but not un-healthy.

"Can you tell me what's going on?"

The line was silent for so long I almost asked if he was still there.

"I can. But not today. Tell me about Meera Murphy."

"I was going to ask you the same. It appears that the woman who's been saying she was Meera might not be."

"That's odd."

"I'd say. We can't understand what's going on. Inspector Winters is here too. Do you care if I put you on speaker-phone while we talk about it?"

"Not a bit."

I pushed the speaker button and set the phone on the table.

"Hello, Edwin," Inspector Winters said.

"I'm here too," Tom said.

"I'm listening in," Rosie added. "There are no customers here at the moment."

Edwin said, "What is this about Meera Murphy?"

Those of us around the table shared glances, wondering who should start. I was the one to tell him what had happened since I'd met Meera, including what Gunter had said about her being out all night and her strange disappearance.

"The hotel said Meera canceled her reservation day before yesterday, Edwin," Inspector Winters said when I was finished. "Did she call you?"

"No. We only corresponded via email, but I don't have access to my email, haven't for two days. I'm sorry about that."

"Tell us what you know about her—how it came about that she was invited and if you'd have any inkling who the woman is who is claiming to be Meera," Inspector Winters said.

"Going backwards, no, I have no idea who she might be. But my correspondence with Meera was with an intelligent, creative young woman who simply loved books. I remember this part—she said she loved books more than she could express in an email, that I should want to meet her so I could see her passion in person. It was all very charming."

"In the file, you note that she has a lovely spirit," Inspector Winters said.

"Aye. That's the best I can tell you. She was lovely via her emails."

"That's not who we've been dealing with, I'm pretty sure," I said.

"Did you get a picture?" Inspector Winters asked.

"No, I never ask for pictures."

"I've requested her driver's license from Ireland, but that might take some time. The phone number Delaney gave me—I don't see it in the file."

Edwin sighed. "It would be in the emails but, again, I have no access."

"Does Rosie?" I asked.

Rosie shook her head.

"No one does. I shut everything down," Edwin said. "I can't go into detail, but . . . well, the best I can share with all of you right now is that I've been a victim of theft. I'm in London, obtaining some assistance for that. That's all I can tell you for now. I'm so sorry."

"Do you need to file a police report here in Edinburgh?" Inspector Winters asked.

"No, not now. I wish I could tell you all more, but I don't want to do anything to jeopardize what is being done to fix my predicament. You are all in my thoughts, and I would like to know if Meera is okay and who you've been dealing with, but I just can't tell you everything that's going on here. Hamlet is fine. I brought him along to assist me and help keep my mind and the facts straight."

"Do you have legal counsel?" Inspector Winters asked.

Edwin laughed once. "More than anyone should have to have."

"I'm so glad you're okay," I said after everyone was silent a long moment.

"I am right as rain, lass. Rosie told me my credit card was declined. You'll be reimbursed for all expenses, I promise."

"I wasn't worried." I hadn't even thought about it again, in fact.

"Nevertheless . . ."

"Thank you, Edwin. Be safe and let us know if we can do anything."

The call disconnected and I sighed and slumped with relief. "I know we didn't get answers about Meera, but it was good to hear Edwin's voice."

"Aye," Rosie agreed.

"Give me a second." Inspector Winters stood from the table and then left the bookshop. If I leaned to my right, I could see him outside in front of the shop's window.

I straightened again and looked at Tom. "What in the world is going on with . . . everything?"

"Great question."

"I should check in with the others." I grabbed my phone from the table and sent a group text to the three remaining members. They all responded—they were fine and planning on finding haggis for dinner in an hour or so. I sent them the address of a restaurant that was reputed to have delicious haggis and told them I'd try to join them.

Inspector Winters returned. "I've got a phone number of a Meera Murphy in Dublin—there's only one, surprisingly. The number is not the same one you have. Let's give her a ring."

A woman answered after three of the longest rings of my life. "Hello?"

"Meera Murphy?" Inspector Winters asked.

"Um, who's asking? The words 'law enforcement' came up on my screen."

"This is the Edinburgh police. I'm here with coworkers of Edwin MacAlister. You were supposed to be in Edinburgh right now for the city-literature tour?"

"Oh, yes, I was. My mother fell ill, so I've had to stay home. I canceled my hotel reservation. Did I wait too long? Do I owe a cancelation fee of any sort?"

"No, that's not it. We've had the strangest thing happen. A woman is in town proclaiming to be you."

"What? I don't understand."

"Frankly, we don't either, and we're just trying to figure it out. Do you know someone who might pretend to be you?"

"No. I can't . . . I have no idea. Should I be worried?"

"I don't know." Inspector Winters crossed his arms in front of his chest.

I would have been much less suspicious-sounding if I'd been the one to make the call, but it was his job to get the answers, even if he had to be less than conciliatory.

"What do you want me to do?" Meera asked. "Wait, is this real?"

"I assure you, it's real," Inspector Winters said. He looked at me.

I jumped into the conversation. "Meera, my name is Delaney. I work with Edwin. We're here in the bookshop."

"Oh." She paused. "He did mention you and Rosie in the email. What's the cat's name?" she asked.

I got what she was doing. "There's no cat, but there's a dog named Hector."

"Okay, well, that will do for now. What should I do?" she repeated.

"Think about it a minute. Do you know of anyone who would pretend to be you, and if so, why?" Inspector Winters said.

The line was silent for a few moments. Then she returned, "Not a soul."

"Okay, well, is there any chance you'd text me back a picture of yourself?"

"That feels very odd."

"I agree, but it really would help," Inspector Winters added.

I leaned closer to the phone on the table. "The woman who is pretending to be you has dark hair and blue eyes. Are those your features?"

"Well, my hair is dark, and my eyes are blue."

Inspector Winters said, "We are working to obtain your driver's license, but would you mind sending a quick picture, just so we all know what you look like? Although I acknowledge that sounds strange, I promise it's just so we can make sure we're doing all the right things. I can give you an email or you can send it to my mobile."

I remembered sitting around the back table yesterday after introductions, exchanging numbers. None of us had any reason to be suspicious. I jumped in. "Meera, do you know this number?" I read off the number that I'd been using, the one I got from Rosie.

"No, I don't."

I looked at Rosie, who nodded and then turned to make her way back toward her desk.

"Text us a picture then?" I said.

Meera sighed. "Sure. Give me a second. What number?"

Inspector Winters gave her his mobile.

The ping of a text came through a moment later. He slid his finger across the screen and opened it. It was a picture of a young woman with her hair pulled back. Her pale skin and blue eyes were free of makeup as she semi-frowned. Her hair was dark, but not as dark as the woman's whom we'd been calling Meera. There was a stove right behind her.

"There you go," she said.

"Same coloring, but you don't really look like the woman pretending to be you," I said. She kind of did, but not enough to mistake the two of them.

"Right," Meera said. I could hear a sense of finality in her voice. "Anything else?"

"Thank you, Meera," Inspector Winters said. "We'll stay in touch, all right?"

"Sure, but I need to go now. My mom could use my help."

Inspector Winters said, "Best to your mother and thank you again."

"Why did you need the picture?" I asked when the call ended.

"I'll compare it to the license. We still don't know for sure who's lying about what."

I didn't want to think that the sweet young woman we'd just been talking to might have been lying, because that would only add more layers of mystery to whatever was going on. "Good point."

Rosie rejoined us. She was studying a piece of paper. "I jotted these all down yesterday. Edwin did not supply me with any numbers. He left too quickly." She set it on the table.

We all looked at it. It displayed all the same numbers I'd been using, the same ones the group had given me.

"Hmm," Inspector Winters said. "Rosie, if you talk to him again, would you ask if he is able to access his email for the number Meera gave him, or if you could?"

"Aye, I can try."

By the tone of her voice, I could tell even she thought Edwin's priority wouldn't be checking his email. It sounded like he had enough on his plate, but I'd encourage her to give it a try.

"Thank you." Inspector Winters fell into thought again.

I didn't want to disturb him, but Rosie said to him, "What is it?"

"Well, obviously someone is lying. I just have to figure out who."

"Do you think that answer could solve what happened to Geoff too?" Tom asked.

Inspector Winters sighed. "I can only hope."

Inspector Winters left the bookshop with the promise that he'd be back in touch and that, of course, we were to call him if anything else noteworthy happened.

"Rosie," I said when he was gone, "are you okay?"

"Och, I'm fine, lass. I just want Edwin to come home and to be done with all of this nonsense."

"Care to share more of what's going on with him?"

"I would love to, but I dinnae think he'd be pleased." She paused. "I wonder about your mystery woman, though, and if there might be a tie to Edwin's issues, though I cannae imagine how. What has this woman been up to? Maybe she realized that what she was doing was wrong, so she found a way to leave the group. But why join in in the first place, and why then disappear? I cannae understand why she would have bothered impersonating Meera, or how she ever even heard about her. Technically, though, has she done anything illegal?"

"Good questions," Tom said.

"See if he can check his email, get a phone number to Inspector Winters?" I added.

"Aye."

I was sure the police were pondering the same things, but I realized that if I wanted any answers to Rosie's good questions, I had three people who might be able to give me some clues. Maybe they even knew about the woman pretending to be Meera.

"You two want to join along with the group for dinner? They're having haggis, but I know the restaurant serves other things."

"Sounds good to me," Tom said.

"You two go on without me. I'll close up the store in a wee bit, and Hector and I will head home." Rosie looked at me.

"Will you tour tomorrow?"

I shrugged. "I don't know. I feel like we've been scammed, but no one in the group has been hurt. I'll see what everyone else has to say."

"Aye. Nevertheless, be careful, lass." Rosie looked at Tom. "Make sure she's careful."

"Always."

Tom and I bid Rosie and Hector good night and made our way to the restaurant with the others. They'd all ordered haggis. Even Tom ended up ordering it, which, since I disliked it so much, might have been our first marital betrayal, I decided.

I ordered my favorite, fish and chips, and wasn't disappointed in the least.

CHAPTER TEN

The mood was even more jovial than it had been at lunch. The remaining three tour group members seemed to like each other very much and got along like they were old friends. Again, I was impressed by Edwin's skills at putting together a convivial party. When I told them what more we'd learned about Meera—and the real Meera—they seemed to lighten up even more, convinced that the woman they'd met wasn't someone they wanted to know anyway. Or else they were just working hard to move past all of it.

The lunchtime sampling of liquor had been more regulated than the whisky shots that everyone but Tom and I were now indulging in, though it wasn't too out of hand so far.

"I can't believe she did that," Luka said, circling the conversation back around. "That person pretended to be Meera. Why?"

"I wonder—everyone wonders—the same thing," I said.

"She didn't hurt anyone, I suppose," Kevin added.

"No, but, well, do you all remember when you came down to the bookshop yesterday?" I asked. "Our first meeting?"

They all nodded.

"Can anyone remember how alleged Meera became a part of the group?"

"I was the first one in the lobby," Luka said. "I was just going to head to the bookshop when I overheard Kevin—though I didn't know her name at the time—asking the front desk people for directions to the bookshop, so I waited until she turned around—"

"Yes, and we introduced ourselves to each other and decided to walk down together," Kevin continued.

"When I came out to the lobby, I think the three of us just came upon each other," Gunter said. "It seemed natural."

"Okay, what about the woman who said she was Meera?" I asked.

They all fell into thought.

"I'm pretty sure she came into the lobby right after Gunter," Kevin said. "She said she was part of the group. . . . No, that doesn't feel right."

"No," Luka said. He looked at Gunter. "You had everyone's names, right?"

"I did. I asked for first names in case I needed to work on pronouncing any of them. Edwin had emailed them to me."

"He didn't do that with me, but now I remember," Kevin jumped in again. "You asked where Meera was, and then she somehow appeared from behind us or something."

"It was seamless, whatever it was," Luka said. "Nothing was strange. We made a group and went together. We were all excited."

"Do any of you remember what Meera said on the way to the bookshop?" I asked.

Again, they all fell into thought. Gunter spoke first. "I don't think she said anything."

"That seems right," Luka said. "I don't remember her saying anything either. I just remember she seemed friendly." He shrugged. "Everyone seemed happy and friendly."

"Yes," Kevin said. "I wish I could tell you something suspicious about her, other than her disappearance today, but I have nothing. I thought she was quiet, and her not going with us to the bar last night was odd, but I didn't find it suspicious."

"Gunter and I saw her coming into the hotel this morning, but I bet we assumed the same thing, that she'd been out all night, not that she wasn't staying there at all," Luka said.

"That's what I thought," Gunter agreed. "I even told Delaney about it."

It was my turn to think.

"Delaney, what is it?" Luka asked a moment later.

"I don't know. I guess I feel like I should have picked up on something sooner." I sighed.

"I don't know how," Kevin said. "We all only just met."

I nodded and sat up straighter. "Okay, are we continuing the tour tomorrow?"

"I would like to," Kevin said.

"Are *you* sure?" Gunter asked me.

"I am. Alleged Meera is on the run, but you're all fine, and you're here."

"Will we do the things we missed this afternoon?" Kevin asked.

I shook my head. "No, we have to move along to what's already scheduled. I'll try to fit everything in, though."

"Let's do it!" Luka said.

Gunter gave a thumbs-up.

"Okay then. Let's meet at ten again, in front of the bookshop?"

Though the mood was still positive, the information I'd shared about the woman who'd claimed to be Meera *had* turned everyone a bit quieter and more circumspect, with the laughs and smiles a little forced, though everyone seemed very excited about continuing the tour.

As we ate dessert, Tom and I tried to steer the conversation away from Meera, asking more about the three others. Kevin's bookshop was running fine with her daughter, but she was always anxious to get back; Gunter still really wanted to meet Edwin and discussed extending his trip a few days with the hope of connecting with his longtime pen pal; Luka was thrilled to be in Edinburgh and had already made plans with Kevin to visit her bookshop in London. He'd decided to add some days to his vacation and travel more in the UK.

After dinner Tom and I walked the three of them back to the inn. No one was at the front desk as we stepped inside, and there was no police presence anywhere. I was sure they were investigating, but they'd let the inn continue to stay open for business . . . which was maybe a good sign? I wasn't sure. I appreciated that they didn't want the inn to suffer financially, but also hoped they were being thorough.

We all bid each other good night and reinforced the plans to meet in the morning. Once Tom and I were alone in the lobby, we sent each other matching raised eyebrows.

"They're fine, lass," he said.

"I know. It's just all . . ." I shook my head. "Need to stop by the pub?"

"No. It looks like Rodger got it all buttoned up nicely." He'd glanced over there as we'd walked by.

"Home?"

"Home."

It wasn't until later that night, in the middle of bothersome dreams, that something occurred to me.

It was true that no one in the group had been harmed, but someone had, in fact, been hurt—one person was dead.

I looked at my sleeping husband. It was far too late to venture out and back down to Grassmarket, but it suddenly seemed more important than ever to try to understand what had happened to cause a man to go off the roof and a young woman to be hurt so badly that she was in the hospital in a medically induced coma. Sure, the police were investigating, but were we all missing something that the rest of us should have picked up on? We'd been right there, after all.

I had more questions, and they centered on the fact that alleged Meera had, for a reason none of us could even guess, slid her way into the tour group. How did that tie into the tragedies? Surely there was some connection. I just had to figure out what it was.

I couldn't wait until the morning.

CHAPTER ELEVEN

"You're up early," Tom said as he joined me in the kitchen.

"You have no idea. I've been awake for hours."

"Aye. I'm not surprised. Your brain going a mile a minute?" He paused. "Lass, are you scared?"

I shook my head. "Not even a little bit, but maybe I should be. I don't know. Here, come, have coffee." I grabbed the carafe and poured him a mug.

Over eggs, toast, and plenty of coffee, I told him about my restless night and how I was wondering if alleged Meera had anything to do with what had happened at the inn.

"Did you leave a message for Inspector Winters?" he asked.

"Not yet. I . . . I'd like to go talk to someone at the inn first. If I talk to the police first, they might tell me they've got it handled and I should leave it alone."

Tom smiled. "Aye, and that might be true."

"Yes, and I don't want to hear that right now. I've been awake for hours telling my curiosity to calm down, but it just hasn't. Want to come with me? Rodger still okay?"

"I do want to come with you. I'm sure Rodger is fine, but we'll stop by and see him since we'll be right there."

"I like this plan."

We finished breakfast and then made our way to the inn in the pouring rain. The weather was going to put a damper on today's tour, but I'd find a way to make it work. I was glad to have the option to ride with Tom. I was becoming used to not taking the bus if his schedule worked with mine.

It was only 8 a.m., but I thought that was a respectable enough hour to talk to someone at the inn. It was at least a better hour than when I'd first awakened. Thankfully, Tom had umbrellas in his car, and we passed by the pub, glancing in to see that Rodger wasn't in yet—he would probably be there by the time we were done at the inn. We made it inside the lobby still relatively dry or at least not soaked.

I didn't recognize the woman at the front desk. Of course, I'd considered that the whole staff could be new—though how they might have managed to hire people so quickly was a mystery.

"Hi," I said as we approached the front desk.

The woman, maybe in her forties, sent us a quick smile, but it was impossible to miss the dark circles under her eyes. "Reservation?"

"No, I'm Delaney Nichols; I'm with the tour group staying here. I . . . well, I want to make sure that everything is going okay, and I have a couple of questions."

"The tour group?"

"Yes, the literary tour? Edwin MacAlister from The Cracked Spine set it up."

"Oh! Yes, of course. I believe everything is fine. Shall I check and see how much the incidentals are adding up to?"

"No, that's okay. Whatever it turns out to be will be fine. My other questions are about the inn's staff."

"Oh?"

"How's Carmel?"

"Aye." The woman nodded. "She's still the same. At least that's what I heard this morning."

"Still in a coma?"

"As far as I know." She bit her lip as her expression turned less friendly and more suspicious.

"Are there any answers regarding what might have happened?"

"To her?" She crossed her arms in front of herself.

"And Geoff."

"You mean, did Geoff jump or was he pushed?"

"Well, kind of. Yes."

"As far as I know, no one has any answers yet." She turned her attention back to the computer screen in front of her.

I sighed and looked at Tom, who nodded me on. "I'm sorry, I know I'm . . . May I ask your name?"

"Sherrie." It was on the name tag pinned on her shirt or she might have ignored the question.

"Sherrie, I'm sorry to bother you, but it turns out that one of the members of my tour group wasn't who she said she was. She said she belonged to the group, pretended to be someone that she wasn't. She's disappeared now, but I'm concerned about what might have happened, and what possible danger the other tour members might be in. I worry she might be connected to these other events."

Sherrie's eyebrows came together. "Danger?"

I nodded. "I saw someone dressed all in black running

from the building the night Geoff died and Carmel was hurt. I'm just trying to make sure everyone else is safe. None of them wants to move to another hotel."

The way Sherrie scratched at her neck as she fell into thought—instead of telling us to just leave—made me think there might be something she'd like to share.

She sighed. "I've told the police what I know, but I had nothing to tell them about someone impersonating a tour group member or someone in black running away from the building—I don't know anything about either of those things. In fact, if I'd known about the person running away and thought they might have hurt Carmel, I might not have agreed to stay on. I used to only work a couple nights a week. They're giving me lots of hours, and it's exhausting."

"What did you think happened to Carmel?"

"I guess I just thought she fell and hit her head. No one told me more than that, and that she was in the hospital with a head injury. The earlier news just said she was hurt. I thought Geoff jumped and . . . well, I just didn't know him well, but . . . of course that was shocking, but it somehow didn't seem too surprising, you know what I mean?"

I shook my head. "Not really."

"I'd heard he was in trouble around here, though I don't know what for. Honestly, I just try to mind my own."

"You don't know why he was in trouble?"

She shook her head and pursed her lips as if she was done speaking.

I nodded. "The man running away might not have had anything to with Carmel's injury. Was something going on here that could be a possible reason for all the tragedy?"

Her mouth relaxed. "Like I said, I work—well, worked—a couple of nights a week only, just so they have someone here. I barely even knew Geoff." She rubbed her finger under her nose. "But . . ."

"What?" I pushed.

She shook her head again, but didn't stop talking. "It's probably nothing, but I always thought it was strange, you know."

"Okay."

"I'm not sure. Well . . . a few months ago, Geoff started not allowing us to let customers stay in one of the rooms. We're not huge, and there are many times we need all the rooms. At first we just went along with it, but then he told us to lie about it if we were asked by the corporate owners. No one from corporate ever asked me because I'm only here part-time, but I did tell everyone I wouldn't lie."

"What did Geoff tell you to say?"

"That we just didn't have the customers to fill the hotel, which was simple bunk. Of course, we're not always full, but we're in Grassmarket. We are in high demand, and we are full much of the time.

"Anyway, the losses started piling up. Last week, I was told to forget it, to go ahead and rent out the room." She paused and bit her lip as she looked at me. She continued, "He was apologetic, but he was also a mess. Emotional, anxious."

"Did you tell this to the police?"

She frowned. "I didn't. I guess I didn't think it through all the way. I mean, I knew he was upset, but until you just asked me about it, I hadn't given it much thought. I . . . I just didn't know him that well. I still don't know if that has anything to do with anything. I . . . You think I should tell them?"

Tom and I answered at the same time. "Absolutely."

"I didn't know about . . . everything you've told me, or I would have. Probably. A man in black? Carmel assaulted? Goodness."

"Now you do," Tom said.

She looked at him. "Right."

"What was going on in the room?" I asked, almost not wanting to hear the answer.

I'd heard the stories about hotels and motels being used for human trafficking, and I feared the worst. Was this all adding up to something as awful as that?

"I couldn't tell you, but I do know that Geoff's wife was involved."

"Oh," I said.

"What?" Tom asked. "How?"

"I don't know. I was just told that if Tillie came in, she could go into that room."

"Did she ever have people with her?" I asked.

"I never saw her once. I was grateful that whatever was going on seemed to be happening more in the daytime." Sherrie sighed. "I've enjoyed my night shift here. Sure, there's a blathered guest or two, but it's not been bad. Most of the time it's quiet, and I'm allowed to let my eyes shut if I feel the need. It's been a lovely job, until they added more hours. I hope I can go back to how it was before."

"You should definitely tell the police," I said.

She frowned at me. She'd wanted her life to go back to the way it was, not be further changed by a visiting bookseller and pub owner. "Okay, I will."

"Sherrie, what does Geoff's wife look like?" Tom asked.

"I'm not sure I've . . . Oh, aye, I remember her now. Pretty. Blue eyes, dark hair. Irish, through and through."

"Oh no," Tom and I said together.

I'd taken a picture of the tour group outside the bookshop that first day. I grabbed my phone and scrolled to it. Alleged Meera was there, though she was hiding half of herself behind Gunter. I held up the phone toward Sherrie. "This her?"

Sherrie squinted and then put on the glasses that were hanging on a chain around her neck. "Aye, that's Tillie. Who's . . . Is that your group?"

I nodded.

"Well, those people haven't caused me any problems whatsoever," she said, as if that made everything better.

My heart sank. We had some answers, but they created even more questions.

"Excuse us," I said to Sherrie. "Tom and I are going to give the police a call. I'll send them over to talk to you, too."

"Of course." She frowned even more deeply. "Of course."

She turned and headed back toward the office in which I'd overheard Carmel and Geoff talking. I hoped there wasn't a back door she might try and escape through, but I was too focused on calling Inspector Winters to worry about it.

Tom and I stepped outside and stood under the hotel's front awning as the rain fell. Inspector Winters answered on the first ring.

"I know who our Meera is," I said.

"Who?"

I told him as much as I could get out in one breath. He said he'd look into my suspicions and then call me later. He was appreciative of the information, even sounding pleasantly surprised by the revelations.

I always tried to stay out of the way, and I always tried to help. Maybe this time I'd actually managed to do both.

CHAPTER TWELVE

"What?" Rodger said. He held a bottle of gin in one hand and a bottle of whisky in the other.

"Our Meera was actually Tillie," I said.

He set the bottles on the bar. "I would bet that's why she didn't come into the pub, took off to a shop on the Royal Mile two nights ago." He paused. "She probably saw me in here, and she knows I know her." He looked at Tom. "You didn't recognize her?"

"I didn't know her," Tom said. "I never met her. She seemed timid when Delaney introduced us. Looking back, I wonder if she thought I might recognize her and mess up her plans, whatever they might have been. I didn't know her at all."

"How did you know her?" I asked Rodger.

"I just did. We weren't close, but I met her through Geoff, saw her around Grassmarket." He frowned. "Maybe saw her a couple times when Carmel and I were dating. I don't know exactly."

"How long ago did you and Carmel date?" I asked.

"Six months or so."

"Something weird is going on over there, Rodger." I nodded the direction of the inn. "Any chance Carmel said something about . . . anything?"

Rodger thought a moment. "Back then, she mentioned that she used to like working there, but things hadn't been as much fun as of late. She didn't want to leave or anything, though."

I jumped in, "I overheard her telling one of the other employees that she wasn't going to do something they'd asked her to do. Gunter heard the same thing, too, when she was in his room, changing the bedding. Does that ring any bells for you?"

"I don't know. Maybe." Rodger rearranged a towel on the bar in front of him. He looked up at us. "She might have said something once about not being paid enough to do what they wanted her to do. But I didn't ask her what that was. I just moved on to something else, I'm sure." He sighed. "We didn't know each other well enough for me to want that sort of information. She seemed to get familiar much more quickly than I would have liked, but I don't think that had anything to do with the inn."

"What about noticing anything over there?"

"I never noticed anything suspicious," Rodger said.

I thought about what Rodger had said about Meera's not going into the pub the night everything had happened, when she allegedly chose to head up to the Royal Mile instead of going with everyone. If she'd never met Tom, she wouldn't have been concerned about him remembering her, but of course she'd been worried that Rodger would have. I seemed to have a vague recollection of her craning her neck to peer inside before letting me know she wasn't coming with us. I couldn't be sure, but maybe that had really happened.

Rodger nodded. "If she was pretending to be someone else, it would be risky to do that in front of her neighboring business, in front of me."

"Maybe she ran off to push Geoff off the roof," Tom added.

"I think that's becoming a more distinct possibility," I said. "But the timing. I don't know. It was almost too fast for her to make it up to the roof."

"Brutal." Rodger reached for another liquor bottle to place on the shelf behind him. "I didn't know any of them well enough to have any indication, but if Tillie killed her own husband . . . Brutal."

"Why . . . Oh, so many 'why's" I said.

"Does anyone know how Carmel is doing?" Rodger asked.

"The same, according to the woman we talked to. Sherrie."

"I don't know anyone named Sherrie over there. I do hope Carmel recovers. I would never wish anything bad for her."

"Same." I scooted up to a stool. "Do you know where any of them live? I mean, Geoff and Tillie and Carmel?"

"Just Carmel," Rodger said. "Hang on. Right, well, not completely. I walked her home, just up the road, a flat above Greyfriars Bobby. I remember Geoff telling me once where he lived, I can't . . ."

"The flats over on Heyward!" Tom said. "I remember him mentioning that too now."

"That sounds about right."

"Wait," I said. "Back up. The flats above Greyfriars Bobby?"

"Aye. When I walked her home, she went through a red door at the side of the pub. She said her flat was right up there. I didn't go up with her."

"Good to know."

Tom looked at me. "Didn't the police talk to Tillie the night of Geoff's death?"

I nodded. "Yes. Inspector Winters told me that he was the one who spoke to her. Even if she did push Geoff off the roof, she must have gone home afterwards, not up to the Royal Mile at all."

"She reappeared the next morning, not seeming upset," Tom added.

"A cool cucumber."

"I'd say," Rodger added.

"Maybe she was trying to set up an alibi," I said. "The timing is off just enough for it not to work, though."

"Who knows?" Rodger said.

I nodded. "This might sound out there, Rodger, but the way Sherrie next door was talking, the idea of human trafficking came to me. Have you seen anything that might make you think that might be happening?"

"I haven't. I'm imagining what that would look like, and I would probably notice people being moved in and out if I was paying attention. My God, that sounds awful."

"It does," Tom added. "I haven't noticed anything either."

My phone buzzed. It was a text from Gunter.

"Kevin is not well. Can you meet us in the lobby?" I read aloud. I flew off the stool and headed toward the door.

"You good, Rodger?" Tom asked.

"Of course, fine. Go."

Tom followed me though the now lightly falling rain to the inn. We went through the front doors just as Gunter and Kevin were entering the lobby.

Kevin was upright but holding on tight to Gunter's arm. Her face was ashen, her mouth pulled down at the corners.

I ran to them. "What's going on?"

"You got here fast," Gunter said.

I nodded. "Kevin?"

"I really don't think it's anything, dear. My stomach was upset, and a headache came upon me quickly. I felt like I just wanted some fresh air. Let's step outside."

"It's raining," I said.

"I don't care. I need some air, and I'm used to the rain."

Tom opened an umbrella over Kevin as we stepped outside. He sent Gunter into the pub to grab a stool. Seconds later Kevin was sitting on the stool and breathing deeply. I could see the color in her face normalize.

"Oh, that's much better," she said. "Yes, much."

Rodger, now wearing his apron, joined us too, bringing Kevin a glass of water. "Didn't think something stronger was needed this early, but I could be convinced otherwise."

Kevin took the water and sipped. "No, this is perfect. Thank you. I'm feeling much better."

"Do you want to see a doctor?" I asked.

She thought a moment. "No, this . . . happens sometimes. I'm old, but I'm in grand shape. Sometimes I just need some fresh air." She smiled in a way that I could only have described as "perfectly British," then turned to Gunter. "Thank you for coming to my rescue so quickly." She faced the rest of us. "Same to all of you."

"You're welcome." Tom smiled as Rodger nodded and then went back inside.

"Are we still touring today?" Kevin asked me. "I would be terribly disappointed if we don't."

"Kevin, are you sure?" I asked.

"Please, yes."

It seemed the signs telling us this tour should not go on were only multiplying. I didn't like that the group was still staying at the inn. I wished I'd insisted they move last evening. By now, they'd be settled in a new place, one that hopefully hadn't recently seen someone propelled off the roof. However, I knew what Edwin would do in this situation.

"It's up to you three. You decide," I said.

"I want to continue. I feel better, truly," Kevin said.

I looked at Gunter, who appeared to be working hard not to look at Kevin with too much concern or questioning in his eyes.

Finally, he nodded. "If Kevin's good to go, I am too."

I glanced at the time: about fifteen minutes until ten. I texted Luka, who was still game and who joined us in the lobby a few minutes later. From behind the counter, Sherrie watched us briefly before she disappeared into the office again.

We all gathered around. I grabbed umbrellas from the pub and then passed them out to everyone and summoned my good cheer again. If we were going to do this, I was going to at least be in a good mood about it. It's what Edwin would have done. "Are you all ready to go to Hogwarts?"

They were definitely ready.

Our first stop was close by—Victoria Street, in between the inn and the pub. It possessed a new and real sense of danger since Geoff's horrible demise, but it was still a sight to behold.

"It's said—and we have to remember that not all of this is truly substantiated, though if you use your imagination it seems pretty valid—it is said that this street and these charming shops along a cobblestone-paved road on the way up to the Royal Mile were the inspiration for Diagon Alley."

I reached into my bag and pulled out a handful of wands. I handed each person, including Tom, their very own. Even grown-ups who'd been thrust into less-than-desirable situations of late couldn't resist the implied magic that came with a wand. They all smiled.

"Can you see the shops? I bet Ollivander's would be right there." I pointed with my wand. "Maybe Weasleys' Wizard Wheezes there, and then the bookshop, Flourish and Blotts, right there."

I didn't know how Edwin would do this. Rosie told me he always handed out wands, but I suspected he managed this part with more flair, even while using fewer specifics. His accent, his ability to dramatize even the simplest things—his eyes, even. You could see that he was seeing what he was narrating. If anyone's imagination might run more amok than mine, it was his.

The props lent nicely to the whole idea, and though we were all adults standing there with wands, nothing about the scenario felt weird in any way. In fact, passersby did nothing more than smile and nod our direction as they continued on.

"I've seen the movies," Luka added. "I will read the books now too. But do you all think the castle on the hill was the inspiration for Hogwarts?"

I waited as they discussed that idea for a moment.

"Actually," I finally said, "there's another building that's rumored to have been an inspiration for Hogwarts, and it's the reason Edwin likes to schedule the tours this time of year. We get to go inside. It's a real school, and they aren't in session right now."

"We do?" Kevin said.

"Yes, we do. Bring your wands and come along."

Honestly, when I first heard about the wands, the word that came to mind was "hokey," but Edwin had once told me that every single person he'd given one to said they loved them and would keep them forever. I got the same impression from these three.

It was about half a mile's walk to our next destination, and again I made sure Kevin felt like she was up for it. In fact, she seemed a new person. The rain had stopped, the umbrellas were all closed, and she had a pep in her step. I hoped our good fortune would continue.

We moved down the market and past the bookshop, waving at Rosie as we went by. She was playing along and was dressed as Professor McGonagall. Even Hector wore a tiny wizard cap that everyone thought was adorable.

"I do love that Maggie Smith," Gunter reiterated.

Again, everyone laughed.

We made our way up Vennel, climbing a bunch of stairs that didn't seem to be too difficult for anyone, Kevin included. We stopped at the top, at the Vennel Viewpoint, and took in the sight of the castle on the hill from that vantage point.

The view of the castle from the bookshop, from the whole of Grassmarket, was good, but this one gave us an even wider look.

"Did anyone tour it yesterday afternoon?" I asked.

"We all did," Luka said. "We had a great time."

"I'm glad to hear that."

"That castle has been here forever," Kevin said. "It's so hard to believe how much time and how many people it has seen."

"Maybe not forever," Gunter said. "The eleventh century."

"Almost forever." Kevin smiled.

"Good point," Gunter agreed.

We continued and turned onto Lauriston Place. Soon we were at a grand entrance to vast grounds and an impressive building.

"This is right in the middle of the city!" Kevin exclaimed. "I had no idea. I would have expected something out in the country."

"Even the entrance is incredible." Luka looked over the gates, solid and ornate.

I said, "Yes, the school is an amazing example of Scots Renaissance architecture, displaying lots of stone carving from the early seventeenth century, much of it done by"—I paused for a tiny bit of dramatic effect—"William Wallace, who was the King's master mason, until he died and another mason took over."

"Braveheart William Wallace?" Luka asked.

"Yes, and though the movie probably didn't get the facts exactly right, the spirit of his bravery was portrayed accurately, I think," I said.

"William Wallace was a mason?" Gunter asked.

"Yes. A fierce warrior too, but also a mason. The lineage of the school dates back to its foundation in 1628. It was named for George Heriot, famed jeweler to James the Sixth and Queen Anne, because of a very generous donation.

"The school was originally entered through Grassmarket, but as you all have now seen, that street where the entrance once was proved to be a good spot for other shops and buildings."

The stone and ironwork gate we stood next to were in themselves impressive enough, imitating a portcullis as well as small towers on each side. Above the gates was what looked like a coat of arms, but it was actually a face.

"Look up. Who does that look like to you?" I asked.

"Dumbledore!" Kevin exclaimed.

It did and it didn't. It was the face of a bearded man, but in Edwin's notes he mentioned that by now the power of suggestion would have taken over and everyone would be sure that Dumbledore was watching all those who entered. I smiled and silently told him he was right again.

The school was a turreted structure surrounding a large quadrangle. It was built with sandstone, and was so large and impressive that it *was* difficult to believe it was truly right in the middle of town. It reminded me of a cross between a castle and the estate in *Downton Abbey*.

"Ready to head inside?" I asked.

Everyone nodded.

We traveled down the walkway over the expansive grounds, mostly made up of well-manicured and very green grass. Clouds still filled the sky, lending a perfectly ominous sensation to the journey.

I knocked on the front door, surrounded by more carved stone. Moments later, it opened wide. A man glanced over us, his smile falling into a frown. "Edwin here?" he asked.

He was a very tall man dressed in regular street clothes. His appearance verged on unkempt, his clothes slightly wrinkled, his hair a bit long and unbrushed. He didn't appear to be old, but his hangdog brown eyes and the jowls that went with them made his age impossible for me to distinguish.

Edwin had mentioned that O'Shea—the only name Edwin had ever called him—though not willing to don a costume, had been wonderful over the last few years in making sure the tour groups got to see whatever it was they wanted to see. Edwin had never explained what O'Shea did at the school, but I had been under the impression that he was a security guard. Now, I no longer thought that was the case, but it didn't feel appropriate to ask for his job title.

"I'm afraid he's been called away," I said. "I'm Delaney. You're O'Shea?"

"I am. Where'd Edwin get called away to?" He was obviously disappointed and somewhat suspicious.

I smiled as best I could. I probably should have called beforehand, but that hadn't even crossed my mind. "It's a long story, but I work with him, and we're still here for the tour. That okay?"

He had to think about it a few moments. His eyebrows came together tightly. "Where's the other one?"

"The other tour member?" I asked.

"Aye, there're always four. If you're here for Edwin"—he looked at Tom—"and I recognize you from the wee pub, where's the other one?"

Tom nodded and smiled. "Good to see you again."

If O'Shea's words hadn't sounded so accusatory, Tom probably would have stepped forward and shaken the man's hand, but it was clear that the man in the doorway wasn't interested in that sort of greeting.

I could have said that the missing tour member was also a long story, but instead I went with "There's just three this year." No one contradicted me. In fact, they all nodded along.

O'Shea's features became friendly a moment later, and he stepped back from the doorway to let us inside. "Apologies. I just wanted to make sure. I think I'm just rattled not to see Edwin and disappointed not to get to say hello to him. Come in. Please."

There was much history to the building—details about who built which wings and when they were completed—but that wasn't what this tour was about. Instead, with O'Shea's nod of approval, I led the group directly to the places I thought might continue to spark their imaginations: a council hall and the dining hall. O'Shea stuck close to the group. I felt under extra scrutiny, as if he was judging how I did things against how Edwin had done them. His expression of bothered dismay only confirmed for me that I would never be as compelling as my boss.

The inside of the building and its wings and hallways did not contain moving staircases or animated portraits, though it wasn't any less interesting because of that.

You could sense a story inside the school. Even if it wasn't one of witches and wizards, its mere existence for so many centuries seemed magic enough.

As large as the building was, the tour inside it was limited to the two rooms Edwin had thought were the most interesting. They both seemed the perfect spots for wizards, witches, and their professors. We ventured inside them and soaked in the sense of ceremonial education that seemed to seep from the checkerboard tile floors and the ornately carved wood doorways, the tall paned windows. O'Shea tagged along the whole way and then seemed to sweep us somewhat hurriedly back toward the front door, when I'd been hoping for a more leisurely stroll so the others could take a look at anything thing else that might have interested them. It wasn't to be. O'Shea hadn't been unpleasant, but I thought he wanted us gone. Maybe he wanted to find a phone and try to reach Edwin.

I ended up being the last one out.

"Pleasure having you," O'Shea said, his hand pushing the door as he spoke.

"Uh, thank you," I said to the closed door. I turned to the others. "Okay, well, there's more to see, and we're not far from it."

Noises and rumbles of excitement spread through the group.

I stepped down the stairs, happy to see it wasn't still raining. "This way." I signaled that we'd be heading off the grounds a different route than we'd entered, through a side gate.

"Do you know him? O'Shea?" I asked Tom as he sidled up next to me and the others followed behind, the three of them having their own conversations about the stories we'd been discussing.

"I don't, but he's been in the pub a time or two. He makes quite an impression with his height. He's not talkative. I've never seen him be anything but quiet, keeping to himself."

"He's likely trying to call Edwin right now."

"Probably won't reach him."

I nodded.

"It's going well, lass. You've no worries."

"Thank you." I smiled and nudged his shoulder lightly with mine. Then I turned and walked backward again. I was about to speak when I noticed O'Shea making his way toward us, a jog to his quick steps.

"Delaney!" he exclaimed as he waved what looked like an envelope in the air.

I made my way through the group and met him.

"Aye, ta, lass," he said, seeming much more cordial than he had inside the school. "Give this to Edwin, please." He handed me a card, the envelope sealed and Edwin's name written on the outside.

"I'd be happy to. Thank you for letting us tour today."

"You're welcome. Best to Edwin." He turned and in only a slightly slower pace made his way back to the school.

I tucked the card into my bag and then turned to the group.

"So, remember yesterday when we first stopped by the statue of Greyfriars Bobby?" They all nodded. "Today, we're actually going into the cemetery where Bobby's master is buried. We'll stop by Auld Jock's memorial, but there's something more pertinent to today's theme to see."

"A cemetery in Scotland. How fabulous!" Kevin said.

"Lead the way," Luka joined in.

We wended our way off the school grounds, over a walkway, and onto the Greyfriars Kirkyard cemetery.

I gave everyone a chance to slow down and move at their own pace. They all seemed to love cemeteries and reading the stones as much as I did, so it wasn't a hurried journey. I liked the pace much more than the one we'd taken inside the school.

I stopped next to the first stone I wanted them to pay attention to. "Once again, there's no proof that this was the inspiration, but it's difficult to believe it wasn't, considering so many other things about where and when the books were written. Take a look."

Carved onto the slab that was a part of a full stone wall were the words:

To the memory of Thomas Riddell, Esq. of Befsborough. In the county of Berwick who died in Edinburgh on the 24 Novm, 1806. Aged 72 years. Also of Thomas Riddell, Esq. his Son Captain of the 14 Regiment, who died at Trinidad in the West Indies on the 26 Septm.1802, aged 26 years.

"Thomas Riddell! Tom Marvolo Riddle," Kevin exclaimed. "The spelling isn't the same, but this must be where the name came from. It just must be."

I knew people liked to believe it was. "I think so too."

"Wait, who is this?" Luka asked.

The others looked at him as if he'd grown horns.

"You don't know?" Gunter asked. "Even I know."

"The actual name of He Who Must Not Be Named." Kevin smiled. She looked at me.

I nodded.

"Wait. Oh! Voldemort?" Luka asked. "I don't remember that part specifically in the movies. I guess I'll have to read the books."

"This is fun, Delaney," Gunter said.

"Edwin puts together good tours."

From behind the group, Tom smiled at me and sent a quick thumbs-up. I sent him a quick nod of thanks.

"All right, off to see Auld Jock's and Bobby's graves?" I asked.

They were all eager to see both graves. We made our way toward two more stones. They weren't quite as magical as Thomas Riddell and his son's, but having learned the story the day before, the tour members enjoyed reading one more time about Auld Jock, whose name was actually John Gray. His simple stone said: "Master of Greyfriars Bobby." And then there was Bobby's, which said, "Let His Loyalty and Devotion Be a Lesson for Us All."

Kevin, Luka, and Gunter all had to dab at their eyes a little bit as we stood near the dog's stone. The emotion of the story, the devotion, the fact that they were still spoken about and revered even after all these years was so much more than a gimmick. This was part of the history that made Edinburgh the place it was.

It was my experience that Scotland simply did not disappoint, and I was witnessing this once again. I loved my new country, and I was glad it was my home.

We all spent a few more minutes in the cemetery, reading the stones and talking about the sadness that mixed with beauty in graveyards. The history. I think we all felt it that day.

"Lunchtime?" I asked when it seemed everyone had had their fill.

They all agreed.

CHAPTER THIRTEEN

We walked through Grassmarket, up Victoria, and to the Royal Mile again. We passed by St. Giles one more time too. Edwin had noted that he choreographed the tours to have a little overlap because not only did people like to learn new things, they also liked to recognize things they knew.

As we passed by the cathedral, I had to once again give him credit.

"The Luckenbooths!" Luka pointed.

"I can still see them," Gunter said.

Kevin and Luka nodded in agreement.

Tom was with me behind the group as we made our way up the now familiar road.

"Relaxing some?" he asked.

"I am." I paused and looked at him, gauging how he might feel about my next thoughts. Tom was the best of sports, but he was also the one to temper my overenthusiasm sometimes too. Nevertheless, I continued, "It seems that Geoff is more on my mind today, though, as if my psyche is finally processing that someone did, indeed, die."

"You haven't behaved as if you're distracted."

"Oh, I'm distracted. The afternoon is a scheduled free time for the group, and I was hoping you and I would venture over to Geoff and Tillie's flat."

Tom hesitated but spoke up soon enough. "Do you think she'll be there?"

"I keep vacillating on that. It would be crazy for her to stick around after she pretended to be someone else, but she's also weirdly bold, and now the police know she was impersonating Meera. She might have been told to stay put. I need to try to talk to her. I need to try to understand what she was up to. I can't help myself."

"I'd love to go with you."

"Deal." I squeezed his hand and then moved toward the head of the group again. "Here's where we're lunching. Deacon Brodie's Tavern. Sound familiar?"

"Well, there's a sign right here that tells us all about Deacon Brodie." Luka pointed, maybe trying not to sound sarcastic, but not pulling it off completely.

"Good catch," I said, playing along. "What's it say? Or just the gist of it if you want."

"All right." Luka cleared his throat. "William Brodie Deacon of Wrights and Masons of Edinburgh was the son of a cabinet maker in the lawnmarket. He was born in Brodies Close and hanged near St. Giles, both places being only steps from the tavern that now bears his name. Brodie's business inspired Robert Louis Stevenson to write that famous classic— *Dr. Jekyll and Mr. Hyde*. By day William Brodie was pious, wealthy, and a much respected citizen and in 1781 was elected Deacon Councillor of the city. But at night he was a gambler, a thief, dissipated and licentious. The annals record his cursing and audacity were unsurpassed.

"Brodie was hanged from the city's new gallows on October 1st, 1788. Ironically, he had designed the gallows that were to eventually seal his fate."

"Fabulous!" Kevin said. "Jekyll and Hyde. I love it."

I'd had my own experiences with the famous story, but I didn't share those details now. Instead, I said, "Well, some do say there were other inspirations for the story, but this one feels pretty solid."

"That's why you brought us here?" Kevin asked. "Jekyll and Hyde?"

"No. Can anyone guess the real reason?" I asked.

Rosie mentioned that this part tripped people up sometimes, or at least that's what Edwin had told her.

"Well," I said. "As I was mentioning earlier, there is some overlap here. In *The Prime of Miss Jean* Brodie"—I emphasized the last name—"the main character actually mentions this."

"I think I remember," Kevin said. "It's not . . . Oh, maybe I can't remember exactly. Remind us."

"Jean is talking to Sandy and Jenny about the Kerr sisters' treatment of Mr. Lowther. She feels as if the sisters were starving the man, and in a huff she says"—I unfold a piece of paper that I'd been keeping in my pocket—"I made short work of those Kerr sisters. They were starving him. Now it is I who see to the provisions. I am a descendant"—I pause to make sure they're all listening. They are—". . . do not forget, of Willie Brodie, a man of substance, a cabinet maker and designer of gibbets, a member of the Town Council of Edinburgh and a keeper of two mistresses who bore him five children between them. Blood tells."

I look at them all again and then continue, "I'm skipping ahead a little here. Jean goes on to say that he died cheerfully on a gibbet of his own devising." I clear my throat. "She doesn't say anything of his poor reputation. Why do you all suppose that is?"

"She didn't know? The writer, I mean," Luka said. "No, that wouldn't work. The book was written in the 1950s; the author would have the whole story by then, surely. I don't know, maybe because we don't look poorly on family?"

"Maybe." I shrug. "But I think it's more."

"Oh, I do too," Kevin said.

"It gives us an insight into Miss Brodie," Gunter said. "She turns out not to necessarily be a . . . how is it said? A good guy."

"That's what I think too. The power of words. Right there," I said, holding up the quote from the book.

"Ah, well done." Luka sent me a wry smile. "Books—they're something else."

"Yes, they are." I smiled satisfactorily. After they'd had a few moments to chatter about Deacon Brodie, Jean Brodie, and Edinburgh, I said, "All right, let's eat!"

The three tour members made their way inside, but Tom lagged behind. I turned to him.

"You're amazing, lass." He kissed my forehead.

"I wouldn't say amazing, but I love it here. I figure I've got that going for me. If I can share that love, it's all good."

Tom smiled and, as so often happened when he did, my heart swooned.

CHAPTER FOURTEEN

Lunch was even livelier than the other meals we'd had. It seemed everyone was working hard to forget the bad things and was simply enjoying their time in Scotland and getting to know each other. As we ate, we learned about Gunter's wife, who had died ten years earlier. She'd worked for the German government and, though he wasn't at liberty to give exact facts, she'd been a spy of sorts, living adventures that he'd written about (well, vaguely) in his letters to Edwin. He shared some of the adventures with us at lunch. We were a good audience for such wonderful and seemingly far-fetched tales. I didn't even care if he was telling us the truth. It was just fun to hear the stories, and a welcome distraction.

After lunch, we made our way back to the bookshop. Rosie was still in costume, but Hector had tired of the tiny hat, and it sat on a corner of Rosie's desk as he came forward to greet us all.

"How did it go?" Rosie asked with a bright smile as she

joined me in the back while the others searched the shelves for new books to read.

"It went well," I said. "You seem happy. Is there good news from Edwin?"

She nodded. "You can see right through me, lass. Things are going well for him, too, and he and Hamlet should be home soon—maybe tomorrow, maybe the next day. He was hoping for today, but no such luck."

"I'm so happy to hear that!" Relief spread through me. Though I'd been assured he was in good health, I wasn't going to let go of that worry until I saw him.

"Me too."

Though Edwin had never intended the tours to be a tool to sell more books, and he gave more away than were purchased, shopping was inevitable, and everyone, including Luka, left with a few new reads, then were off to have their afternoon to themselves. Kevin was going to relax with her books, but Luka and Gunter weren't sure what they were going to do next.

Tom and I told them we'd meet up again for dinner. I'd given them a list of restaurants to choose from. They were to let us know which one they chose, and we'd be there. Maybe Rosie would be able to join us too.

Shortly after the group left, Tom and I set out to stop by the pub and check on Rodger. We found Luka inside, enjoying a drink before heading off to the Writers' Museum. The rain started lightly falling again, which was perfect timing, I thought. We spent a few moments checking on things and then left Luka in Rodger's good care.

"I want to see if Sherrie is still at the inn, or if there's an update on Carmel," I said to Tom when we stepped outside.

"Aye. Let's go."

Sherrie *was* still there, appearing even wearier than she had before.

"Hello, Sherrie," I said.

"Ah, hello again."

"I'm sorry to bother you," I continued.

"Are you really?" Sherrie asked. She cleared her throat. "Apologies. I'm tuckered out."

I nodded. "No problem. Any new word on Carmel?"

Surprising me, Sherrie smiled and nodded enthusiastically. "She's better, I've been told. They are taking her out of the coma, but I don't know if she's awake yet."

Even more good news. "That's great!"

"I agree." She paused. "And I did talk to the police, told them how Geoff was upset. They were glad I rang."

"Thank you, Sherrie. Your call might help solve the mysteries."

She shrugged, and her eyebrows furrowed.

"I guess everyone's waiting to hear what Carmel has to say about what happened?" I said.

"I guess so," she said doubtfully.

"What?"

"Something was going on here, lass, and I wasn't privy to what it was. I hope I wasn't unwillingly a part of something unsavory. I . . . Well, what happened to Geoff was terrible, and . . ."

"Are you concerned for your safety?" Tom asked her.

"Aye! I need the money I get from this place, but I asked the police if we were in danger."

"What did they say?" I asked.

"They didn't give me a straight answer. Someone else should be in soon to cover the next shift, but I might not come back."

"I'm sorry you're scared. I don't . . ." I was going to say that I didn't think she needed to be afraid, but I wasn't so sure.

"Did you tell the police you were frightened?" Tom asked her.

"No."

"I think you should. Maybe they will send someone over to watch the place."

Sherrie nodded and her eyes lit, as if she'd just heard the best idea ever. She nodded. "I'll ring them again right now."

She turned and disappeared into the office. I looked around, wondering how many employees actually worked at the inn and where they all were. Was Sherrie's shift going to end, or was it just going to go on and on?

I looked at Tom and said quietly, "I'm not sure what I was expecting, but not that."

"Sherrie's afraid. Geoff might have been afraid. Something's going on here that's causing fear."

"Should we move the tour group to another hotel? For safety's sake and . . . well, just because."

"I don't know. If the police do come watch the place, it'll be pretty safe. Tomorrow's the last official day of the tour, right? I do think everyone likes being settled in, but let's ask tonight at dinner." Tom paused. "Do you still want to drive by Tillie's place?"

"I do."

"Let's go."

Geoff and Tillie's Heyward apartment was located in an up-and-coming part of town. I'd heard about the Heyward flats mostly because of their location near to an old and abandoned lighthouse I'd attempted to see the inside of a few months ago. I'd been on a walking excursion with my friend Joshua. He worked at the National Museum, and we'd become friends over not only museum displays but walking tours, where we investigated the insides of old historical buildings. Or tried to. We hadn't made it inside the lighthouse. I glanced at its cordoned-off grounds as Tom drove by it before parking outside the Heywards. It appeared that visitors still weren't welcome.

Near the water, the flats were sought after, even though they weren't high-end. Their style and affordability, as well as the location, contributed to their popularity. There had been a huge demand and then a waiting list. I'd heard stories about people paying others ahead of them in line just to get a better spot.

They were attractive, in an angular, contemporary way that would never be any match for my old, little blue house by the sea.

Tom and I stood in front of the three buildings that made up the complex. Each building had four stories. The wind was always stronger near the water, and I had to hold my hair back with my hand.

"We didn't get a flat number, did we?" I said.

"I doubt anyone would have given it to us."

"Right. Should I call Inspector Winters and ask him?"

"Only if you want to risk him telling you to go home."
Tom smiled.

"No. Don't want to do that."

A man came through one of the building's front doors. He wore a black trench coat and was whistling a tune. His longish dark hair moved with the wind, and he had a newspaper tucked under one arm. He was tall and just as angular as the buildings.

The second he came through the front gate, I said hello.

"Oh, aye? Hello to you two, too. Do I know you?"

"No," I said. "We came to give our respects to Tillie Larson, but we've never visited her and Geoff here before, so we don't know her flat number. Do you know it?" It was weak, but I tried to sound confident enough to be truthful.

"Aye, I know who you mean—my neighbors. But she's not there. She left, back to Ireland, I presume."

I was surprised that the police had let her go.

"I'm sorry we missed her."

"We don't know her address in Ireland," Tom added. "Do you?"

"No idea."

"Maybe we'll mail her a card here and it will forward. Would you mind telling us her flat number?" I asked.

He didn't know us, but I was sure we seemed harmless enough. I watched doubt cross his face and then . . . something else gleamed in his eyes. Suddenly, there was something unfriendly to the set of his shoulders, his squint. I nearly gasped and had an urge to take a step backward, but I didn't. Tom must have felt the same thing, because he slipped his arm around my waist and pulled me a little closer.

The man smiled, but still wasn't friendly. "Seventeen, in the first building," he finally said.

"We were lucky to catch you then," I said. "Thank you."

"Aye." He hesitated. "Did you hear anything more about Geoff? Did he jump or was he pushed?"

"I don't know if the police have determined that yet," I answered.

"He was a good fellow." He paused. "Mostly."

"Mostly?" Tom asked.

"Aye. You knew Geoff—that temper. They both liked to yell. I talked to them about it, and they said they'd quiet down, but they never did."

"Goodness, that's not a side we've seen," I said. "What were they yelling about?"

The man shook his head. There was still something about his demeanor that wasn't normal, whatever that might mean. It was almost as if he was pulled taut, as if he could unload and start swinging at any second. He wasn't old, but he wasn't young, either. I'd seen such behavior in teenage boys before, but never on someone, like him, who was probably close to forty and appeared, with his long trench coat, to be a fellow just out for a walk.

"Aye, they fought," he repeated.

Tom and I waited silently to see if the man would tell us more. We were rewarded.

"Mostly the fighting was about Geoff's son, from his first marriage."

"I see." I'd loosened some from Tom's grip, but I noticed his hand at my waist.

"Aye, the lad had come back into Geoff's life, was disrupting everything from what I could discern."

"How old is Geoff's son?" Tom asked.

"Mid-twenties, I think. He'd been coming around here at night, knocking on their door. Tillie would never let him in, but Geoff would."

"I think I remember Geoff talking about him a time or two. Lad's name is Max?" Tom asked.

"Aye. That's right. At least that's what I've heard them call him." Suddenly, the man relaxed, as he smiled sadly. "It's all bad news, you know. You could feel the emotion swirling over there. It was uncomfortable, and now Geoff is dead."

"Have you seen Max over the last couple of days?" I asked.

"No, I haven't seen him for at least a week. I've been thankful for the quiet because of it." He cringed as he might have thought his words inappropriate because of Geoff's death, but he didn't retract them. Instead, his demeanor softened; he was much less threatening.

I looked at the building and back at the man. He suddenly seemed so non-threatening, and I wondered if I'd imagined his body language earlier. "Are you sure Tillie's moved out the whole way? Maybe she's coming back."

"I don't know." He shrugged. "Go in if you want. Here, I'll open the building door."

"Thank you," Tom and I said once we were inside, as the man turned and walked off, whistling the same snappy tune.

"He was different," Tom said when the building door had closed all the way.

"I felt like he wanted to hit us, or just someone."

"I got the same thing, but just for a few seconds."

"I don't feel like we aren't being careful. We're being careful, right?"

"We are." Tom stepped to a window at the side of the door and looked through. "I don't see him at all."

"He got away quickly."

"Aye." Tom turned, and I noticed his furrowed brow.

"You okay?"

"Aye, but something isn't right."

I nodded. "Let's go check seventeen."

"Let's." Tom turned and led us down the hallway.

We knocked on the door, but no one answered.

"I certainly don't think we should break in, but I'm going to try the knob," I said.

"Okay."

"I don't think she's in there anyway." I was trying to rationalize, for Tom's sake and my own.

Tom wasn't thrilled—I could see it in his eyes—but he didn't stop me.

The knob turned, and to both our surprise the door swung open easily, almost of its own accord, giving us the view of a still furnished, if sparsely, apartment space. There were even pictures on a mantel above a small fireplace.

"Tillie?" I called.

There was no answer.

"Tillie, are you here?" I tried again, and again there was no answer.

"We're not going in there," Tom said.

"No, even I can't do that," I conceded.

But then we heard a noise, something that might have been a groan of someone in pain.

"Stay here, lass." Tom stepped in front of me.

"We'll go together." I followed right behind him.

"Tillie?" Tom called as we made our way through the front room and past the small, utilitarian kitchen, still with appliances and storage bins on the countertops. It did not appear that anyone had moved or was in the process of moving out of this flat. "Tillie?"

The groan sounded again, seemingly coming from the next level, which was up some modern suspended slat stairs. Tom and I both took them two at a time.

Tom pushed through the first door we came to. It led us into the master bedroom, which featured an unmade bed and a few articles of clothing strewn about.

"Help," a tiny voice came from the master bath.

We hurried, and found Tillie on her back on the floor, a trail of blood oozing from her head.

Tom and I reached for our phones at the same time.

"Okay, you call 999. I'll see if I can stop the bleeding," Tom said as he stood to grab a towel from a wall rack.

I pressed the numbers, and then crouched next to Tillie as I waited for an answer.

"What happened?" I asked her. "Can you tell us anything?"

"He . . . he was here," Tillie said.

Or I thought that was what she said. She was slurring, and her words came out in one big stream.

"Who?" I asked.

She said something unintelligible.

"I've called for help," I told her.

"I'm here. What's the emergency?" an operator said from my phone.

Sounding very much like I had with Carmel, I told the woman about the injured Tillie.

"She's still conscious?" the operator asked.

"She is. Should I leave her be or keep her talking?"

"Don't shake her or move her, but if you can keep her talking, keep her awake, that's good. Do not move her, but try to put something on the wound to stop the bleeding."

Tom was doing exactly that with a long white towel. The wound was bleeding a lot.

"Got it. Tillie, tell me whatever you can about what happened," I said.

Her eyes were having trouble focusing, but I was sure they landed on me with a big question. *What in the world was I doing there?*

It was a good question, but certainly not important at the moment.

"Who hit you?" I asked.

"Maaan."

I shared a look with Tom. Oh no. I was pretty sure he was thinking the same thing. The man we'd spoken to, the one who'd gossiped so easily. Had he been the one to hurt Tillie?

"Black trench coat, longish hair?" I said to her, though I didn't think she could truly catch what I was saying. She didn't nod or shake her head. "What's his name?"

She didn't answer.

"Tillie, you're going to be okay," I continued. "Stay awake. Come on, Tillie."

Her eyebrows came together as if she wasn't so sure.

I suddenly noticed that she'd been hit very close to the same spot on her head that Carmel had. Did that matter? A head wound was a head wound, right? I didn't know if location on the head meant anything important.

The man with the newspaper, though tall, hadn't been the same person I'd seen running from the hotel, I was sure. My frantic mind sifted through all the information I had, and I realized that the runner must have been young. It was in the way he'd moved—agile, quick—and in the way he was built. It would be difficult for a man over the age of twenty-five or so to move that way.

The sounds of sirens came closer, and relief spread through me when the officers rushed inside and Tom and I could step away from Tillie. I didn't recognize any of the first responders from earlier.

The situation had been almost a duplicate of what I'd gone through with Carmel. Was there some sort of pattern here? Was I part of the pattern or was it all just coincidence?

A slew of questions were directed at Tom and me, but neither of us was arrested.

Who were we?

What did we see?

How did we know the victim?

We just opened the door?!

We answered every single question honestly. Of course, we had to include the fact that Tillie had been impersonating someone else, which made it all so much stranger. We told them about the man we'd talked to outside the building and described him as best we could. We told the police what he'd said about the loud arguments, about Geoff's son, Max, and then about Geoff himself. It was as if the tragedies just kept building upon themselves.

Finally, when it was all finished, I called Inspector Winters and told him what was going on. I took my phone to the officer who'd been asking most of the questions to see if he wanted to talk to my friend, a police inspector. With an incredulous glare my way, he took the phone. The conversation eased his irritation but didn't get rid of it completely.

Tillie was still conscious when she was taken to the hospital, and when I finally checked the time a hundred years later, I saw that only an hour had passed since we'd opened the door to the flat.

As we were dismissed, I remembered the photographs on the skinny, modern white mantel above a gas fireplace. I veered quickly toward them.

Geoff and Tillie smiling—in Edinburgh, outside the inn. There were also some shots in the Highlands. But it was the young man in a couple of the pictures I was most interested in.

I assumed the young man who looked like Geoff, though thinner and taller, was Max. I didn't know how old the picture was, but there was no doubt in my mind that this kid could have been the person in black I'd seen running away from the inn. He was obviously tall, a good six inches taller than his father.

I didn't want to tell anyone my suspicions about that yet because I was still feeling the trauma of coming upon Tillie and my mind was on overdrive, working to try to come up with so many answers. Was I even thinking clearly? I would first talk to Inspector Winters.

What in the world was going on?

"Lass?" Tom asked from behind me.

I grabbed my phone. "That must be Max."

"Aye," Tom said.

I snapped a photo of the picture. "Have you ever seen this guy around?"

"Not that I remember." He studied the picture a moment longer. "No, he doesn't seem familiar."

"Did you notice that Tillie was hit in the head in very close to the same spot Carmel had been hit?"

"Not really, but that would be a difficult thing to pull off on purpose. I'm not sure how you'd manage it."

"Me neither." I put my phone back in my pocket and then looked at all the pictures on the mantel again.

"Sir, lass, you need to go," an officer said from the doorway.

We nodded at him and then left. Once outside, we both looked the direction the man had gone, but of course he wasn't anywhere to be seen.

"I couldn't even guess where he might be," Tom said.

I shook my head. "He might not have been the one who did that to Tillie, but something tells me he was. I don't think she fell and hit her head. I don't think the police think that, either."

"I agree. And, believe it or not, if we hadn't come by, they might never even know about him, about her. She might have died. Then again, if Tillie didn't see him well, or if she doesn't remember everything . . ."

I nodded. "Why do you suppose he talked to us, told us to go check the flat? I mean, he could have just stuck with his story about her leaving or not have offered to let us inside."

Tom shrugged. "Maybe he wanted Tillie to be found, or maybe he was proud of his handiwork. He probably just wanted to get rid of us so we wouldn't know where he went, or follow him. He might have been lying about them being loud, about Max. I don't know, but I'm glad we told the police everything."

"Almost."

"Aye?"

"Based on the pictures on the mantel, Max could have been the person I saw running away two nights ago. I need to call Inspector Winters and tell him."

"You don't want to tell the officers inside?"

I shook my head. "There's just so much . . . I'm going to call Inspector Winters."

I grabbed my phone again and made the call.

CHAPTER FIFTEEN

Though none of them admitted to hating haggis, no one was interested in eating it again. Instead, everyone chose a place with cheeseburgers and chips, or as I called them, French fries.

It was a few steps up from fast food and a place that Tom and I enjoyed, but I was surprised the rest of the tour group was intrigued by such an American-style menu. I noticed Gunter swoon a little when he saw banana cream pie available for dessert.

The dinner and dessert conversation had been about the sights they'd seen and the places they'd visited that afternoon. All three of them had explored a few closes. Kevin had spent time in one furnished with flowerpots and benches. She'd bundled up and sat under an awning for a while, reading a book and enjoying the quiet. Gunter had explored the Writers' Museum, and Luka had simply walked around, sampling whisky from a few different pubs.

Rosie had joined us for dinner, and like Tom had, regaled our visitors with stories about growing up in Edinburgh. She also shared with them about when she first started working for Edwin, and how different—though still as wonderful as he was now—he'd been back then, with energy to spare and more good ideas than hours in the day to execute them. Even Tom and I were intrigued by those stories.

Once dessert was finished and everyone either had coffee or something a little stronger, I told them all what had happened over the afternoon, and then asked again if they wanted to change to another hotel.

As I looked at the surprised expressions around me, I quickly said, "I'm asking because I want to make sure you are all okay with staying there. I don't want you to feel unsafe."

"We've got each other," Gunter said, his German accent adding strength to his proclamation.

"I never thought about not feeling safe," Kevin said. "Even with all the strange things."

"I'm good. We're good," Luka added.

"It's fine, dear," Kevin added.

I'd been particularly worried about her. She looked better now but had been pale again when I'd met them at the restaurant. She'd insisted she was feeling okay, better every minute.

"It's a lovely place," Gunter added. "I don't think we are in danger."

"Okay." A big part of me still wanted to convince them to move, but I understood where they were coming from. "Well, how about tomorrow, then? The schedule got off a bit, but are you up for another half-day of touring?"

"I am not," Luka said, and then he smiled. "In fact, I would like this to go on for at least a few more days, not just half of another, and this is coming from someone who doesn't like to take vacations. It's been perfect."

"Thank you," I said.

The others agreed that they wished the tour could go longer. Rosie sent me a knowing nod. We'd talked about the fact that that's what most of the tour groups said at about this point. She was letting me know I was still on the right pace, despite all the bizarre diversions. I appreciated it.

"What I would like to do," Kevin said as she turned to Tom, "is be finished here and have a drink or two at your delightful pub before I retire for the night. The last time we were there, it was under dire circumstances. I'd like for this to be a happier occasion."

"A wonderful, plan," Luka said. He lifted his whisky. "Also, a toast to Delaney."

Everyone else lifted their drinks too.

I wanted to wave away the accolades, but I couldn't deny that I was very pleased that they were all happy. I wasn't looking forward to its being all over either, even if I knew my workload would decrease substantially.

"Oh!" Dramatically, Luka put a hand in front of his eyes. "Goodness, that's blinding."

"What?" I looked behind me.

"Your locket," Luka said with a laugh. "The light hit it just right and the glare got me."

I looked down at the monocle that I'd put on again that morning. The flap that covered the glass had somehow swung open. I closed it and saw how a fixture on the ceiling above had created the glare.

"It's a monocle," I said, and then I told them the story of how I'd obtained the new jewelry.

"It had the name 'Tom'?" Kevin said. "That's so romantic."

"I thought so too. I've come to love it already."

"It's beautiful, dear, and I promise you, there will come a day when it will be useful, too. That day is a ways away for you, but time always flies much faster than we want it to," Kevin said.

"True." I smiled.

Tom drove Rosie home, saying he would meet us at the pub, and I walked with the others back toward Grassmarket. Tom beat us there and was sending Rodger home as we arrived. Rodger looked tired but was trying not to. He'd be back the next day while Tom helped me again with the tour.

Drinks were handed around and conversations were resumed, or new ones ignited.

As Tom worked and the rest of us enjoyed the fun, Kevin sidled up next to me. "Want to go up to the roof?"

"What do you mean?" I asked after taking a big gulp of my soda.

She nodded. "The roof of the inn. I went up there today. There's no one stopping anyone from doing so. And the door at the top is unlocked. Sure, I propped it open with a rock just to be safe, but it's not locked." She looked around. "I couldn't venture far when I was up there, but your young knees would allow you to. I thought you might be curious."

Always. "What did you see?"

"Come with me and look for yourself."

I sent her a side-eye, but I tried to temper it with a little humor. She wouldn't hurt me, would she? She wouldn't hurt anyone.

"Let's go," I said.

I told Tom the plan. He wasn't overly thrilled by the idea, but he couldn't leave the pub unattended to join us. He glanced at Luka and Gunter as if considering asking if they'd go, but both of them seemed too inebriated to attempt a trip to any rooftop.

"I know I don't need to say it, but be careful, lass." Tom looked at Kevin. "Both of you."

"Will do." I leaned over the bar for a quick kiss.

There was no one at the inn's front desk when we entered the lobby, and we hurried through quickly in case someone came out from the office to investigate. I felt both ridiculous and sneaky, but I didn't stop Kevin from leading us up the switchback flights of stairs, all the way up to a door that said ROOFTOP. Her knees had done just fine.

"Even the sign is charming." Kevin pointed at the old wooden hand-carved block hanging on the door.

She pushed through and grabbed the large rock that had probably been left up there, as she'd already guessed, for the purpose of propping open the door.

My mind conjured that someone could still grab the rock and leave us stranded, but Tom knew where we'd gone; we'd be rescued eventually.

The rooftop wasn't what I expected. Even though I knew the front façade of the building was turrets and peaked windows, I had it in my mind that the rooftop would be flat, perhaps with an asphalt floor and HVAC units clunking away somewhere. It wasn't like that at all.

It wasn't flat but covered with several pyramid-like peaks, each about five feet high. It felt like a strange maze.

"Why is it made this way?" I asked.

"I don't know," Kevin said. "I wondered if it was storage, drainage, or just something to dissuade people from coming up here."

"That would be my guess," I said. "It's intimidating."

"This is as far as I go," Kevin said. "But I bet you could manage more."

Slowly and carefully, I stepped onto one of the peaks and climbed up it, my feet holding me just fine.

I climbed up to the top, which wasn't as pointed as I'd assumed. I could balance pretty well.

"What's up there?" Kevin asked.

"Not much of anything. However, it's intriguing, considering someone went off the side of the building."

"Just yell if you're pushed off the side," Kevin said to me. "I'll save myself, make a quick escape, and go tell Tom. He's sure to come help."

"Okay," I said with a wry smile. "I can't resist going a little farther."

"My dear, if I didn't have these knees and ankles, I couldn't resist either."

I slid down the other side of the thing I'd climbed atop of and then climbed the next one.

"You came up here alone?" I said, raising my voice a little to reach Kevin.

"I did. I like a bit of risk in my life. What do you see?"

"This is a great view. I can even see the George Heriot school we visited. The building and the grounds."

At night, lights formed an even pattern around the perimeter of the grounds, and a couple of windows were bright with yellow light. I couldn't make out anyone inside. "Pretty. And the castle view is stunning."

"I bet. You okay over there?" Kevin called.

"Fine." I looked at the castle again. I'd seen it a million times by now, but this was a one-of-a-kind view. "Wow."

I turned my attention to the spot where Geoff must have gone over.

Around the odd peaks, indeed the whole rooftop, I saw security bars. At first I was looking for something that might be evidence—maybe a piece of fabric, footprints; something tangible—but I soon realized that wasn't the most important consideration here.

I muttered to myself, "I wonder . . . could anyone feasibly jump from this rooftop?"

"What's going on, Delancy?" Kevin called.

"It seems almost impossible to get close enough to the edge of the building to actually go over."

A moment later, Kevin said, "What do you mean?"

"Give me a second."

I surveyed again. If Geoff had tried to jump from up here, he couldn't have made it over the security fence by himself. Now, if he could have climbed that fence he might have made it, but there was no place along the edge to get purchase.

I made my way back to Kevin and shared my conclusions with her.

"But not completely undoable, I would guess?" she said.

"No, but difficult." I paused. "I didn't see the body."

"I didn't either. Well, I looked away quickly."

"I wonder what shape it was in because, well, I looked at the location where it landed. Victoria Street curves but also inclines up toward the Royal Mile, right?"

"Yes."

"Okay, well, if he managed to get to the corner over there and he jumped, there's a chance he could have survived it. I mean, yes, at that spot it's about three stories up, but . . . Have you seen the Indiana Jones movies?"

"Sure."

"Just like in one of the films, there's an awning right over the side." I nodded that direction. "It would have stopped any jump he could make. There's simply not enough foot space to get a running start or leap far enough to miss it."

"So, what are you saying?"

I shook my head. "I'm not exactly sure, but the only way my brain can make sense of all of it is to think that either he was boosted up or thrown off—and I don't know exactly how that would work either, but I can see it—or he was already dead before he hit the ground. Did someone see him actually fall?"

"I don't know. That's a good question. I know you're friends with a policeman. Maybe you could talk to him about all this. I mean, maybe he already knows, but it's . . . I don't know, the questions seem pretty obvious."

I nodded. "They do. This is pretty good, Kevin."

"I'm so fascinated by crime. I'm one of those people who listens to all the true-crime podcasts. I like to think about how things could be done. My nosiness has gotten me in trouble a time or two."

I laughed. "Me too."

"I'm not surprised."

I looked around one more time. I wouldn't have minded a more thorough search, but it truly wasn't the safest of places—not because it was easy to go off the side, but because the peaks made it difficult to maneuver. Sprained ankles were probably the biggest concern, though. "Anything else we should look at?"

"I don't think so."

"I'm going to call Inspector Winters."

"You are?"

"Absolutely."

Kevin smiled. "Well, then be extra careful getting back to the pub. Let's not hurt ourselves now."

We put the rock where it seemed to belong and went through the doorway. I sent one more glance out at the rooftop before I shut the door and followed Kevin back out of the still empty lobby and to the pub.

CHAPTER SIXTEEN

I didn't have to call Inspector Winters. He'd come to the pub looking for me and was none too happy when Tom told him where we'd gone.

"That wasn't safe," he said as we made our way inside. Tom was sending me apologetic eyes.

"We're good, and I think Kevin is actually onto something," I said. "We'll tell you everything."

Inspector Winters might not have been pleased with what we'd done, but he had a potential murder to solve, so even if he did it with stern eyes, he was going to listen to everything. I hoped the contribution wouldn't turn out to be useless.

He listened as Kevin and I sketched the roof on an unfolded napkin and then shared our theories.

"I haven't been up there," he said. "I'd heard there were strange angles, but no one has mentioned that it might be difficult to jump off unassisted. I know that there's not one speck of evidence of anyone else being up there. I'll have another conversation with the officers and crime scene investigators who examined the roof, see what they think."

"A cause of death hasn't been determined for Geoff?" I asked. "I mean, maybe he was dead before leaving the roof."

"Blunt force trauma is all we've got. There was no sign of anything else, but the injuries could have come from a fall or jump, or from a violent act that was then made even more calamitous by his landing on the road below." He frowned. "I do wonder about the distance now. I'll check it out."

He'd moved past being worried about or angry at us and onto wanting to get back to the investigation, no matter how late it might have been. Taking Kevin's sketch with him, he gave everyone a distracted goodbye and left the pub.

I turned to Tom. "I didn't even find out why he was here in the first place. Did you? Did he say anything about Tillie?"

Tom shook his head. "As far as I know he just stopped by. He didn't tell me anything specific. Maybe he sensed you were up to something you shouldn't have been."

"A good possibility."

It wasn't much later that the group members—all of them "zonked," according to Luka—said they wanted to go back to their rooms. They also wanted to confirm that the tour was on again the next day. I assured them it was.

While Tom remained at the pub, I escorted them across the street and into the inn. There was still no one at the front desk as I bid them good night, after they'd assured me they'd make sure everyone got into their room okay.

I hurried back to the pub, anxious to help Tom clean and close up before it got much later. He didn't act as if he was tired and he didn't look as worn out as Rodger had, but I was sure he was anxious to get back to his regular schedule.

As we worked, we couldn't help but replay the events of the day, and then wish we'd asked Inspector Winters for formal updates on both Carmel and Tillie. Just as we turned out the lights and Tom was putting the key into the front door lock, my phone rang. I fumbled in my bag for it and answered. It was Gunter.

"Come quick, Delaney—it's Kevin!" he exclaimed.

We took off toward the inn. There was still no one in the lobby. Tom and I ran up the stairs to Kevin's room. The door was open, and all of the tour members were inside. Kevin was sitting up on the edge of the bed, sipping from a glass of water, her skin once again ghostly pale.

"I don't feel well," she said to me as I crouched next to her.

"Let's get you to a doctor."

Kevin sighed. "I think that's for the best. I'm so, so sorry."

Everyone told her not to be sorry. She insisted that we not call an ambulance but just let her climb down the stairs and run her to the hospital ourselves. I was worried about her trying the descent, but she did fine with Tom on one side of her and Luka on the other. We went through the still empty lobby and stepped outside. It was cool but not raining. Kevin took in a couple of deep breaths.

"Oh, see, that's better," she said. She blinked at us all. "Is there somewhere I could sit?"

Tom unlocked the pub's door and grabbed a stool. Just like she had the first time she hadn't felt well, she took a seat, sipped some water, and breathed in the fresh air.

"I don't understand this," Kevin said a moment later. "I feel almost back to normal. I would feel silly going to a doctor now. What would I say?"

I looked at Tom, who seemed to be on the same page I was—there was something wrong with Kevin's room. I wasn't ready to speak the words aloud, but Luka didn't hold back.

"There's something in Kevin's room," he said. "I thought there was a funny smell in there, but I couldn't place it. And, you know, you smell something odd, you don't want to say anything. But I think there's something in there that might be making her sick."

"I don't think I noticed," I said.

"Come with me." The others remained behind as Luka led Tom and me back to Kevin's room.

"Sniff," Luka said as we stepped though the still open doorway. No one had thought to even close the door.

Tom and I sniffed.

I smelled some of Kevin's perfume, but there was something else too, something familiar.

"What is that? It's not . . . unpleasant, but not nice either." Tom sniffed deeply. "It's alcohol."

"What?" Luka and I asked at the same time.

I stepped farther into the room. "Of course! It's rubbing alcohol. I should have recognized it immediately. Where's it coming from?"

"I think we'd better call Inspector Winters back," Tom said as he touched my arm.

I nodded, and without asking for further clarification, I placed the call. Inspector Winters said he'd get there as quickly as he could.

CHAPTER SEVENTEEN

In one of the most peculiar things I'd ever seen, ten small plastic bottles of rubbing alcohol had been tucked between Kevin's bed's mattress and box springs. There was also a good supply of sandpaper there. Three of the bottles had cracked or come open, probably from pressure when Kevin had lain down—probably one of them that very night; two other bottles were empty, but were surely the culprits in her earlier issues.

"I have an odd sniffer," she said when told what had been found. "I'm sensitive, but can't always distinguish what I'm smelling. The scent of rubbing alcohol has always been an issue for me. I just didn't know that's what I was smelling. I'm sorry."

We all laughed nervously, just relieved that she was okay, and told her again that she had nothing to be sorry about.

Inspector Winters and three other officers, along with an alert German shepherd, arrived quickly. Since no one from the inn was around, they took it upon themselves to search

Kevin's room, which was located at the end of the hallway on the second floor.

It took only moments for them to find what was causing the problem—and I didn't know what to make of it, at first.

The rest of the hotel was then searched from top to bottom. No one was thrilled to be roused from their relaxation or sleep, and no one liked the police searching their rooms, their things. I wasn't informed as to whether they found anything else suspicious. In fact, for a while I was baffled that such a search needed to be conducted. For alcohol and sandpaper?

But then it was explained to me as Inspector Winters and I stood in the lobby.

"They are things frequently used in identity theft," Inspector Winters said. "Alcohol and sandpaper are sometimes used on driver's licenses, to clean them so other information might be printed onto them."

"And that works?" I said.

"Well, it used to. It's a little more difficult now, but sometimes doable."

"Huh." I looked at him. "You know Kevin isn't stealing identities, don't you?"

"What makes you so sure?"

"Inspector Winters . . ."

He held up his hand. "Aye, Delaney, we know. We checked all of your tour group."

"You checked their records?"

"Aye, we checked everyone staying in the hotel, and we'll check the staff too. Your guests are clean as whistles."

"That's good to know."

"Aye."

"Does everyone have to leave the hotel now?"

I'd already configured in my head where the tour group would sleep at our house. It would be a tight fit, but they would all be welcome.

Inspector Winters shook his head. "They do not. We're confident in the dog's abilities, and there was nothing else to be found."

"Any more specific idea where it came from?"

"Not yet, but it's another piece to add to the puzzle. We're looking very closely at the hotel staff and previous guests."

"So anything to help with a motive for killing Geoff maybe?"

He shrugged. "Anything is possible, but the rest of the hotel is clean, and I'm leaving an officer in the lobby tonight. We're trying to get ahold of , , , well, of someone with the inn."

"May I go back to my room?" Luka asked as he approached.

Inspector Winters looked toward one of the other officers. "In just a few minutes."

"You're welcome to come to our house," I said.

"No, thank you, I just want to get back to my room."

I nodded. I understood. I'd have rather stayed in my own hotel room than at someone's house too, but I wondered when it might all become too much for any of them. If this place wasn't jinxed, it had at least been disturbing.

I stepped away from Inspector Winters, and Tom and I extended the offer of our home to everyone. Even Kevin just wanted to go back to her now searched and cleaned-out room, though she was forced to move to another one. Since no inn staff was around, the police rounded up room keys and carried all of her things over to her new room.

As Tom and I were just about to head to our car, a man showed up. He was so tall that the motorized scooter he rode at first appeared extra small. He'd thrown a terry-cloth robe over his pajamas, and it wasn't until he removed his helmet that I recognized him.

"O'Shea?" I said.

Tom looked that direction too. "That looks like him."

"Hello!" he exclaimed to the police. "I'm Barney O'Shea. You are trying to reach someone with the inn? Is everyone okay?"

Tom and I looked at each other. What in the world was going on? This was most definitely the same man who'd shown us around the George Heriot school. Was he maybe a security guard there—and here?

"I can't leave yet," I said to Tom.

"No. Let's see what happens."

We stepped closer and hung around the periphery of the activity as we tried to eavesdrop.

After he spent some time talking to the police, O'Shea apologized to everyone and told the officers that he would make sure all the guests were comped the night's stay, that he'd figure out a way to make it right with everyone. He had no idea about any sort of alcohol or sandpaper or driver's licenses, couldn't understand their use even as the police tried to explain it to him. He was too rattled to focus, I thought.

By the time the police were done with him, O'Shea, still in his robe and pajamas, took it upon himself to man the front desk. The remaining officer didn't seem to even notice as Tom and I marched toward it.

"Mr. O'Shea, I'm Delaney Nichols with The Cracked Spine," I said as I approached. "We met just yesterday. This is my husband, Tom, from the pub."

"Ah, aye, the tour group. Edwin's group. I'm so sorry about everything. I will make it up to you all."

I didn't know what to make of anything, so I just jumped in.

"Mr. O'Shea, I don't understand your tie to the school, the inn." I looked at Tom. "Or to Edwin, for that matter. It might be none of my business, but I'm very surprised to see you here this evening."

He nodded but didn't answer, though he seemed to sober back to the much more reserved person we'd met at the school. "It has been a few days. So much—and a death even."

I nodded. "I'm . . . sorry for your loss. Do you work here?"

"Not usually, but it looks like I am tonight."

When he didn't continue, I was at a loss again.

"Why are you here then?" Tom asked.

He looked at Tom. "Oh, I'm a partial owner of this place."

"Of the school too?" Tom asked.

"No, not at all. I'm a benefactor there. I've given them lots of money over the years."

The pieces, vague though they still might be, came together in my mind. O'Shea was one of Edwin's rich friends, or maybe just acquaintances, and helped him with things that involved the tour.

"You and Edwin are friends," I said. It wasn't a question, though he answered as if it were.

"Aye. We go back a long way." He finally gave me his full attention. "You didn't know?"

"I didn't understand. It all makes more sense now."

"I see." O'Shea smiled sadly. "Yes, it does all make a little more sense. Is Edwin all right? I've tried to ring him."

"He's fine. He was called away. He'll be back very soon. Again, I'm sorry about Geoff."

"Ah. Thank you. I . . . I'm ashamed to say that I didn't know the lad much at all. I am not in charge of anything here." He looked around. "But no one answered their phones tonight. Somehow the police found me. I have no idea what's going on. I hope the police figure it out."

I debated saying what was on my mind, and then just went with it. "Mr. O'Shea . . ."

"Everyone just calls me O'Shea."

"O'Shea, did you hear about Geoff's wife today?"

"No."

"Tillie was attacked. Hit over the head like Carmel was— Carmel's an employee here."

"Is she okay? Tillie?"

"I don't know."

"How terrible."

"Did you know that for a while, Geoff asked that a particular room not be rented out to customers?"

"Lass, I'm not involved with the day-to-day here." He paused. "But that might explain why revenues fell some."

"I would bet so."

"Someone should get to the bottom of all this."

"Who would that someone be?" I asked.

"I don't know, lass. I just don't know."

Did he truly not know, or was he just keeping it to himself? Why would he tell us anyway—it wasn't our job to figure this out. But it sure sounded like there had been no one minding this store for at least a while now.

O'Shea didn't behave like he felt bad about much of anything except maybe being called into the hotel to work at its front desk. I'd noticed his reserved personality at the school, but I hadn't chalked it up to him having money or not caring about the "little people."

I got some of that sense of snobbery now, though I wasn't sure that was fair.

Maybe it was as simple as that he just didn't like to become involved in any way but with his money. That reluctance, at least, was confirmed in the next few seconds.

"Excuse me," he said before he turned and went into the office. This seemed to be a convenient escape for those behind that counter.

Tom and I stood there a long moment. I looked at him to see if he was bothered by what I'd done. He certainly looked bothered, but not at me, it turned out. He signaled me outside.

The police, except for one officer on watch, were gone. The guests were in their rooms. Grassmarket wasn't completely quiet, but there wasn't much going on. We made our way to Tom's car.

"Tom, you said that you've seen O'Shea in the pub."

"Aye."

"Did you know he was a man of means?"

"Lass, unless he'd been talking to me about his money, I wouldn't know how to recognize something like that. And he never spoke to me about any such thing."

He had a point. Edwin never talked about his money, but it was clear he had lots of it. Well, it was clear to me.

"I'm overthinking Mr. O'Shea. I'll ask Edwin about him. Hopefully sooner rather than later."

"Aye. Let's go home, lass. We've a big day tomorrow."

I fell asleep in the car on the short trip back to the blue house by the sea. And, once home, I conked back out the minute my head hit the pillow.

CHAPTER EIGHTEEN

I plopped my hands on my hips. The others were gathered around me, and we all looked down the long street. "Welcome to Princes Street, a place where a wonderful chase scene from a very popular book and movie, both called *Trainspotting*, was filmed. Princes Street is an amazing place that you just must see when you come to Edinburgh." I nodded toward the statue. "Mostly, in my humble opinion, because of this incredible tribute and work of art, the Scott Monument."

A tall Gothic towered monument filled the middle of the grounds. It had been built over a statue of Sir Walter Scott. The monument had been commissioned shortly after Scott's death and was one of the most popular tourist destinations in Edinburgh.

I continued, "It's one of the largest and most impressive monuments to a writer in the world."

We all glanced up. The weather wasn't terrible, but it certainly wasn't sunny. Clouds filled the sky, though I'd yet to feel any rain.

"Scottish people love their writers," Luka said.

"Yes, they do," I agreed. "So I'll give you some brief background. Scott was born on August 15, 1771, in Old Town Edinburgh in a small apartment located in a close. He was the ninth child, six having died in infancy, of Walter Scott and Anne Rutherford.

"A childhood bout of polio in 1773 left him with a lifelong pronounced limp. It was a condition that would affect his life and his writing. In 1773, he was sent to live in the rural area called Scottish Borders, to stay with his paternal grandparents' family in Sandyknowe. Here, he was taught to read by his aunt Jenny Scott and learned from her the speech patterns of the area and many of the tales and legends that later showed up in his work.

"He spent some years traveling back and forth from the country, then enrolled in the Royal High School in Edinburgh. By then he was able to walk fairly well and visit many places throughout the city and the countryside. He loved reading chivalric romance, poems, history, and travel books.

"His parents sent him back to the country when they thought he needed to rebuild his strength again, and he met James Ballantyne and James's brother John, who would later become his business partners and printers.

"I have some lines here from *The Lay of the Last Minstrel*. Kevin, would you read them aloud please?"

I'd thought about having Tom read them to the group. My husband had a delightful voice with a perfect Scottish accent, both when reading and singing. If he'd worn his kilt and read aloud, the experience could not have been any more genuine. However, I knew that Kevin enjoyed words so much that reading them aloud was something she would enjoy doing.

"I would love to." Kevin took the sheet of paper I handed her and cleared her throat.

She was well-rested, or rested enough. We hadn't rushed getting started today. I'd let everyone sleep in, and then we'd had a small lunch with sandwiches brought into the pub. Everyone was in good spirits. I'd been informed that though they all deeply regretted Geoff's demise, the tour had turned into the stuff of legends. There would never be another one like it.

For so many reasons, I truly hoped they were right.

Kevin read:

Breathes there the man, with soul so dead,
Who never to himself hath said,
This is my own, my native land!
Whose heart hath ne'er within him burned,
As home his footsteps he hath turned,
From wandering on a foreign strand!—
If such there breathe, go, mark him well;
For him no minstrel raptures swell.

"Well, I have no idea what that meant, but it was lovely," Luka said.

"Made even more so by you reading it," Gunter said to Kevin.

I thought I might have seen her blush a little.

"Thank you." She tilted her head graciously.

"This is where you'll miss Edwin the most," I said. "Of

course, I've read some Scott, but Edwin has read—devoured, I might say—every single word the man wrote. He can quote and bring tears to his eyes at the drop of a hat. He loves Scott."

They all smiled my direction.

"Well, my favorites are his *Tales of a Grandfather*," Kevin said. "In them, Scott tells his six-year-old grandson the history of Scotland. The stories are lovely and make history much less dry than it can be."

"I love those stories too," Gunter added. "Though I'm surprised you might find history dry."

"Oh yes."

"Shall we climb up?" I looked that direction.

Everyone, even Kevin, despite her knees, was excited to do so.

Still taking our time, we ascended the monument's 287 steps. It wasn't overly crowded today, but the climb couldn't have been speedy even if we'd wanted it to be. At the top, everyone enjoyed the panoramic views of the city.

Trying to keep my words just amongst us, I said to our small gathering, "Just over two hundred feet tall, it was designed by the winner of a monument contest in 1838 and then was built with sandstone from a quarry in West Lothian."

"This is even better than the rooftop view," Kevin said.

I nodded. We were all a little winded from the climb, but taking in the expansive sights gave us a few moments to recover. Today, without the sun, it seemed all the colors were a touch more vivid. There was no glare anywhere.

"Didn't Scott discover the crown jewels or something like that?" Luka asked. "I remember reading about it."

I nodded at Tom.

"Aye. Well, *re*discovered them. The sword and scepter—

which are on display in the castle—had been locked away in an iron box in the castle for over a hundred years. George the Fourth was so impressed with Scott's works and how he managed to weave Scottish history into his stories that he asked Scott to lead the group that rediscovered the box and opened it."

"How wonderful."

"A couple other fun facts—he invented the word 'glamour' as well as the genre of 'historical novel,'" I added.

Another few minutes later we made our way down the stairs. We continued down Princes Street, and Tom and I pointed out and discussed places of interest—the Waverley train station, named for Scott's *Waverley*; the Ross Fountain; the Floral Clock; and many other Edinburgh favorites. The tour group's favorite turned out to be the Wojtek the Soldier Bear statue, which was built in 2015 to commemorate the brave men, women, and children who fought in World War II. Not even the oldest of the group, Kevin and Gunter, had experienced World War II firsthand, but they'd both been born shortly after VE Day, and we all felt their emotions along with our own at the remembrance.

There was only one more part of the tour left. It was Edwin's favorite part, but I thought it could be left out if the group wasn't interested or was too tired after the previous evening's events. The afternoon had passed quickly, and the light lunch we'd had wasn't quite enough.

"We've got one more place to visit after dinner, but I want to make sure everyone is on board. It's the underground. If anyone is tired or wants to just stay in the pub after we eat, do not feel obligated."

"The underground? After dark?" Luka asked.

"When the ghosts are most likely to be roaming them? Absolutely," I said.

"I'm here for all of it," Luka said.

"Me too," Kevin and Gunter agreed.

"All right then—off to our meal at the very end of the world," I said cheerily.

We set out to the World's End pub. We were met with, if not the biggest surprise of the tour, certainly the best. As we wove our way to a table that had been reserved for us, my eyes first caught Rosie sitting there, sending me a smile—and then, as my breath caught, Edwin and Hamlet with her, the three of them all looking just fine and very happy to see the rest of us.

I worked hard not to burst into tears of joy and relief when I saw them. Tom put his arm around me, and I sniffed a little as I dabbed at my eyes before I hugged them all.

CHAPTER NINETEEN

It was impossible for me to grab a moment alone with either Edwin or Hamlet. Hamlet was his normal fascinating self, and Luka fell into a conversation with him that had something to do with trains, or maybe just the transportation back and forth to London. I couldn't quite follow.

Everyone had wanted so much to meet Edwin. They'd all had their own email exchanges, their own impressions. They all felt they knew him and had craved meeting him in person. They all wanted their own moments with him, and those moments were far more important than the questions I had. I'd get my time with my boss and coworker, but for now I was just glad they were okay.

As always, Edwin was gracious as well as apologetic. He didn't explain his absence to the group, and no one came out and asked him specifically why he was gone. He said that Rosie had filled him in on most of the week's happenings, and he asked everyone if, despite the various misfortunes, they were having a good time. They all assured him it was a great tour. He said that he'd known I could handle it.

When we told him about our visit to the Scott monument earlier today, he entertained everyone with his well-known Scott quotes, his voice, tone, and accent all perfect. Though I never found his accent too difficult to understand, when he quoted from Scott, or any other old Scottish writer for that matter, he always deepened the brogue and peppered in just enough of the Scots language to make it all the more intriguing.

"Did you know the inn manager?" Luka asked, moving the conversation back to the other goings-on.

"Geoff? Aye, I knew the lad fairly well," he said, surprising everyone, me the most. "We went out to dinner once a month, just he and I. He was very intrigued by the rare manuscript market and wanted to know how he could dabble in it without spending much money."

"Did he ever buy or sell anything?" I asked.

Edwin shook his head. "Not to my knowledge. Not with me." He paused. "I really think he just liked talking about things, probably more than spending the money to acquire them. I understand that—it can be an expensive undertaking. I enjoyed the conversations. He was a quick study, a nice lad."

"Did you know his wife or son?" I asked.

"I never met Tillie, but they were only recently married, within the last year or so, I think. I met his son once. Hamlet knows Max."

We all turned toward Hamlet.

"Aye, Max and I met at university. We both took a bus to Grassmarket one day. When we disembarked, we talked about both of us working in the market, hit it off, had a pint or two at a pub near the university. But I haven't seen Max for a few months now. I thought about him the other day, wondered what had happened to him."

"Is he tall?" I asked, though the pictures had confirmed that he was.

"Aye. Very."

"Agile?"

"I don't know, Delaney. He looks as if he could be."

"Why?" Edwin asked.

"I saw someone running from the inn that night."

Though Rosie had shared with them what had happened, she hadn't given them all the details. I filled in more of the blanks.

"Goodness, I wonder if Max was up to something." Edwin looked at Hamlet.

Hamlet's eyebrows rose. "I don't know. Maybe."

"What?" I asked, my attention moving between the two of them.

Edwin shook his head. "Nothing."

I nodded and turned back to Hamlet. "Did Max seem . . . I don't know, troubled in any way?"

Hamlet shook his head. "I don't think so. It's been a while." He looked at Edwin and then back at me. "The last time we spoke, he seemed tired, but not troubled. I wished I'd popped into the inn to inquire about him, but I didn't."

The air seemed to hold a bunch of unanswered questions. Fortunately, everyone was far too polite to allow any uncomfortable silences to go on for too long.

The table fell into conversation again. I caught bits and pieces. Luka was describing his plans for a pub, and Tom seemed genuinely impressed by his ideas; Hamlet and Gunter were laughing about something; Kevin and Edwin were discussing literature, from what I could gather; and I had Rosie all to myself.

"You are as relieved as I am," I told her.

"I am, lass. Edwin will share what happened later. I don't think it's my place."

"I understand." I sighed. "However, we're doing the underground tonight—they still want to go. Do you think Edwin will lead the way?"

Rosie laughed. "I think he'd be delighted to."

She was correct. We sent Tom to work so Rodger could have some help, and Rosie and Hamlet went home with promises to be at the bookshop bright and early the next day. Edwin led the way, and I was able to just enjoy the ride for the night.

He was so much better at this than I was, but thankfully no one pointed that out.

There was a reason the World's End pub was scheduled on the tour the same day as the underground excursion. The pub was located at the spot where the city had once ended. It had been enclosed by the stone walls, so the population was, in theory, protected and guarded. However, those close quarters made for overcrowding and then ultimately a perfect petri dish of sorts for the spread of the plague—twice.

People needed someplace to live when everything aboveground was occupied, so the underground was carved out, built to house people—and, again, unknowingly allow the plague to spread easily and decimate the population.

Buried below the ground in Old Town was a network of narrow alleyways and abandoned one-room homes. The underground was a source of many a ghostly tale—in fact, I had my own unexplainable experience in a tunnel one time—but as a tour guide Edwin avoided the paranormal and stuck to the facts.

We'd gone inside a building on the Royal Mile, and then down some stairs. The tunnels were the real deal, though the decorations, including clothes hung on lines here and there, weren't from the original time. They did, however, lend an authentic flair to everything.

"It was crowded—it was stinky up there," Edwin said, his head almost touching the carved-out stone ceiling as electric torches, looking very much like the old fire ones, cast shadows and yellow light throughout the cavern. "The richest people lived on the top stories of the buildings aboveground, which meant that the poorest lived on ground level, where sewage was simply thrown everywhere.

"It was almost by accident that this underground world was created—a close was accidentally buried under houses that were being built. But, oddly, those who had done business in the close or lived there carried on even when it was buried, still needing the space no matter what. This underground world was not desirable, though. No windows, no fresh air. Ultimately, when the plague rolled through in 1644, the wealthiest Edinburgh residents fled the city, but not those down here, for the most part. They were all gone shortly after that, either somehow lucky to get out and away or having died."

"Is it haunted?" Kevin asked.

"Many say it is. I love our ghosties, but I can say I haven't experienced one down here." Edwin looked at me but didn't bring up my Christmastime experience.

"No matter what tour you choose to take down here, it's always fascinating. Let's look around."

Again, Edwin had gotten special permission for the evening tour. There were plenty of professional tour guides to show people through the underground, but Edwin was given full access and was allowed to be an unescorted guide all on his own.

Imagining life under the city always left me feeling melancholy. Edinburgh was such a spectacular place—now, with the advent of modern plumbing, at least—that I wished everyone who'd ever lived there had the gift of the experience I'd had.

But I knew better. That's not the way history worked. I knew that most of the time, but those moments of melancholy had me thanking the universe for the life it had sent my way.

We traveled along the uneven length of walkways as Edwin continued to talk about the misery of life lived down here.

"It was a place for thieves and other sorts of lawbreakers to hide, a place where so many people died, mostly because they couldn't get enough fresh air to have a chance at recovery. Activities of all sorts of unsavoriness occurred down here." He stopped and pointed inside one of the small cut-out rooms where a good old-fashioned pillory had been set up, a skull resting atop. The device had been used to secure a victim's head and wrists so they might be tortured.

"Oh," Kevin said.

"Is that a real one or a reproduction?" Luka asked.

"I believe the pillory is authentic, the skull probably not." Edwin paused. "Though I don't know for sure."

Edwin pointed out troughs that had been used to feed cattle that had been kept underground with the people. He told stories peppered with criminals and their activities, and others who'd just tried to make a life for themselves but didn't have the resources.

The time flew by, and, before we knew it, we were done and headed back into the real world. When we emerged from the vaults, we all took deep breaths of fresh air.

"Fascinating, but I really wouldn't want to live there," Gunter commented.

"I agree," Kevin said.

"I'm not ready to leave Edinburgh." Luka looked around. "There's so much more to see."

"I agree," Kevin said again.

We walked slowly back to Grassmarket, offering suggestions for those who truly wanted to spend more time in the city. Ultimately, everyone decided that though they wanted more, they were tired enough to call it quits for the night. Edwin and I made sure everyone got to their rooms safe and sound, and that there were no bad smells in any of them.

Sherrie was at the front desk, but she didn't seem to want to spend any time talking to either Edwin or me. After we told her all was well and thanked her for taking care of everyone, she disappeared into the back office again. I hoped there was something good in there to entertain everyone.

"They will have to hire more staff quickly," Edwin noted.

I wanted to ask about O'Shea, but I felt like I needed to ease into my curiosity about everything with Edwin. He was in a good frame of mind, but he'd been through some sort of wringer. I knew we'd talk about everything when he was ready.

"I guess so."

For a long moment, we both stared at the vacant space

behind the counter. I thought I saw Edwin fall into serious thought for a moment, but it didn't last long.

Finally, he turned to me. "A drink, lass? Tom's pub?"

"I hoped you would ask." Maybe he was ready to talk now.

Edwin laughed. "Come along."

"My identity was stolen—it's both that simple and that complicated," Edwin said.

We were sitting at the bar. It was just us, Tom, and one customer, seemingly in no hurry to head home but also not interested in our conversation.

"How did you know?" I asked at the same time Tom asked, "How did it happen?"

"I went to purchase groceries online." Edwin shrugged. "I love having my groceries delivered, but when I attempted my last order, the card I most use was declined. And then my others were declined as well. And, when I went to log into my bank accounts, they were all either showing a zero balance or locked, and I was unable to access them."

I swallowed hard. "That had to be terrifying."

"It was. For a time, Delaney, I had nothing, not a dime, other than the few bills I carried in my wallet. I made a call to some of my attorneys in London, but I was too anxious to sit and wait for them to do their work. I grabbed Hamlet just in case I needed some assistance and, frankly, a valid credit card—of course, I'll pay him back too—and we made our way south. We sat in attorneys' offices, bankers' offices, and watched them work."

"I bet that didn't make them happy," Tom said.

Edwin laughed again. "Not even a little bit, but I didn't care. I had to know what had happened to my money."

"And what *had* happened?" I asked.

"Somehow, a hacker—which is a terrible word, by the way, but so appropriate—hacked into my accounts and drained everything."

"How is that possible? And how did you get it all back?" I asked.

"I still don't understand how it's possible, but I'm insured— very, very insured," Edwin said. "I was certain the banks would attempt to fight my claims, but they were all helpful and took care of me well. There's an international group investigating. It's rather exciting. Well, now that I have my money back."

I blew out a heavy breath. "Edwin, that's awful, and, of course, now a relief."

"It was scary, but it's truly all good at the moment, though I suspect I'll have a nightmare every now and then. Even if I hadn't gone to London, I don't think I could have conducted the tour, Delaney. I was a wreck."

"I've never seen you a wreck. You're always so in control."

"I wasn't this time." Edwin shook his head. "However, the tour seems to have gone perfectly."

"Other than the issues, I suppose."

"Aye. But they all say that they will never forget their trip to Edinburgh."

"No." I sloshed the ice and my soda around in the glass.

"You helped, I think," Edwin said.

"Helped? With the tour?"

Edwin laughed. "No, lass, with the international investigation."

"I don't understand."

"Well, the first time I discovered the trouble was with my groceries, but when you went to ask the inn how things were going, they let you know my card didn't go through. That transaction predated the attempted grocery purchases. Rosie found the records, and the investigators now think that the initial transaction after the theft was with the hotel. That will help them track down the thieves."

"Right. It's impossible not to think something was going on at the inn. We told you about the items found in Kevin's room and what they could be used for?"

"Aye, though it's hard to believe that bottles of alcohol and some sandpapers are somehow tied to the sophistication that was needed to steal all of my property." He paused. "It does seem like an odd coincidence, though. I can't deny that."

"It does. And maybe what got Geoff killed—or caused him to jump off the roof?"

"It's a possibility. And, so you know, from that moment of discovery, the team in London has been working with Inspector Winters."

"He knew what was going on with you?"

"Aye, and I know that will bother you, that he didn't let you in on things."

I thought about the fact that he hadn't really seemed worried about Edwin, or even inquired about him. It was because he already knew where he was. "No. That's not his job . . . well, maybe a little." I smiled and then shook my head. "No, it's good. But do you think Geoff or someone else over at the inn might have been stealing identities along with even bigger things?"

"I don't know, but that's where my first issue seems to have occurred. I would never guess that of Geoff, but who knows? People are full of surprises."

"There are other people over there. Tillie and Max and the other employees. I wonder if the police have found and talked to Max. And Barney O'Shea."

"O'Shea?" Edwin said. "Oh, of course! I always forget he's a partial owner of the inn. He's got his hands in so many things."

"I do know he had to work there last night."

"I can't imagine."

"I don't think he could have either."

"Ah, it's good for him, I suppose. How was he at the school?"

"Fine. Bothered you weren't there. Oh! He gave me a card to give to you. I'll bring it to the bookshop tomorrow. I put it in my bag and forgot all about it."

"I'm sorry he was bothered I wasn't there, but that would be like him."

I nodded, wishing I had the card, if only so Edwin might open it in front of me.

Edwin took a deep breath. "Tell me, what's been your favorite part of the tour?"

I thought about it a moment and then smiled. "That's easy. Getting to know the people. They are delightful."

"You didn't like the cemetery the best? I'm surprised."

"I love any good cemetery, Edwin, you know that, but, no, it's the people."

"Aye, I do too."

We spent another hour at the pub, enjoying the company and conversation. We didn't do that enough.

As Edwin stood to leave, he asked if I wanted to visit the hospital with him the next day. I was momentarily confused, but he clarified quickly, saying that he wanted to check on both Carmel and Tillie, perhaps give Tillie his condolences, even though he seemed bothered that he couldn't understand why she'd impersonated Meera. I read between the lines—he was doing some investigating of his own. I answered immediately that I would go with him, and wondered what strings he'd pulled to be allowed to talk to either of them.

It didn't matter. I wasn't going to miss out.

"That was odd," Tom said after Edwin was gone. "But maybe it's the neighborly thing to do, visit Carmel and Tillie."

I shook my head. "He's not being neighborly."

"What then?"

"I'm not sure, Tom, but I'm looking forward to finding out."

"Aye." He paused. "Give me a few and we'll head home ourselves. It's been a long few days."

I smiled. "I'd say."

Though Edwin had been the one to say he'd probably have nightmares about what had happened to him, the theft of his identity weighed on me all night, images of Edwin and Hamlet moving through my anxiety-riddled dreams. Again, I was glad when it was time to wake up and get going again.

And, maybe, if we were really lucky, get some answers that would keep all future nightmares at bay.

CHAPTER TWENTY

When Edwin picked me up the next morning, he called an audible. We weren't going to the hospital first.

"Lass, first we're off to talk to Barney O'Shea."

"Okay. I'm game." I reached into my bag and found the card O'Shea had given me. I handed it to Edwin. "Want to open this before we go?"

"No, I'll check it later." Much to my disappointment, he set it on the backseat of his car. "What did you think of O'Shea?"

"He was . . . a surprise. I'd assumed he was with the school, maybe a security guard, but that wasn't what it seemed when we got there. He didn't like that you weren't with us. And then, last night, riding in on the scooter . . . It was just all a surprise. How long have you known him?"

"He moved to Edinburgh about five years ago. We met at a function. He told me he was an investor in the inn, at the time it was being sold. I told him about the tour group and that that's where they'd been staying for years. He said he could get us inside the Herriot school if I wanted to add that to the itinerary. Before, we'd just toured the grounds."

"I bet you could have gotten inside if you'd wanted to."

"Until O'Shea mentioned it, going inside didn't even cross my mind. But I think it's been a good addition."

"Why are we going to see him this morning?"

"I've had the night to think over things more. I wonder if he might give us more insight into what could have been happening at the inn. Was there something like driver's license fraud going on? Was there something more sophisticated? It might be a complete coincidence that all of what has occurred happened at once—my identity, my money, Geoff, Tillie. I'd talked to Geoff, who'd run the card for the deposit, but something else occurred to me only last night after talking with you and Tom. I took myself back to the moment that I gave him the card number over the phone. He said it went through and all was well."

"But it didn't, so . . . Well, maybe he just didn't run it at that moment and assumed all would be fine."

"Or he didn't run it for another reason."

"And that reason could have something to do with stealing your money, your identity?"

"I have no idea. I'm far too trusting, lass. In a million years, it would never occur to me that Geoff would take advantage of our friendship—or maybe even work to create that friendship simply for the goal of taking my money, ruining me. Without even thinking, I read my card number and its particulars to him over the phone. I'd like to believe he had nothing to do with what has occurred and that maybe someone was listening in, but that feels naïve. Honestly, it's probably a good thing I was out of town when he died. I might be under some suspicion."

"I hadn't even gone there."

"I also think the investigators looking into what happened to me will track down the perpetrators, but maybe there's something we can learn that will nudge them in the right direction."

"I'm glad you got your money back."

"Again, I'm insured. I'm well-respected. Though for a moment in time I couldn't pay anyone with a check that wouldn't bounce, I have expensive counsel. I'm lucky, don't get me wrong, but I imagine I haven't seen all the damage that's been done yet." Edwin sighed. "Anyway, I do wonder if O'Shea has any insight."

"As a partial owner?"

"Aye, don't let him fool you. He's more in the middle of things than he lets on. There are many George Heriot school benefactors, but few that would do what he's done for the tour group, and I would bet that no one has fought him on it."

"What if he does know something?"

Edwin shrugged. "Again, I think it just might help things along." He glanced over at me, almost sheepishly. "Lass, I'm deeply curious, and though I've criticized you for being such, I can't help myself."

I smiled at him. Edwin had mulled things over, and he was angry, and probably hurt. He'd had lunches with Geoff, shared his rare manuscript knowledge. Though Edwin would never feel someone owed him anything for that, he certainly wouldn't think that he should be taken advantage of, if only because of the friendship.

"O'Shea is a part of the Fleshmarket Batch," Edwin continued. "I suspect the card is about something he'd like to bring to our next gathering. It's the way O'Shea has always done things, a card instead of a formal email to all of us. It drives Birk a little crazy."

Both Edwin and his good friend Birk were part of a group that enjoyed buying and selling very expensive items. I'd been to a few of their auctions by now, and they and the people there were fascinating to me. All the members were very well-off and, somehow without being snobbish, had enough money to spend as if the auctions were simple carnival events, maybe bingo games.

I hadn't seen O'Shea there once. I tried to picture him among the others, and it wasn't easy. He was tall, sure, but he was also much younger than most of the members. Off the top of my head, I couldn't think of one member I knew who was younger than sixty. O'Shea was probably in his late forties or early fifties. There was something about the older crowd that gave them a distinct personality that I couldn't see O'Shea fitting into.

Edwin stopped the car in front of the Greyfriars Bobby pub.

"He lives here?" I said, my eyes going to a red door.

"Aye. In a small flat above the pub. He once said that he's not here much, said he only wanted some place small. He travels back and forth to Ireland."

"Edwin, this is also where Carmel lives—the woman from the inn who was hurt the first night."

"That might make sense. A neighbor who needed a job.

I've been to O'Shea's, but I saw no evidence that he lives with anyone. There's a flat across the hall . . ."

"Let's see if that's her place."

We went through the building door and climbed one flight of stairs to a landing that held two other doors and a picture window looking out to the cemetery I'd taken the tour group through so recently, though it felt like ages ago now. There was another flight of stairs that led up to a top level.

"Do you know how many apartments are up there?" I asked Edwin as I pointed upward.

"Just one. A penthouse of sorts. I don't know the family who lives there, though. I don't know who lives in that one, either." He nodded to the door across the landing from O'Shea's as he knocked on O'Shea's door with a few friendly raps. O'Shea appeared, and looked at me a long moment, then cocked his head. "I know you . . ."

"Delaney Nichols." I extended my hand.

"Of course. We spoke just last night. You are married to the pub man."

"Yes, Tom is my husband."

He seemed to *almost* frown as he studied me another moment. I realized that Edwin must have called O'Shea before we'd arrived to tell him he was coming but must not have mentioned me.

"Good to see you, O'Shea," Edwin interjected.

O'Shea lifted his chin and then nodded. "Same to you. Come in, have a seat. I'll grab us some teas."

It was the way he spoke—clipped and very close to monotone. He didn't add any other sounds—differing pitches, laughter, guffaws. He wasn't really unfriendly—he just wasn't . . . immediately cheery, I thought. I decided that he hadn't been being anything but himself at the school.

The layout of the flat reminded me of Rosie's, though it wasn't decorated with nearly the same number of bright colors that she always enjoyed.

The front main space was attached to a small kitchen. A door on the other side of the kitchen led to the other rooms, which, if the layout was like Rosie's, were probably two bedrooms and one loo. Both places were cozy, but O'Shea's black-and-white, sleek-lined décor wasn't as comfortable as all of Rosie's cushions and throw rugs.

"How's the bookshop, Edwin?" O'Shea asked from over the kitchen counter. "You were away? Did all go well?"

"Aye, all is well. We are happy with our corner of the bookshop market."

O'Shea brought a tray around with a teapot and three mugs. The flowery and colorful tea set seemed to brighten up the room immediately, and I knew Rosie would enjoy the decorative pot.

Once our mugs were full, O'Shea sat in a chair as Edwin and I took the couch.

"I did miss you the other day. To what do I owe the pleasure of today's visit?"

"I have some questions. They might feel intrusive," Edwin said.

O'Shea sighed. He looked weary. "Ah, the bad business happening. I can't imagine they would have ever kicked out your guests . . ."

Edwin shook his head. "I'm glad it didn't come to that,

but aye, I'd like to talk about the bad business." Edwin sipped from his mug.

O'Shea nodded. "I understand and I appreciate your curiosity. I'm still trying to figure it all out, but I am almost certain that the manager, Geoff—did you know him?" Edwin nodded, and O'Shea continued, "I am almost certain he didn't jump off that roof. In fact, I think he was killed before he was thrown off it, and that it probably took a couple of people to do the deed. I talked to the police just this morning and asked again if the cause of death had been determined." He took a sip and then fell silent.

My eyes went wide. I was surprised by O'Shea's conclusion, as well as by his openness. He seemed to be comfortable sharing.

"What did the police say?" Edwin asked a long moment later.

"Oh. They said they'd call me back. I'm still waiting to hear." He shook his head.

"I was up on the roof, O'Shea," I inserted. I'd already told Edwin about my explorations with Kevin, and Inspector Winters had told me about Geoff's cause of death being blunt force trauma.

"You were? Why? How?" he asked, a distinct frown now pulling at his mouth.

"The door to the roof was unlocked and one of the tour group had explored up there. She came to the same conclusion you did, or at least suspected it."

"Aye?" O'Shea shook his head. "I feel like I should have been more involved, even if that truly wasn't my place. Maybe I could have prevented something, even if I don't know what, exactly. I'm the only local investor, so my investment group tasked me with checking on things every now and then but told me that they didn't expect me to be a part of any sort of day-to-day operation. I . . . I guess maybe I should have been."

"Don't blame yourself," Edwin said. "Something was definitely going on over there, but I think the police have a few different angles to explore. I doubt you could have stopped much of anything. You're not a hotel man, are you?"

"Oh no. I'm just an investor. I fell in love with Edinburgh and wanted to spend some time here." He shrugged.

I nodded. "Do you know the young woman who was hurt—Carmel?"

"Of course. She lives right across the hall from me. I'm the one who suggested she apply for a job there."

I nodded again, feeling like I was on to something that should either lead to an answer somewhere or at least rule out a line of investigation, though I couldn't know which. "Did you talk to her about Edwin's group?"

O'Shea shook his head a long moment later. "No. I don't think I've had many conversations with her—certainly nothing about Edwin. I know she was hurt, and I'm concerned for her, but I don't know her well." He sighed again, the only thing that interrupted his continually clipped words-sighs. "Yes, I am just an investor, but I'm also observant. I called Geoff a year ago and told him I thought he should ask the staff to—of all things—dress better. I stopped by one day and no one was wearing any sort of uniform. It wasn't easy to tell who worked there. Maybe I'm old school, but it seemed important. My concern was dismissed, and I didn't feel it was my place anyway, but, because of all of that, Geoff and I talked every now and then, mostly when I was walking through Grassmarket and we happened upon each other."

"Did it bother you that your concerns weren't taken seriously?" Edwin asked.

"Not even a little bit. I have money in lots of different places, and I'm a small investor with the inn. As I said, I've never been in such a business. What do I know about it anyway? Mostly, I just shrugged it off."

"I heard Geoff might have been in trouble, his job maybe in jeopardy, not that long ago," I said, noting to myself that O'Shea seemed to be contradicting himself some. Was he involved or wasn't he? It wasn't easy to determine.

"I have no knowledge of any of that," O'Shea said.

Edwin nodded.

"Now, of course . . . Well, I wish I'd been paying better attention to many things," O'Shea added.

I cleared my throat. "When Geoff told me about Edwin's card being declined, it was Carmel who pointed out that there was also a note from him about throwing out the guests. Geoff wasn't pleased she shared that part."

"No, I can't imagine he was." O'Shea looked at me a long moment. "Do you think Carmel and Geoff got in some sort of argument, maybe a physical fight?"

I had wondered about that, about the timing of everything, but I couldn't make it all work. "I have no idea, but I don't think so. I guess I just wonder . . . who did Geoff report to? You were an investor, but surely Geoff had a boss?"

O'Shea shook his head. "I couldn't tell you. I have no idea."

"The police haven't asked that?"

"They haven't asked me."

"Maybe you could do some research, let them know," Edwin said.

"I don't even know where to begin, but I will see what I can see." O'Shea studied Edwin. "Why? Is there more to your credit card issue?"

Edwin nodded a long moment later. "Aye, a wee bit, but I'm not at liberty to share the details."

"Oh. Well, yes, I will dig deeper."

"I overheard Carmel telling Geoff that she wasn't going to do something he wanted her to do. Gunter, a guest at the hotel, said he overheard the same sort of thing."

"What did he want her to do?"

"I have no idea. I've been wondering that since it happened, and"—I glanced at Edwin and then back at O'Shea—"since *everything* happened."

"Did you tell the police?" he asked.

"Of course."

O'Shea sat back in the chair and rubbed his finger under his nose. Finally, when he looked up again, he said, "She's awake, you know. Carmel."

"I'd heard," I said.

"I wonder if she can shed some light on all of these matters," O'Shea added.

"I'm sure the police hope so."

Edwin and I shared a look, but neither of us mentioned where we were headed next.

"I will see if I can find out anything more," O'Shea said.

"Thank you," Edwin said.

We left O'Shea's flat only a few minutes later, O'Shea seeming even more distracted, Edwin appearing not as relieved as I'd hoped he would.

I remembered that my bookish voices had been oddly silent.

My intuition couldn't even pick up on what might be happening between them.

"I can't read that man," I said once we were inside Edwin's car.

"Aye, I wonder if he really doesn't know who Geoff reported to."

"As just an investor, it might make sense."

"Lass," Edwin said, looking over at me, "that's the thing—he feels like more than just an investor to me. He knew about my credit card issue. Why?"

He sat there a long moment, his fingers on the key but not turning the ignition.

"That's a good question. Someone told him. Not the police, so it might have been Geoff or Carmel before . . ."

"Aye. Why would they tell him?"

"He was more involved but doesn't want you to know? He's embarrassed by all that's happened."

"Now, that I can see." Edwin reached to the backseat and grabbed the card. He opened it and handed it to me. "Has nothing to do with the auctions."

It was a simple card, blue with no printed words on the inside, just a quick scribble of words. "*Edwin—apologies for the credit card mix-up. We would never have kicked out your guests.*" I closed the card. "Someone did let him know."

"They wouldn't have bothered if he was just an investor, aye?"

"I don't think so. You think he knows what's truly going on?"

"I think he at least suspects. Let's hope he calls the police."

I nodded. Edwin was pretty good at this investigating, and it was fun for me to be with him.

"The hospital?" I said a few moments later.

"Aye." He returned his hand to the key, turned it, and pulled out into traffic.

The hospital, a large, mostly white building with many different wings, took up a lot of real estate. Edwin had called someone to let them know we were on our way. We entered through the front doors and were met immediately by a man in a white coat.

"Edwin." He nodded. "How are you today?"

"I'm well, Dr. Phillips. This is my coworker, Delaney."

We shook hands.

"I'm here to visit Tillie Larson and someone we know only by the first name of Carmel—I regret to tell you that neither of us knows her last name."

I wished we'd asked O'Shea.

"So you mentioned on the phone earlier." Dr. Phillips frowned. "I'm sorry to tell you this, but even you can't just visit people here. There are many privacy laws in place. We are a secure facility, and we must respect patients' rights. You must have their permission to visit any of them."

It had been a difficult speech for the doctor to make, and my heart went out to him. Edwin had probably given the hospital a lot of money.

"Aye, doctor, I understand completely," Edwin said, causing the doctor's eyebrows to raise with what looked like surprise and relief. "May we call them and ask if we could visit?"

"Oh, well, one of the patients is in the ICU, so no, but the other one is awake." He paused. "I suppose we could ask her."

"I'm the person who waited with her," I said. "I saw her come out of the inn when she was hurt."

I cringed inwardly after I spoke the words. I wasn't looking for kudos.

I cleared my throat. "I just mean, I've been worried about her and would love to talk to her."

Dr. Phillips looked at both Edwin and me as if he wanted to be kind and understanding but wasn't sure that's what the moment called for.

Finally, he sighed and nodded once. "Give me a moment."

He disappeared behind a door off to the side of the front reception counter.

I looked at Edwin. His expression was pained. "You okay?" I asked him.

"Tillie's in the ICU. I'm saddened by what has happened, and if it has something to do with me and my silly money . . . Well, Geoff and Tillie. I would have given a load of money for them not to be hurt. I'm not even bothered by her impersonating Meera, though I'd like to understand why."

I'd never heard him call his money "silly," and I knew he didn't mean it. I understood even better now why our conversation with O'Shea and this trip to the hospital were important to him.

I put my hand on his arm, meaning to say something to comfort him, but the doctor reappeared.

"Delaney?" he asked me.

"Yes."

"You may go up to speak with Carmel." He looked at Edwin. "I'm sorry, but she only wants to speak to Delaney."

"I understand completely." Edwin nodded agreeably.

I hesitated. The doctor was watching, but I had to ask Edwin, "Is there anything you want me to tell her?"

"Just that I hope she's doing better and see if there's anything we can do for her."

I nodded, and the doctor said to me, "Let's go."

I followed him into an elevator. We were the only two riders.

"You work with Edwin?" he asked.

"I do."

"He's a lovely man. I'm sorry we can't accommodate his wishes to see the patients."

"No problem." I sent him an awkward smile that he returned in kind, and then I followed him off the elevator on the fourth floor.

He led me into Carmel's room. As I stepped through the doorway, my first reaction was that she seemed just fine. She was sitting up and alert. There were no machines attached to her—not even a fluid IV. It appeared that a bandage had been put over her injury, but I couldn't tell if that part of her head had been shaved or just covered. The rest of her hair was pulled back into a ponytail. She didn't appear either in pain or sickly. Relief relaxed my shoulders.

"Hi," I said after the doctor left.

"Delaney, right?" she said.

I nodded and walked closer to the bed. "Yes. Hi, Carmel."

"Hello."

"How are you feeling?"

"Lots better. The doctor said I'm going to be fine. I still have a slight headache and I can't believe they're not letting me leave yet, but I can't complain. I hear you . . . helped me."

"Well, I saw you come out of the inn . . ."

"Thank you. The doctor told me you're the one who made sure I got taken care of. I don't remember that, but thank you."

I nodded. "I was there earlier in the day—to check on the tour group. Do you remember me being there then?"

She nodded. "I think so."

I frowned. It suddenly seemed so wrong being in her room asking her questions, but there I was, and I sure wanted some answers.

"Have the police been in?"

"Aye," she said. "I told them all I could remember."

"Do you know who hit you?"

"No idea. They came up from behind me. I wish I could tell the police something helpful, but I have no idea."

That was disappointing.

I swallowed hard. "Could I ask you some questions about the inn?"

"Sure." She shrugged.

"What was going on there? Why did you guys have to stop renting out a room? It must have struck you as odd."

She shook her head. "I have no idea. I couldn't have cared less. I just worked there, you know?"

"Did anyone tell you who could go into the non-rented room?"

"Sure. Tillie and Geoff."

"And you didn't wonder why?"

"Of course I wondered, but no one was going to tell me. I just needed the paycheck." She gave me a long look. "I wasn't a bad employee. I did my job well, but I don't need that drama, you know? Life is dramatic enough." She pointed at her head.

I thought about what Rodger had said about her and her dramatic ways. I decided to keep that to myself. "I overheard you saying something in the office to Geoff, something about you refusing to do something."

Her eyebrows came together. "Okay, well, I'm not sure I remember exactly what that was, but Geoff is a jerk. Was." She blanched. "Sorry, but he really was. He was always asking people to do things they didn't want to do."

"Like?"

"Well, let's just say he didn't like cleaning the rooms, which, okay, that wasn't his job. It wasn't mine either, but sometimes we had to pitch in." She fell into thought again. "There's a chance I was telling him I wasn't going to clean up a room that had held a rowdy party the night before. That was probably it, but I can't remember exactly."

"You have a housekeeping staff?"

"Sure, but like everyone else, they don't always show up, particularly after big parties."

"What's the last thing you remember?"

"Just talking to Geoff, probably being irritated by him. No specifics."

"He was there, with you?"

"Yeah. I don't remember the moment of being hit, though. That's what the police wanted to know, if I remembered any-one else there with us. I don't."

"Do you remember changing a customer's bedding that day? He said it smelled too strongly?"

"Oh, sure, that happens." She smiled. "I do remember him, though. A lovely German man. Yes."

"Accidentally, he heard you saying the same sort of thing to someone on a call, that you weren't going to do something. Do you remember that?"

"Oh. I don't . . . Wait, maybe I was talking to my mother on that one. She wanted me to go home this summer." She snorted. "There's no way I'm doing that."

I swallowed again. "Why not?"

"My family is crazy. I'm from Inverness. I left two years ago."

I nodded. "Have you been okay? Has it worked out?"

"Up until the other night when some fool hit me over the head, for a reason I can't begin to fathom."

She wasn't lying. Or, at least, I didn't think she was.

She continued, "I'm a good worker. Sure, I don't make much money, but I can pay my rent, eat just fine, and that's all I care about."

I nodded again. "Do you know a guy named O'Shea? He's a partial owner of the hotel, or something like that."

"My neighbor? Sure. He recommended I apply for a job at the inn."

"Do you know much about him?"

"Not much at all." She paused. "Before he suggested the job, I'd seen him around, of course. I did see him talking to Geoff last week."

"Where?"

"At the inn. Why does that interest you?"

"Just trying to figure things out, I guess. Did you hear what they were talking about?"

She shook her head. "It wasn't friendly, I didn't think. I asked Geoff about it later. He didn't share the details, but he didn't seem bothered by it for very long." She paused. "It was just the way Geoff was, you know. I didn't think anything of it. He was a little too dramatic about everything."

"Do you think he could actually jump off the roof and kill himself?"

Carmel laughed, without humor. "Nope, and I've told the police as much. He was too much into himself—what's it called, a narcissist?"

"Really?"

"He could be really friendly, pull you in, then get crazy angry, and he thought of everything from his point of view. He had a higher regard for himself than anyone else did." Carmel shrugged.

"Got it." I wondered if Edwin had ever seen the angry side of him. And I wondered about the man outside Geoff and Tillie's apartment. He'd mentioned them yelling, but I'd decided he was probably lying. Maybe he hadn't been the one to hurt her. I made a mental note to tell Inspector Winters my thoughts. "Do you know Tillie well?"

"Not really. She isn't one to get to know the staff. She is above all that, from what I can tell."

"You know she pretended to be with the tour group, posed as one of those visiting?"

Carmel frowned. "That doesn't make any sense. How could she get away with that? Why?"

"She must have known that Meera wasn't coming."

"Meera?"

"One of the tour group members."

"Huh. Well, I'm not sure, but there's a chance I heard Geoff say that name when he was talking with Tillie."

"Really? Can you tell me more? That could be pretty important."

Carmel's eyes seemed to squint even harder, and I wondered if this was hurting her head too much.

"It's . . . okay," I said. "Only if you remember."

"I don't . . . not at the moment, but I'll try to. Should I tell the police if I do? I mean, I didn't even think about any of this when I was talking to them."

"That would be a good idea."

"So, you're thinking that someone named Meera had something to do with Geoff?"

"Honestly, I'm not thinking much of anything but how confusing this all is. If you remember anything else, it might help."

"Doesn't make sense."

"Maybe Tillie heard about a guest named Meera canceling, and then she decided to pretend to be her?"

"But why?"

"Great question."

Carmel sighed. "Okay, but that's not . . . When Tillie was at the inn, she wasn't interested in anything going on downstairs. Mostly, she beelined for that room and then left later."

"Who else went into that room?"

"I'm not sure. I thought I saw some people talk to Geoff and head up there, but he was good about keeping that on the down low, I guess. Or, as I said before, I just didn't care to pay attention. It's a paycheck, that's really all."

"I get that." I didn't, not really. I'd never had a job that was simply a paycheck. I'd loved them all.

Carmel looked tired, even more so since I'd come into her room. "My boss, Edwin MacAlister, sends his best wishes. Remember when I was there, and his card had been denied?"

"Yes, it's coming back to me."

"Have you seen anything at the hotel to make you think something unsavory like stealing credit cards was going on?"

"The police asked me that too."

"And?"

She shook her head slowly. "I have no idea."

"Would Geoff have truly canceled the reservations if I hadn't come in with another card?"

"Aye. I think so."

"I'm sorry to hear that." I couldn't connect Geoff's attitude to Edwin's problems, at least not solidly. However, that might have been the reason Geoff and Tillie were arguing.

I nodded. "Thanks, Carmel. I'm so glad you're going to be okay."

"Me too. Thanks for taking care of me. I really do appreciate it. I . . . You work at the bookshop?"

"I do."

She nodded. "I'll see you around then."

"Yes." I smiled. "I look forward to it."

As I reached the door, I turned one last time. "And you really don't remember who might have been the person running from the inn?"

"Wait. What?" She sat up some. "Running from the inn?"

I hesitated as my brain stumbled. I walked back to the bed. "I assumed, though I could be wrong, that he was the one who hit you? He was dressed all in black."

"No one has said anything about someone dressed all in black running from the inn. Everyone has just asked if I knew who hit me. You saw someone running away?"

"I saw a figure—probably male—dressed in black, even

with a black cap like a ski mask on, running from the hotel right before you came out."

"I didn't know."

I nodded. How had all of this not been thought through or fully asked? "Yes: tall, thin, agile."

"That sounds like Max. Geoff's son."

"It does?"

"He's always in black, though I haven't seen him in a ski mask."

I pulled out my phone. "I think we'd better clarify this with the police. Do you mind?"

"Go ahead." Her expression turned pained, and her eyes seemed to become watery. I hoped the conversation wasn't further jeopardizing her health, but I felt like we were onto something important.

She watched me as I called Inspector Winters.

CHAPTER TWENTY-ONE

Inspector Winters arrived and didn't say much more than a quick hello before he sent me away. I left him in Carmel's room just as she began to look worn out. I felt bad for probably being the cause of that but was glad for the important information that I'd gleaned. As I made my way back to Edwin, I thought about why the police hadn't asked Carmel if she had seen the person in black. It had probably been that they'd just asked her if she knew what happened and she'd simply said that she didn't remember.

"I saw Winters rush by." Edwin was right outside the elevator doors, waiting for me. "Is everything all right?"

I nodded quickly. "No one had asked Carmel specifically about someone in black. Inspector Winters is getting another statement from her. I described the person I saw, and she said it sounded like Max. But she's doing okay."

"Max?"

"Yes."

He nodded. "Oh dear, but I'm glad she's better. Anything else?"

"I'll tell you on the way," I said.

Once inside the car, I recapped my time with Carmel and asked Edwin if he had any idea where Max could have gone.

"No idea, lass. Geoff and I weren't close enough to discuss Max very often. But what in the world was going on at that inn?"

"Whatever it was, I'm more and more sure that it led to murder, Edwin. Geoff didn't jump—I'm feeling more and more certain of that. Carmel doesn't think he would have jumped."

"Aye. We never really know what's going on in others' lives, but it's all too suspicious."

I nodded.

On the way back to the bookshop, we rehashed almost everything a few more times. Edwin tried to keep a distant view of the circumstances, study them from afar, keep his issues out of it, though that wasn't easy for either of us, while I attempted to put myself in everyone's shoes.

My way didn't work. I had no idea what any of their lives were like. Though I'd grown fond of our visitors, I was relieved that the tour was over and they would all be heading home. They would finally be out of the inn, and, hopefully, harm's way. I also hoped the hotel's goings-on had nothing to do with Edwin's emergencies, but I suspected they did.

The police would have to figure this one out. I'd relaxed into that idea by the time we got back to the bookshop.

But as I'd discovered before, in the words of one of Scotland's favorites, Robert Burns, the best-laid plans do often go awry.

Hector greeted us as we walked inside, but something about his trot was less than cheerful. Edwin and I shared a look. I reached down to pick up the dog as I heard two female voices from the back, one of them belonging to Rosie, neither of them happy.

"What's up, Hector?" I asked him as he half-heartedly kissed my cheek.

Rosie appeared a moment later. "Ah, there you two are. We have a guest, and she's not pleased."

"Aye?" Edwin said.

"Aye."

Another woman appeared from the back. I recognized her immediately, but Edwin hadn't seen the picture she'd texted Inspector Winters.

"Meera?" I said.

"Yes."

"It's Meera Murphy," I said to Edwin. "The real one."

"Aye?" Edwin hurried a smile. "Welcome to the bookshop. I'm Edwin, and this is Delaney."

Meera nodded, but the distinct frown on her face didn't transform.

"Oh, aye?" Edwin said, sobering his tone. "What's wrong, Meera?"

"I'm here on a wing and a prayer, Mr. MacAlister. All my money was taken from my accounts, and I have nowhere to turn other than you. You are the only person I think who might have taken it. I'm here for my money." She crossed her arms in front of herself.

"I see. Well, I didn't take your money, dear lass, but I

promise you, we will find out what happened to it and get it back to you as quickly as possible. Please, have a seat. We'll figure it out."

The pause was long and strained. I was biting my tongue as Hector squirmed in my arms. Meera probably hadn't expected such a quick offer of a solution, and when she heard it, naturally, she was still suspicious. It even sounded suspicious to me, and I *knew* Edwin would do what he could to help her.

"You promise me?" Meera's eyebrows rose.

"I do. Come along, everyone, let's have a seat in the back."

Before we could take one step that direction, the door opened and Luka came through, smiling when he saw Edwin.

"If it's not too much trouble, I've come to see if you wouldn't mind visiting with me for a bit. I've extended my break and don't want to miss a chance . . ." Luka's eyes finally landed on Meera. He'd seen a picture of her too—when I'd shared the one she'd texted, so the rest of the group would be on the lookout. He hesitated a beat before clearing his throat and then continuing, "Aren't you the woman who was supposed to be here?"

She crossed her arms in front of herself. "I am. And who are you?"

Luka started at her tone, but then smiled again. "I'm Luka."

"Luka, please come join us in the back. It seems Meera has run into an issue similar to the one I have. In fact, I would like to explain it and for you to make sure you haven't had the same difficulty." Edwin looked at me and then back at Luka. "We will figure this out."

Luka frowned. "Um. Okay."

For a long moment, it seemed none of us were sure which direction to go. Finally, Rosie moved us along.

"To the back, everyone. We'll sort this out." She waved her arm and led the way.

There was more good news than bad, fortunately, but the bad was certainly pretty darn bad. Edwin shared more specifics with Luka and Meera on why he'd taken off for London, explained more fully what had happened to him. It was a bit comforting to Meera that she wasn't the only one who'd been stolen from, but her relief was temporary. She still didn't have her money.

"And Mr. MacAlister," she said, then corrected herself, remembering what he'd asked her to call him. "Edwin, the only money I had was probably pocket change to you."

Meera's mother *had* been ill. Her reason for missing the tour had been real. Though her mother was feeling better, Meera felt guilty for leaving her in Dublin and needed to get back as soon as possible, but she hadn't been able to stop herself from confronting Edwin in person.

She'd been with her mother for months prior to the tour, the only real transaction on her one credit card being the reservation for the hotel room in Edinburgh, the room Edwin said he would pay for. But the inn had asked her for her own card number, just to keep the room in her name. It wasn't the way it was supposed to have been done, but she didn't think much of it at the time.

Luka called his assistant, who said that the inn hadn't asked for a card number when she'd let them know he'd be there. The assistant was checking on Luka's accounts, but at first glance, everything seemed to be in order.

"Why didn't you just call the police?" Luka asked Meera.

"I don't have time for the police," she said. "Why would they care anyway? I wouldn't be a priority. They wouldn't have come directly to Edinburgh. I need answers. I need my money. They'd take my statement and then take forever to investigate, if they bothered at all."

"You weren't scared to come here and confront him?" Luka nodded toward Edwin.

"I'm more scared of not having my money."

I didn't think Meera feared much of anything. Though petite and delicate looking, she gave a quick impression of being tough as nails.

With all of us still at the table, I again called Inspector Winters, who said he was finished with Carmel and would meet us at the bookshop within the hour. Edwin called some of the people he'd met with in London, attorneys and bankers. It was interesting to hear this side of the conversation and his professional tone—one I'd witnessed before, but rarely.

There was nothing confusing about anything I overheard Edwin say, but there was a lot of information. Numbers, questions, pauses as we all waited for answers from the other ends. Ultimately, Edwin shared that the attorneys and bankers told Edwin that they had no indication that what happened to Meera's money had any connection with what happened to his, but they were going to keep investigating.

"I don't have much money," Meera said when he'd ended one of the calls. "But I need every pence of it."

"Meera, I can help temporarily," Edwin said.

She blinked at him. "You will do no such thing. I want *my* money, not yours. I'm convinced you don't have my money, but now I need to figure out how to get it back." She paused and looked around the table. "Thank you all for helping me."

Edwin nodded. "I understand, but no matter what everyone keeps telling us, this all has to be somehow tied together, and I . . . well, I have plenty of money. Let me make you a short-term loan and we'll both feel better."

Meera studied him. "I'll think about it. Mom rounded up some money for this flight, and she still has some to pay next month's bills, at least most of them. I'm staying with her for now, and she can take care of us both, but not forever. I'm okay for a short while. I'll let you know."

Meera had warmed to Edwin, though her stress was still evident.

"All right. Then at least let me host you. Please stay with me."

"Or me," Rosie piped up when Meera's expression hardened again.

Rosie didn't have the room.

"Meera, my husband and I have a home by the sea. We have a couple of spare bedrooms just for guests. Please stay with us," I said.

"I can stay in the inn—" she began.

We all, even Luka, let out a resounding "No!"

"Something strange is going on over there," I said. "I think we all believe that's where the thefts are originating. Remember we told you that someone impersonated you? That was the inn manager's wife. She's in the hospital now. . . . Anyway, no. If you'd like to stay at a different hotel, we can take care of the arrangements, but I—my husband and I—would both like for you to stay with us."

Meera frowned, but then finally nodded. "Thank you. I would appreciate that."

"And, I'll be happy to host a tour just for you today," Luka added.

We all looked at him.

Luka shrugged. "If it's inappropriate, I won't, but I'd love to revisit all the places that Delaney showed us. I've decided I'm not leaving yet. I might move to another inn, but I'm fine. I did give them my card to extend my stay, but I suspect they've halted whatever it was they were up to, at least for now. I'm going to visit Kevin in London when I'm done here, but I'm just not done yet."

"No, it's all right, if Meera agrees," Edwin said. "That's a lovely offer, Luka."

Though nothing was settled, at least we had some semblance of a plan. Meera wasn't nearly as panicked or angry as she'd been, though we could all see that she was still scared.

Inspector Winters arrived at the same time a few customers entered the shop. We let Meera and Inspector Winters use the table in the back as we helped customers and Luka.

It was all so strange, but I couldn't help but hope that with the theft of Meera's money, more answers were going to be found.

I was glad when Inspector Winters stayed behind after Meera and Luka left to revisit the tour spots.

"Anything new?" I asked him before he could stand from the table.

"I don't know, Delaney. She didn't contact her own law enforcement. I'm not sure there's much I can do except casually check if the theft of her money is tied to Edwin's. I don't have jurisdiction in Ireland, but I do know some people. I'll call them."

"But the thefts took place here."

"We think. Her bank is in Ireland. Edwin's international investigators would be more appropriate."

I nodded.

Rosie asked, "Do ye think she's telling the truth?"

"I don't sense she's lying, but I'm always suspicious. Why do you ask?" he said.

"She hurried to Edinburgh. She has no money, but managed to get here on a plane."

"Aye, but I hope she's telling the truth, Rosie. Even if the police in Ireland can help her, they can't do anything right away. She thought Edwin took her money, and she was determined to get it back from him. She's distraught, and I think that's genuine."

A thought occurred to me. "Inspector Winters, Tillie is from Ireland. That's where O'Shea's investment group is located, where he's from too. So is Meera."

Everyone's attention turned my direction.

"What?" I said.

"You might have a great point, lass," Edwin said. "That's . . . Well, it's not as strange for the rest of us because we're from here. We all know lots of people from Ireland. Valerie is one of them."

Valerie was Edwin's "lady love."

"Aye," Rosie agreed. "I wouldn't think much of it."

"I hadn't even thought about that. Edwin's correct. We all know people from Ireland, know some who've moved there from here. The connection is more obvious to you than the rest of us because we're so used to the back-and-forth. Good job, Delaney." Inspector Winters stood.

"Really?" Despite everything, I was momentarily pretty darn pleased with myself. "I hope it helps."

"I do too," Inspector Winters said. "Anyway, I need to go."

Inspector Winters left the bookshop as Hamlet came inside, the two of them sending each other quick greetings. Edwin didn't leave right away but told us he was going to spend some time in his mostly unvisited office on the dark side. He'd share with us if he heard any news.

Hamlet worked in the back, catching up on bookshop work and schoolwork he'd missed while traveling with Edwin. It seemed we were going to have a steady stream of customers today. I ran over to the dark side and grabbed my laptop, bringing it over to work on the light side so I could be there if Rosie needed help.

I called Tom to let him know about our houseguest. He was intrigued by the new addition to the mysteries and was looking forward to meeting Meera that night. It all seemed like such a normal day at the greatest bookshop in the world, at least for a few minutes.

Once I had a quiet moment, I sat at Rosie's desk with my laptop and started with what I'd figured would be the simplest of searches: "Meera Murphy in Dublin."

Though her name seemed pretty Irish to me, there were fewer hits than I'd predicted. There were several *Mira* Murphys, the slight change of spelling narrowing the options and leaving very little to go on.

I didn't do social media. In fact, the only person I knew who did was Hamlet, and he wasn't as involved with it as he once was. However, I always thought we were an unusual group that way. Most people seemed to have a Facebook or Twitter account or something.

According to what I could see, Meera Murphy didn't have any social media either. I couldn't find her on any of the usual websites. I wasn't familiar enough with anything else to search, and Hamlet was too busy to bother.

During the simple Google search, though, I found something that might be from the Meera Murphy we'd just come to know, in an online obituary for a man named Liam Reynolds. Someone named Meera Murphy had added a comment that said, "Mom and I send our condolences, Brit. We're so sorry. Liam was the best."

But that was it. I couldn't find anything that might tell me what her mother's name was. I couldn't find an address or a phone number. I even typed in the phone number I had for her, but that search came up empty too, or led me to sites that wanted me to pay for them to give me more information.

Though I liked making myself difficult to find via the internet, it was bothersome when others did it and I was trying to find them.

Rosie caught me sighing. "What is it, lass?"

"I can't find anything on Meera. Anywhere."

She shrugged. "Sounds like me, and like you some, too."

"I know, but I sure wish ignoring social media wasn't a thing with the people I'm curious about."

"Aye, well, I wish it would all just go away. We were better off without it."

It went against the tide, but even The Cracked Spine didn't

have much of an online presence. Of course, the reputation of the bookshop and its decades-long existence made it less necessary.

"How about the others?"

"What? O'Shea and Tillie?"

"No, actually I meant the others involved with the inn. Have you researched them?"

"Not really." I poised my fingers over the keys again and began with Geoff Larson.

I found him immediately. The inn did have an active web page, and Geoff was part of the home screen picture, standing next to the hotel with a welcoming and friendly smile. My throat got thick for a moment. More important than anybody's missing money, Geoff was gone, and Tillie was still in the ICU. I was sure everything was tied together, so I kept going.

Geoff also had an easily found Facebook page, and that's where I discovered some good stuff. Pictures of him with Tillie—smiling, seemingly happy. There were no pictures of them at the inn, but there were at other places like restaurants, parks, and even a bookshop I was familiar with but hadn't been inside of yet.

The privacy settings were nil as far as I could tell, so I just kept scrolling over silly memes and light posts—nothing heavy, nothing political.

But a few minutes in, I gasped.

"What is it?" Rosie said as she joined me at the desk.

Hector had been resting at my feet. He sat up and looked up at me.

"I think this is the man."

I took a screenshot and enlarged it on my laptop screen. It

was a picture from inside a restaurant. Geoff was holding the camera up for a selfie. Tillie was sitting on the other side of the table. They were both leaning in toward the middle of the table, smiling over what looked like a plate of flaming sushi. Behind the table, standing there—in an apron, I was pretty sure, though it was difficult to tell because of the flames—was the man Tom and I had spoken to outside of Geoff and Tillie's place, the man we'd assumed had been the one who'd hurt Tillie.

"What man?" Rosie asked.

I replayed the story to her.

"Are you sure?" she asked.

"I'm about eighty percent sure."

"That's good enough to call Inspector Winters, aye?"

"Oh yes."

I called him yet again and told him what I'd come upon. He had me text him the picture and then asked me to keep looking through Geoff's Facebook page, and any other social media if I had the time. He'd put someone on it at the station, but more eyes were always better.

I didn't mind the task at all. So, for the rest of the afternoon, in between helping customers with Rosie, I lost myself in the worlds of social media.

I found pictures of Geoff's son, Max, on Geoff's page. They were simple smiling pictures with no distinct location. I couldn't find pages for Max or Tillie.

My next search was for Carmel. I found her last name on Geoff's page, under his Friends list. Carmel Roberson was on all the sites I knew about: Facebook, Twitter, Instagram, and TikTok. Her Facebook page was public and had links to all her other social media sites. There had been nothing posted for about a week, but before that she'd posted frequently.

However, I couldn't find one post about the inn—about any of the people she worked with or the hotel itself. It seemed she had lots of friends, but I was glad not to find anything about Rodger.

As the bookshop's closing time came around, Rosie stopped at the desk again.

"Lass, do ye mind locking up? I'd like to get home, put my feet up a wee bit." Rosie lifted Hector, who'd remained sitting by me.

At some point, Rosie had put a sweater on him that matched her scarf, and they were adorable together. Edwin and Hamlet had left an hour or so earlier, telling me goodbye, but I'd been so into my computer that I'd barely even looked up to return the farewells.

I pulled my eyes away from the screen and smiled. "Of course."

"Did you find anything else helpful?"

"I don't think so. I'm not even sure if the picture I did find was helpful in any way." I shrugged. "Inspector Winters might have just wanted to keep me out of trouble, keep me here."

Rosie laughed. "Meebe."

I stood from the table and followed Rosie to the door. "Meera texted me that she and Luka would be having dinner tonight and she'd be at my house later. I hope it was okay for Luka to spend his day entertaining her."

"He's a nice lad."

I heard something in her voice. "Oh, hang on. What did I just hear? I don't think you truly mean that."

"Oh, I do, but why is he still here, Delaney?"

"He wanted to spend time with Edwin?"

"Wasn't he the one who was upset to miss work? I dinnae ken, lass, but I just wonder . . ."

He hadn't known Meera was in town until he'd come into the bookshop that morning, so I didn't think it was because of any interest he might have had in getting to know her. He'd mentioned that he was having a good time, that he wasn't ready for the tour to be over, though, yes, he'd also wanted to get back to Australia, back to work.

I shrugged. "I just don't know."

"Me neither." She smiled as she pulled the scarf around her neck a little tighter. "I think ye've changed me, lass. I'm much more suspicious of everyone than I ever used to be."

I laughed. "Maybe Scotland brings out the mystery in everything."

"Hmm."

"What?"

"I dinnae mean this in a bad way, but maybe it's not Scotland, lass; maybe it's you."

"Hmm," I repeated her tone. "Maybe I should work on that."

"As long as you're safe. It has certainly been interesting."

Rosie, with Hector tucked in her arm, left the shop.

I watched them reach the bus stop and then wait the minute or so until the bus arrived.

I looked up toward Tom's pub. There wasn't a line of customers out the door like there were some nights, but I could see shadows play on the walkway outside the window. He would be done for the day soon. I decided to head up there and grab a ride from him.

I hurried back to the laptop to shut it down. As I went to close it, though, I accidentally scrolled down the screen, going even farther into Carmel's Facebook page, back to a date just over a year earlier.

A close-up of her kissing a boy filled the screen. It might have been no big deal, but this boy was familiar. I was almost one hundred percent sure she was kissing Max.

I sat down on the chair with a plop and enlarged the picture on my screen.

"Is that you, Max?" I said.

When no one answered, I screenshotted the picture, then scrolled even deeper. I didn't see any other pictures that might be him. I shut down the laptop, locked up the bookshop, and hurried to the pub.

CHAPTER TWENTY-TWO

The pub was busier than I'd expected it to be. Busy enough that I hopped behind the bar to help Tom and Rodger, something I'd only recently begun to do. I couldn't mix drinks yet, at least not with any speed or accuracy, but I could pour a mean draft. I could also clean glasses to a sparkling shine when necessary.

After about thirty minutes, it began to clear out, which was a frequent weeknight pattern. The crowds stuck around longer on weekends.

Once we got things in quick order, I filled Rodger and Tom in on what had been going on and showed them both the pictures I'd saved, setting my laptop up on the bar.

Rodger wasn't bothered in the least by the picture of Carmel kissing the man we all thought might be Max, though he had no recollection of Carmel and Max ever dating.

"I scrolled down a bit more to look for other pictures. I didn't find any, and this one isn't tagged, plus I couldn't find any social media for Max. There weren't many comments, which might have helped me figure out if it was him. Carmel posted so many things, but this is the only picture I found of her kissing anyone."

"And no one commented with anything like 'cute couple' or 'relationship goals,' those sorts of things," Rodger said.

"I can't figure out if that means this was just a random occurrence or if all of Carmel's friends were so used to the two of them being together that no one said anything," I said.

"Or maybe they didn't have anything complimentary to say." Tom shrugged.

"When I talked to Carmel in the hospital and she said that the tall man in black could have been Max, she didn't add that he was or had been her boyfriend. I've been trying to replay those moments in my head, wondering if maybe I missed a hint of something, but I can't pick up on anything."

"According to the date, the picture was taken just over a year ago," Tom added.

Rodger nodded. "I do remember that Carmel took pictures of our food and of the two of us at dinner. It struck me as odd, but I was just getting to know her, so I didn't say anything." He paused. "I'm not into any of that either."

"I didn't see any pictures of you," I said.

"That's good," he said. "I hope she's able to get back to a normal, healthy life."

"Me too," I said.

"Hang on." Tom pointed at the picture of Geoff and Tillie. "I know this place."

"The restaurant?"

"Aye." He held the laptop toward Rodger and pointed to a print that hung on a wall in the background. "Does this look familiar to you?"

Rodger concentrated a moment. "Oh, aye, Landon's, down by Holyrood."

"That's what I was thinking too," Tom said as he put the laptop back on the bar.

"I should let Inspector Winters know." I grabbed my phone. "You really think that's it?"

They looked at each other and nodded. Tom said, "I'm pretty sure."

I texted the information to Inspector Winters and then fell into thought.

"What is it, lass?" Tom asked.

"I guess I'd like to run over there, but that's not my job, and that guy we ran into was so . . . creepy that I have no real desire to run into him again. I also think Meera will be at our house soon."

"She's already there. Luka dropped her off about an hour ago. I had Artair go over to let her in. I thought you knew," Tom said. "Artair said he was going to let you know, but he must have forgotten."

I sat up. "No, I didn't know. I should head home."

"Both of you go," Rodger said. "I've got the rest of this."

We helped with another quick wipe-down of the bar and the tables and chairs, and then I put my laptop in my bag. By the time we were walking to Tom's car, I noticed that Inspector Winters had texted me back saying he'd check it out.

"He's going to hire you away from the bookshop," Tom said after I read aloud the return text.

I laughed. "Never."

When we got home, we found Artair reading on a chair in the front room and our guest fast asleep on the couch. He'd covered her with one of Rosie's crocheted blanket gifts, and now he put his finger to his lips as we came inside.

We retreated to the kitchen in the back of the house and spoke in whispers.

"She was exhausted. I told her she could head up to a bedroom, but she asked if she could just rest on the couch for a while." Artair shrugged. "She fell asleep quickly, so I just covered her up."

"Thank you for taking care of her," I said.

"She's lovely . . . but haunted," Artair said.

"Aye?" Tom said.

"Aye. There's something about her eyes. The lad who dropped her off was polite but seemed to want to get out of here. It felt like maybe the two of them didn't quite get along, though neither of them said anything. I sat with her for a few minutes. Briefly, we talked about why she was here and what had happened. She's very worried."

"Edwin will find a way to get her money back," I said.

"Aye," Artair said doubtfully.

"What?" Tom asked.

"There's more than that going on. None of my business, of course, but there's more."

"Her mother's been ill," I suggested.

"That could be it. I just don't know."

"Well, thank you for letting her in and staying with her," I said.

"My pleasure."

We made our way, still quietly, to the front room again. But we all stopped in our tracks once we got there, almost comically accordioning together.

Meera was no longer on the couch. She wasn't in the living room. The blanket had been thrown aside. The front door was wide open, a cold wind blowing in.

"Meera?" I called toward the stairs. "Maybe she just went upstairs."

But even as I hurried up to the second floor and frantically searched the rooms, I knew she wasn't in the house. I knew she'd left. Why else would the front door be open?

While it was completely her right to come and go as she pleased, this was weird. We hadn't seen her leave. We all wondered if she had left on her own or if someone had come into the house for her. I tried to call and text her, but the calls went to voice mail, and there was no response to the texts.

Finally, for what felt like the millionth time that day, I called Inspector Winters.

"I can't see any cameras anywhere that might have caught something," Inspector Winters said as he came back into the house after looking around the neighborhood.

This time there wasn't much good news, and we couldn't be sure how bad the bad news was. We didn't know why Meera left or if she went with anyone, but we knew she wasn't answering her phone. It went directly to voice mail each time Inspector Winters tried the number.

"I've got an all-points bulletin out for her," Inspector Winters said.

"That sounds . . . serious," I said.

"It is." He paused. "The coroner determined that Geoff was killed before his body went off the roof. It was murder, and it has something to do with that inn, we're sure. Meera's arrival and now her disappearance are too tied in with the inn to discount them. The airport and ship ports are on alert too. We'll find her. Even if she just wanted to leave, we need to know what's going on."

"What else, Inspector?" Artair said. "Is there any more you can tell us?"

He looked at us all and then shook his head. "No, not yet."

"I didn't want to worry about them anymore, but I received texts from the tour group earlier this evening. They're still staying at the inn. I'm not sure when they're all going home, but they all seem to have extended their stays."

Inspector Winters frowned. "Tomorrow, tell them to move if they're staying in Edinburgh. Everyone needs to stay away from that inn."

"Okay." I considered texting them tonight, but it was late. "They'll be okay until tomorrow?"

"I'll send someone over there."

Inspector Winters and Artair left a few minutes later—Artair with a concerned crinkle to his forehead and Inspector Winters with an exhaustion I'd never seen on him before.

"Murder," I said to Tom.

"Aye."

"Do you think we should wake everyone and bring them here?"

"No, the police will make sure they're safe tonight. Tomorrow, though. We need to get them moved."

"I'll miss them when they do leave, but I sure won't miss worrying about them."

My dreams that night were filled with Meera and Tillie,

running from people trying to grab them, me standing a distance away and unable to reach them no matter how close it seemed they got. Frustration dreams.

It was an awful night, and I was again thankful when it came time to wake up the next day. I always loved going to work, but today called for even more important tasks.

CHAPTER TWENTY-THREE

"Well, I'm off to the airport right after breakfast," Kevin said as she cut her bagel in half.

I'd met Kevin, Luka, and Gunter at the restaurant across from the inn, and we'd amicably crowded around a corner table. It appeared the only one I was going to have to ask to move from the inn was Luka.

"I'm going up to London in two days to visit Kevin," Luka had said.

"That's wonderful!" I enjoyed hearing of their continuing plans.

"My plane leaves this evening, but I've scheduled a time to come back and visit with Edwin in a couple months," Gunter said. "I'm heading up to the castle until it's time to go to the airport. I'd like to see the royal jewels again."

"Enjoy," I said.

I looked at Luka. "You're welcome to stay with Tom and me while you're still here."

"Thank you, but I'm fine where I am."

"Inspector Winters would really like for you all to be out of there." I paused and looked around. "It has been determined that Geoff was murdered before his body went off the roof."

"I knew it!" Gunter exclaimed.

"Goodness, it must have taken two people to push him over the side," Kevin said.

"I didn't ask Winters, but that's surely what the police are thinking," I agreed. I looked at Luka again. "I can't insist, of course, but would you at least think about moving somewhere else?"

Luka nodded, but his eyes were unconvincing. "I'll think about it."

"Thank you." I looked around. "As crazy as this week has been, I'm going to miss all of you."

"Us too!" Kevin said. "I'm coming back next year, would have even if Edwin hadn't offered."

"I'm so sorry about . . . I mean, murder? Of all the horrible things," I said.

"Dear, you didn't kill anyone," Kevin said.

"No, but . . . Well, it's been so good to get to know you all, and I hope we stay in touch."

"You won't be able to get away from us," Kevin said. "Expect at least weekly emails from me."

They all seconded that.

Luka, Gunter, and I got Kevin and her luggage loaded into the cab she'd arranged for.

"Would either of you like to visit the castle again?" Gunter asked Luka and me after we'd waved farewell to the departing taxi, Kevin smiling out the back window.

"I'm afraid I have some work to do, but thank you. Do you need a ride to the airport?" I asked.

"I've already scheduled an Uber." Gunter looked at me. "I'll be back in a couple of months, but may I hug you good-bye right now?"

"Of course!"

We hugged like we were old friends, and I felt a silly tear come to my eye. Maybe this closeness I was feeling was the product of having gone through trauma together, or maybe I just liked them.

"Such a pleasure, Delaney. I will miss you and hope to see you again soon."

Gunter and Luka shook hands, and then we watched Gunter disappear up Victoria Street.

I turned to Luka. "Really, promise me you'll think about relocating."

"I will."

"Do you have time to walk me to the bookshop?"

"Of course."

We set off to cross the market. "I didn't tell the others, but Meera disappeared from my house last night."

"The Meera I was with, or the one who'd pretended to be Meera?" he asked, sounding genuinely confused.

"Right. It seems to be a Meera thing, doesn't it—disappearing. The one you were with yesterday. That's part of why Inspector Winters wants everyone out of the inn. Something really off, and probably dangerous, is going on there. I got the impression he was close to shutting it down while they investigate."

"I'd say. Okay, yes, I'll move."

"Thank you, but I was also wondering if you would tell me

about your time with her. My father-in-law mentioned you might have been in a hurry to drop her off."

Luka cringed. "I hope I wasn't rude."

"No, my father-in-law is just very perceptive." I didn't much care if Luka had been rude. Meera would take the cake in that category anyway.

"Okay. Well, she was very quiet. She went along with everything but didn't seem overly interested in what I was pointing out. We had a quick bite to eat at the takeaway"—he nodded across the market—"but she didn't seem to want to have any sort of conversation. It was fine, but I thought maybe I'd offended her."

"I doubt it, Luka."

We'd made it to the bookshop, where Luka held the door open for me.

We were greeted first by Hector, who'd come to like Luka enough not to ignore him, but everyone else was there too. Edwin, Rosie, and Hamlet were all sitting in chairs around Rosie's desk, enjoying mugs of warm drinks. Hamlet gathered a couple more coffees, and Luka and I joined them. I welcomed my beverage.

I recounted everything for everyone, including the confirmation that Geoff had been murdered.

"That hasn't hit the news yet," Hamlet said.

"Och, Inspector Winters trusts us. We'll keep it to ourselves," Rosie said, then looked at Luka.

"Oh, my lips are sealed." He locked his lips with his fingers.

I looked at him. "You said Meera was quiet, maybe uninterested in the tour you gave her?"

"I got the impression that she would have rather done it all by herself."

"Really?" Edwin said.

"Yes, she was . . . bristly, but I tried not to take it personally. She doesn't even know me."

"Did she make or take any calls while she was with you?" Edwin asked.

Luka thought a moment. "No, but there was a time when we weren't together."

"Where? When?" I asked.

Luka sat back in the chair and held the mug on his leg. "Well, this is odd. I hadn't even thought about it until now, but it was at the same place where we originally lost the first Meera."

"Over by the whisky restaurant?" I asked.

"Right. The old, abandoned gasworks building. That's where the woman pretending to be Meera disappeared."

I nodded. "We even called the police to come look for her. That was the beginning of us figuring out that she wasn't who she said she was."

"I know the place. It's known as a spot for drug transactions," Hamlet said.

I turned to Luka. "Do you think she bought drugs?"

He shook his head. "No, I found her right outside the front fence of the abandoned building. Last time we were there the fence had fallen down, but it appeared to have been reinforced since then. Meera was just looking at the building. She'd had no interest in the whisky, so we'd eaten quickly. As I paid for the meal, she went outside. It's an intriguing building; I thought she just found it interesting."

"Very similar to Tillie," I said. "There must be something about that place . . . I wonder what."

"Do you think Meera knows Tillie?" Hamlet interjected.

I shook my head. "Inspector Winters asked her. She said she didn't know Tillie. He determined that Tillie must have just seen Meera's canceled reservation and used it as an opportunity."

"An opportunity for what?" Hamlet asked.

"I don't know. I can only conclude that either Tillie was trying to escape from something and saw that as a way, or she was trying to interject herself into the tour for a specific reason, which I could only think was Edwin."

He nodded. "Something to do with my identity being stolen?"

I shrugged. "I guess."

"But why did the real Meera disappear too?" Rosie asked.

"The Ireland connection," Edwin said. "Delaney brought it up. Maybe there's really something to it."

"Edwin," I said, "how did Meera—the real one—get in touch with you regarding being a part of the tour?"

"Just like I mentioned—she emailed me. We corresponded for a while."

"How did she get your email?" I asked.

Edwin laughed. "I never ask. Word about the tour gets around."

"Luka?" I asked.

"I read about the bookshop, an article where Edwin said things about reading books that I just couldn't buy into. I imagine I had my assistant find his email, but I don't remember the details."

"Right. It's an organic process, something that, in a way, I leave to the universe to sort out, but . . ." Edwin rubbed his chin.

"What?" Rosie asked.

Edwin stood. "Excuse me a moment."

We watched as he made his way toward the stairs and then climbed them. We looked at each other with raised eyebrows. Hector took the moment to trot over to Luka and jump up so that his front paws were on Luka's leg.

Luka smiled and picked up the dog, settling him on his lap. "You're willing to put up with me now?"

Hector curled into a contented ball on Luka's lap.

Edwin reappeared only a few moments later and sat again.

"I have a few different emails that I use," he began. "I'd all but forgotten that Meera had written me on my business email, not anything I keep for personal use. In fact, I don't load it on anything but my desktop here, and then I always sign out of it when I'm not reading it."

"But you said it was all word-of-mouth. She could have gotten it anywhere," I said.

"She could have, but she's the only one on this tour who used this one. And, since it's my business email, it is the one I use for things like reserving the hotel rooms for the tour."

"So, Geoff had it?" I asked.

"Well, people at the hotel had it."

"That doesn't mean they gave it to Meera," Rosie said thoughtfully.

"No, but no one else has ever written me on that email regarding the tour. Honestly, I don't even remember thinking it was odd, but I'm pretty sure that Meera is the only tour person to have ever used it." Edwin looked at Rosie.

"Aye, if someone calls to ask for your email address, I give them the one that you use for personal things, not business."

"Everyone else used the personal one. Meera also didn't email me that she couldn't make it to the tour, which is somewhat odd. She said she had. I might not have noticed because of everything else going on, but I just checked and there was nothing in writing from her canceling either."

"That's interesting," I said.

"Maybe not, though." Rosie shrugged.

I sighed. "We all want Geoff's murder solved, Edwin's money mysteries figured out. Maybe we're working too hard to make all these mysteries tie together. Forcing the connections."

"Aye," Hamlet said. "But this group of mysteries certainly feels connected, even if we don't know how."

I nodded. "Maybe."

Though Luka still wasn't ready to leave town, he did leave the bookshop, telling us that he was going to spend some time just walking around the city, adding that he'd return later, and that he'd move to another hotel before the day was over.

"I don't think he's ever going home," Rosie said after he shut the bookshop door behind him.

"He's meeting Kevin in London in two days," I said.

"Aye, we'll see," Rosie said with a good-natured laugh.

"He's a good lad, though. He's too much work to do in Australia, but we might have adopted another one, at least temporarily." Edwin turned to me. "Do you think we should tell Inspector Winters all the things we've discussed this morning?"

I nodded. "He's probably tired of hearing from me, but it's important. I'll call him from the warehouse."

I excused myself and made my way to the dark side, where, if nothing else, I might be able to get some work done after I called Inspector Winters. I had to leave a message for him, but it was good to pass the information along, even if I wondered if I was overloading him, or relaying obvious or useless things.

Sitting on the corner of my desk, I looked around the space. I'd straightened it up well, so there was no messiness to bother me, get under my need-to-be-organized skin. But there was plenty to do, and it had all been neglected the last few days. I stood and made my way around to the desk chair. I fired up my laptop and watched my email in-box populate with new messages. Thankfully, none of them needed immediate attention, except for maybe one.

Well, Michael had sent me *two* messages. The first one delineated the value of each of the monocles I'd left with him. Only one of them was anything nearing valuable, and even that one wasn't worth a fortune. I appreciated the full appraisal. The second email from him was him just asking if I'd received the first one. I replied quickly that I had and that I would be by to see him in the next couple of days. I thanked him for his work and then forwarded the appraisal to Edwin, asking what he'd like me to do with the box of monocles.

I still wore the pendant Michael had given me. I held it between my thumb and finger and looked at the engraving and smiled. How in the world did something with the name "Tom" randomly end up with me?

My thoughts stumbled over that for a minute. Tom wasn't an unusual name, but still, what were the odds?

I took off the pendant and set it on my desk, but the monocle itself landed on my phone, bringing it to life and displaying what had last been on the screen—a picture of Meera, the one she'd texted to Inspector Winters and forwarded to me.

I'd picked up on the Ireland connections, but there were other obvious things of note. The monocle enlarged one of Meera's blue eyes. Tillie had blue eyes too, and dark hair. Just as not all Scottish people had red hair, not all Irish people were gifted with the dark hair, blue eyes, and porcelain skin that both Meera and Tillie had been given.

In fact, they did look alike.

Didn't they? Was I forcing something? I slipped the monocle chain back around my neck.

I turned to my laptop again and typed in *Meera and Tillie Murphy, Ireland*. There wasn't one hit with the two of them listed as I'd written. But there was something pretty darn close.

A few things popped up for Meera and Matilda Murphy in Ireland, though no pictures. The three sites my search directed me to were articles that mentioned two sisters, Meera and Matilda, who lived in Dublin, but there wasn't much to any of the posts. One just listed them as being involved with a local charity for a children's hospital. The second was a picture from what I thought was a school, maybe high school. It was a cricket team; the names "Meera Murphy" and "Matilda Murphy" appeared after the words "Not Pictured," below the photo. I stared at the picture a long time, trying to calculate if the women would have been the right age to have been part of the team. I wasn't sure.

The third article was the most intriguing. Sisters Meera and Matilda Murphy were listed as new employees at a bank in Dublin. The article was from two years ago. Again, though, there were no pictures, and I had absolutely nothing that could confirm that I was onto something.

I looked up the bank's phone number and called it. Not surprisingly, the phone was answered with an automated system asking me to dial an extension if I knew which one I wanted. I pressed zero a couple of times and crossed my fingers that someone would answer.

"Central Bank of Dublin, can I help you?" a young-sounding woman said.

"Yes, thank you, I'm looking for Meera or Til . . , Matilda Murphy. Is one of them available?"

"I'm not familiar with those names, ma'am. Are you sure you wanted the Central Bank of Dublin?"

"I am. Is there a chance you could ask someone who worked there a couple of years ago if they know where Meera or Matilda might have gone?"

There was a long pause before she finally said, in a perfectly delightful Irish accent, "Give me a minute."

The hold music was bagpipes. I laughed a little and enjoyed it.

When someone picked up again, it was a different person, a man.

"Can I help you?" he said with a distinctly agitated tone.

"Yes, thank you. I'm trying to find Meera and Matilda Murphy."

"Why?"

"They're old friends from primary school," I said, my accent distinctly American. Hopefully, he wouldn't think too hard about that.

"They haven't worked here for some time. I have no forwarding contact for them."

"Oh. Um, well, shoot," I said, trying to think of what else I could possibly say to get this man to give me more information.

My pause helped.

"Look, I don't know who you are, but if you're in any way tied to those women, we don't want your business here at Dublin Central. Don't call back." He ended the call.

I blinked and then looked at my phone. "Oookay. Huh."

This time I didn't even mind calling Inspector Winters again. Unfortunately, I had to leave another message, but something told me this was a good one, a substantial lead, even if it didn't really make any sense to me, and even if it turned out that Meera and Matilda weren't our Meera and Tillie.

Just as I ended the message, I got a text from Tom.

Want to go to dinner at Landon's?

Yes, I absolutely did. I glanced at the time. The day had flown, and the bookshop was set to close any minute. I hadn't checked in with any of my coworkers for hours.

I texted Tom: I'll meet you at the pub in fifteen.

He texted back a heart emoji, which, of course, made me smile, despite everything else.

I double-checked all my self-imposed security steps—locking my desk, shutting down the computer—and then I locked up the warehouse before I hurried to the other side.

Everyone, including Edwin, was still there. They were again gathered around Rosie's front desk.

"Oh, did I miss anything good?" I asked.

"No, but you've worn off on us," Hamlet said with a smile. "We're all still trying to understand what might have happened.

"Did you figure anything out?"

"No, I'm afraid not," Rosie said.

"Did you enjoy your time in the warehouse?" Edwin asked.

"I did. It felt good to get some work done." I debated telling them all what I'd maybe discovered, but until it was something solid, I'd keep it to myself and Inspector Winters. And probably Tom.

"I got your email on the monocles."

"Yes. Any idea what you want to do with them?"

"I think that donating them somewhere would be good. Does anyone need old monocles for anything?"

"I'll ask around," I said.

"Maybe a museum display? Your friend Joshua? Or the gentleman who did the appraisal. I'd be fine letting him have them. If he can sell them, that is. I'd like for someone to profit from them if that's possible."

I touched the pendant around my neck. "I'll ask them. Thanks. Does anyone care if I take off? Tom's offered to take me out to dinner." I didn't mention where we were going or why, but I saw something in Hamlet's eyes that made me think he knew I was chasing another lead. I smiled back at him, and he nodded knowingly.

"Go and enjoy," Rosie said.

"Luka called and asked if he could bring breakfast over to us tomorrow morning," Edwin said. "I told him it wouldn't be necessary, but we'd love to see him again."

"I'll be here early."

"Us too," Edwin said. "Our best to Tom."

As I left the bookshop, I wondered about Edwin's spending so much time there since he'd returned from London. He'd never been anything but polite to Luka, but I hadn't seen Edwin in the shop this much, ever. Was he worried about Luka showing up without him being there? Maybe he was worried about Meera, too. Maybe he was just there because he wanted to be. I tried to shake it off.

Tom was on this side of the bar, sitting on a stool and talking to Rodger. Only two patrons were there, enjoying drinks around one of the tall tables, but it was Friday and more people would file in soon enough.

"Hello, love," Tom said as he stood and kissed my cheek.

"Hello."

"Before we go, I wanted to tell you that we had a visitor today whom you might find interesting. Carmel stopped by."

"Really? She's out of the hospital?"

"Aye," Rodger said.

"Why did she come in?" I asked. "Did you ask her about the picture, by chance?"

Rodger smiled. "I'm afraid I didn't have a chance, really. She came in to apologize to me for her 'behavior,' and then she left before I could do so much as even accept the apology."

"Really?" I said. "Well, that's . . . interesting."

"I thought so too," Tom said. "We were both surprised to see her. She came directly to the bar, told Rodger she was sorry, and then turned and left. I'm afraid we were both struck a little speechless."

"I bet. How did she look?" I pointed at my head.

"She wore a hat." Rodger shrugged. "It was all very surreal. I mean, it even took me a moment to realize who it was."

I nodded. I'd visited with her the day before, and she'd wanted to go home, though absolutely not to her family's home in Inverness. I knew she'd talked to Inspector Winters again, but, of course, he hadn't shared their discussion with me.

"Well, I guess I'm glad she was sorry," I said.

"I wondered if you talked to her about me, about her and me?"

I shook my head. "Not a word, Rodger."

He nodded as if relieved. "Thanks."

Tom and I bid Rodger and the two customers good evening and left the pub.

"Tom, would you mind us running up to Carmel's flat first?" I asked as we stepped outside.

"You want to talk to her?"

"I don't know what it is, but I feel compelled to go. Do you mind?"

"Not a bit."

Instead of heading to the car, we walked across Grassmarket and up toward Greyfriars Bobby. It took only a few minutes. The red door that led to the stairway was unlocked, just like it had been when Edwin and I had visited O'Shea.

Tom followed me up the stairs. First I knocked on O'Shea's door, but there was no answer.

"It sure seems quiet," Tom said. "I don't get any sense that he's in there.

I nodded and knocked again. "O'Shea, it's Delaney from The Cracked Spine."

A few seconds later, I glanced at Tom and then reached for the knob. We were probably both equal parts disappointed and relieved when it didn't turn.

Tom followed me as I went to the other door. "This is Carmel's."

Surprising us both, this door opened with the first knock.

We stood still and watched it swing wide, exposing an apartment that looked both ransacked and nearly emptied.

"Uh-oh," I said.

"What do you suppose this means?" Tom asked.

I sighed. "I think it means I need to call Inspector Winters again."

"Aye." Tom nodded. "Aye."

CHAPTER TWENTY-FOUR

"This is definitely where Carmel lives," Inspector Winters confirmed as he looked at a message on his phone. Though he'd believed me when I told him, he thought it wise to double-check. I was glad he had.

He, along with a few other officers, had arrived quickly, though confusion reigned for a few minutes.

It was difficult to make everyone understand the connections. Were they supposed to be searching the flat for a person or for information? And why? Because she'd been hurt or simply because this woman lived across the hall from the man who had ownership in the inn?

Ultimately, Inspector Winters took command of the situation and told Tom and me to wait outside as they did what they needed to do.

We found an empty bench outside the pub and waited. It was cold enough that we were about to head inside the pub when Inspector Winters finally joined us.

"Any sign of her or that she was further hurt?" Tom asked.

"No sign of much of anything except that she seems to have left. We've called her family in Inverness, but they haven't heard from her either. We did find this, though."

He showed us an item in his hand. It was a small picture inside a wooden frame. Carmel and Max. There was no doubt about it this time.

"The picture you sent me earlier might make this one important," Inspector Winters said.

"Okay," I said. "But where's Max? Maybe they're together?"

"We're looking for him."

"What about the waiter at Landon's?" Tom asked.

"Aye?" Inspector Winters smiled, but it was a weary expression. "We think we've got a name, though he hasn't worked at the restaurant in some time. And, he has a record—identity theft."

It felt like the mysteries were being uncovered little by little, even though nothing was actually getting solved.

Inspector Winters noticed the look on my face. "This is how it goes, lass: one little bit at a time. You've been a great help. Thank you."

I nodded. It felt weird to say "You're welcome," but I mumbled it quietly.

"What about O'Shea?" Tom asked. "It's odd that he and Carmel live across the hall from each other, aye? We knocked on his door too. No answer."

Inspector Winters continued, "O'Shea's took off for Dublin. That's what he said when I rang him. He has no idea where Carmel took off to."

I searched my thoughts for a question, but the first one that came to me wasn't about Carmel. "Any word on Tillie?"

Inspector Winters nodded. "She's going to be fine. She's asked for an attorney, so we'll wait until that's in place before we interview her."

"I'm glad she's going to be okay!" I said, even if I wondered just how involved she might be with everything. "Meera?"

"No sign of her yet, but we'll get her. Honestly, I believe we're very close to having the answers."

"Even as to who killed Geoff?" I asked.

"I hope so. We're getting closer."

"Any chance you'd tell of the name of the waiter at the restaurant?" I asked.

Inspector Winters smiled. "Afraid not, but . . . I'd like for you to be on the lookout for him. He's a dangerous character, even if he wasn't the one who'd hurt Tillie, though I suspect he was."

"'Dangerous'?" Tom asked.

"Very," was all Inspector Winters said.

I frowned. "What in the world is going on here? And does Edwin's money have anything to do with it?"

Inspector Winters sighed. "If I were to venture a guess, and this is just a guess, mind, I would say that Edwin's being involved bothered someone—maybe Geoff—so much that whatever was going on at that inn, he challenged it. Again, that's only a guess, but we'll get to the bottom of it."

"Someone might have tried to protect Edwin?" Tom asked.

"Aye. Maybe. Have a good night, you two. Be careful out there, but don't hesitate to call or text me with anything else. I'll be looking for your messages." Inspector Winters turned and went back inside.

There was still time for dinner at Landon's, but we weren't

as interested in going now, even though I might have been able to ask someone the waiter's name.

"How about soup and sandwiches at home instead?" I said to Tom as we walked back toward the market.

"That sounds perfect."

So, not only had I had a semi-normal workday, but Tom and I managed a normal evening at home. Sure, we discussed all the twists and turns, all the people who'd come and gone through our lives over the past week, but the dinner was perfect.

It wasn't until I was trying to sleep again that night that I remembered something. What had happened to Sherrie? Did she still work at the inn, and had she seen anything helpful? I grabbed my phone from the nightstand and thought about texting Inspector Winters to ask, but decided enough might be enough.

"Lass?" Tom asked wearily.

"It's nothing. Get some rest."

"You too, love."

CHAPTER TWENTY-FIVE

As promised, Luka brought us all breakfast the next morning—a feast that he'd arranged to have delivered to the bookshop. We used Rosie's desk to set up the buffet and then ate at the back table. I couldn't remember ever having this big a breakfast here in Scotland. I'd had quite a few enormous meals back on the farm in Kansas, but that was when we'd spent the days helping my dad with the harvest. Lots of calories were consumed, and lots more had been burned off.

We'd dug in quickly and were probably about halfway through with the meal when the bell above the front door jingled. Hamlet stood to greet whoever was coming inside. He returned only a few seconds later with the man who had delivered the food. The man looked nervous.

"Sir, may I speak with you a moment?" he asked Luka.

"Of course." Luka didn't stand. "Go ahead."

The deliveryman cleared his throat and rocked back and forth from one foot to the other a few times. Suddenly, I felt like I understood what might be going on. I heard Edwin mutter a quiet "Uh-oh" as if he got it too.

"It seems the card number you gave us . . . Well, it didn't go through."

We were all bothered, but not really surprised. I could sense some anger flare in Luka. The thought occurred to me that this could be the final straw. Maybe whoever was doing this had just gotten too greedy and would now get caught. I was sad about the interruption of the meal, because it really was delicious, but it looked like it was once again time to get the police involved.

"I'll take care of it," Rosie said to the deliveryman. She stood. "Come to my desk. I'll write you a check."

Luka's life wasn't turned upside down like Edwin's had been. All that seemed to have happened was that someone called in to his bank claiming to be him, telling the bank that the card was missing and needed to be canceled. It was either a prank or maybe something done by his assistant to be helpful. It seemed as if it wasn't tied to the other issues, but the timing was certainly odd.

As far as he could tell, nothing else had been touched. Sitting in the bookshop and working on his phone, he changed all his important passwords. He also communicated with his legal and business teams in Australia, telling them to be extra vigilant, and left five messages for his assistant, who seemed to be MIA, though Luka suspected she was just taking some time off.

"Did you use that card in front of Meera yesterday?" I asked Luka after the police left.

"No, only when she wasn't around. I bought lunch, but that's when she disappeared. Afterwards, I went to look for her."

"So, she couldn't have taken the card number?"

"Not during a moment I can remember. Since the police think there's a chance it was just all a big mistake or misunderstanding, I'm trying to . . . Well, I guess that's possible, but considering everything else . . ."

"I'm sorry, Luka."

He smiled at me. "It's fine." He paused. "I've had more fun this week than I can ever remember having, Delaney. You are all marvelous hosts. This isn't as daunting as what happened to Edwin must have been."

"Edinburgh is a magical place."

"Even more so when the people are wonderful."

"Thank you."

"Okay, I'm out of here for the day, I'll check in later this afternoon if that's all right. Then I'll head up to London tomorrow."

"We'll be here," I said.

We all, even Hector, bid him goodbye at the door, and watched him make his way across the market and then around the corner. He was moving with his typical seemingly content and confident gait.

"He's fine," Rosie said.

"I think so too," Edwin said.

Hamlet had wrapped up the food and taken it all over to the refrigerator in the kitchenette on the dark side. It might not ever get eaten, but we'd be covered if any of us got hungry in the next few days.

A moment later, it was only Hector and I looking out the front window. I was enjoying the morning activities, and there were enough dogs being walked through the market that Hector was intrigued too. Well, it was either that or he enjoyed the crook of my arm.

If I hadn't remained standing there, I wouldn't have seen O'Shea leave the hotel. He must have returned from Dublin. Or had he lied to Inspector Winters as to where he'd gone?

He was walking this way, but I doubted it was because he was planning on visiting the bookshop. I didn't want to miss my chance to talk to him, though.

"Excuse me," I said to Hector as I put him down. Edwin had gone over to the other side, and Hamlet and Rosie were both helping customers. I mouthed "I'll be back" to Rosie as I grabbed my jacket off the hook by the front door.

She nodded at me before returning her attention to the customer.

I got outside just as O'Shea turned and made his way past the bookshop and toward the city center. I opened my mouth to call out to him, but then shut it again. Sure, I wanted to talk to him, let him know I was there, but not quite yet. For now, I could follow from a good distance, see what he was up to. It was daytime, and if I got nervous, I'd just turn back toward the bookshop.

He headed the direction I'd taken the tour group the day of the magical sights, up the Vennel Steps and toward the George Heriot school. There was nothing strange about him going this way. Lots of people traversed this path, both locals and tourists, and maybe he was headed to the school again.

When he turned onto Lauriston Place, I muttered quietly to myself, "I bet that's exactly where he's going."

Nevertheless, I was surprised when he did, in fact, turn and make his way through the ornate gates.

I hurried to the entrance, but because there was so much open space between the gates and the buildings, I couldn't risk stepping onto the grounds immediately. If he even glanced around for a moment, he would see me, which would surely be weird. As I watched him make his way, I decided I'd have to pick another day to talk to him. This wasn't feeling right, but I just couldn't make my feet turn around. I couldn't help but wonder what he was up to.

Was I going to try to follow him inside?

No, of course I wasn't going to do that. It was weird that I was following him in the first place.

Except, was it?

Even if you're on the right track, you will get run over if you just sit there.

There they were! A bookish voice was speaking up. They'd been so quiet that I couldn't help but pay attention to this one. My intuition was finally sensing something. It was Will Rogers who spoke, and I always liked hearing his voice in my head.

In fact, for a moment I was so distracted by listening and then trying to understand what he was telling me that I almost missed the person who came outside to meet O'Shea, because the man pulled back into the entryway quickly.

It was a younger man, tall, thin, dressed in black. I was pretty sure it was Max.

It was apparent that I'd been far too bold in my explorations— I'd stepped out and into the open. I couldn't see the young man I thought was Max anymore, but with a wave and a smile, O'Shea started walking my direction. It crossed my mind that Mr. Rogers had been telling me I should probably turn around and leave.

Should I run now? I listened hard for another bookish voice to speak up. I'd been caught, but there was no reason for O'Shea to think I'd been spying. This could have all been happenstance. Right? It would be rude and look even weirder to run. I would just greet O'Shea, tell him I was out for a walk, and then turn and go back to The Cracked Spine. I could handle this. Just don't act guilty, Delaney.

"Delaney?" O'Shea said as he approached, a smile on his face.

I nodded, but should have noted that the smile and the happy tone were indications that something wasn't right. From what I'd witnessed, O'Shea didn't smile easily, and he hadn't sounded happy anytime I'd spoken with him.

I took a step backward.

"I've been wanting to give you a ring. Edwin left something here."

He reached into his pocket and took out what I thought was a credit card, but it was difficult to distinguish.

"Oh. Well, I can take it back to him." I held out my hand, even as I knew I probably shouldn't. But it was then I remembered Edwin and I wondering about the card O'Shea had given my boss. *Edwin—apologies for the credit card mix-up. We would never have kicked out your guests.*

Edwin and I had both wondered how O'Shea had known so much. We'd accepted that he must have spoken with someone, but maybe we should have pondered it more, thought about it longer. How *had* he known so much? Could the answer possibly be something about him being somehow involved in all the bad deeds?

Shoot, I thought.

Still smiling, O'Shea grabbed my wrist and yanked me toward him. A noise came from my throat—a cross between a squeal and a scream—but it didn't last long and didn't get very loud. A few seconds later, O'Shea had me wrapped in his arm, his hand over my mouth, as he dragged me toward the building.

I tried to wrestle myself free, to scream, to bite his hand. But he was so much bigger than me, so much stronger, that I could do little more than keep my feet moving so they wouldn't drag on the ground.

In what seemed both like a matter of seconds and a million years, he had me inside the school's doors, their shutting clanking noises echoing through the empty entryway and hallways.

No one was around—it was as empty as Hogwarts on a holiday. What was even worse was that no one knew where I'd gone. *I* hadn't even known where I was going.

I was going to need some magic to get out of this one.

CHAPTER TWENTY-SIX

As I'd noticed before, the inside of the school wasn't really anything like Hogwarts. That was just one of the things rattling around in my panicked brain—where were the moving staircases, the animated portraits? I didn't know what my thoughts were doing, but I needed them to focus and figure out how to save myself, and whoever else might need saving.

Maybe this was all just a way to deal with the terror—dilute it. And I can say, unequivocally, that I was completely terrified.

O'Shea didn't say anything as he dragged me along. I continued to try to scream, yell, and bite, but I was just burning adrenaline.

We moved down the hallway to the left, to an area we hadn't had access to during the tour, the area where administrators' offices were located.

I didn't see any offices, but I did see through widows at the tops of doors that some of the rooms were classrooms.

O'Shea stopped outside one room. Keeping a hand over my

mouth, he angled himself so he could turn the knob and then propel us both inside. In one motion, he shut the door behind us and threw me toward some furniture. I stumbled and rammed my leg into a couch before falling sideways on top of it. This was neither an office nor a classroom. It was a teachers' lounge.

Noises of despair and anger came out of me, but nothing was forming words quite yet.

"You can yell, you can scream—no one will hear you," a voice from a chair in the back corner said.

I turned to see Max—I was sure it was him now, sitting there with his arms resting on his knees.

I was still trying to catch my breath, but my heart was beating too fast. I had so many questions, but my fear was so big, I still couldn't get words out.

"You don't get to talk," O'Shea said to Max, who frowned.

We were all silent for a long few beats, none of us moving from the spots we were in. Finally, I managed to speak, "Wha . . . what in the world is going on?"

Max huffed a disgusted laugh. O'Shea sent him a look.

"You had to get in the middle of things that were none of your business, that's what happened." O'Shea crossed his arms in front of his bulk. He didn't sound like the same person I'd met before. There was no doubt that the other one, the less effusive one, had been a faked persona. This one had a much bigger personality, and a meaner one too. I'd seen a glimpse of it that first day.

My mouth opened again as I tried to figure out where exactly I'd gone wrong. I'd tried not to be nosy. I'd worked hard on making sure I'd let Inspector Winters know everything I'd observed. Or, that's what I thought I'd done.

Max laughed again, but there was no humor in his tone. It seemed he couldn't help wanting to contribute, no matter the angry looks O'Shea sent his way.

"It's all him, Delaney. It's Delaney, right?" Max said. He didn't wait for me to answer. "This is the man who has been ruining all our lives, your boss's included."

I swung my attention back to O'Shea. "Why?"

O'Shea smirked at Max. "See, that's how little you actually know, Mr. Smarty-Pants. I'm ruining your lives *because* of her boss. It's all his fault."

"Whatever you say." Max smirked.

"Why? What's going on?" I asked yet again. When they didn't answer, I looked at Max. "Why are you here?"

"This is where we meet." He nodded at O'Shea.

"Why do you meet?"

Max looked at me like I didn't understand a thing in the world. He might have been right.

"Money. What else?" Max said.

"You followed me," O'Shea said to me.

My inclination was to protest, but that's exactly what I'd done.

"Why did you follow me?" O'Shea asked.

I didn't want to talk to either of them, but I needed to figure out what was going on and how much danger I was in. I sensed it was a lot. I thought about lying, but that wasn't going to get me out of here, so why not try to get to the root of the problem?

"I guess I was just curious. I thought you were in Dublin."

"I knew I should have hidden longer," O'Shea said.

"Why did you want to ruin Edwin?"

O'Shea finally moved from where he'd been standing, taking a few steps to a table against a wall. He sat on the corner of it as if he were a teacher about to give a lecture.

"Who wouldn't? I mean, I saw an opening and I jumped. He has more money than . . . Well, I know he's very rich."

I shook my head. "I thought *you* were rich."

"I was . . . but, well, things changed."

"He lost lots of money on bad investments," Max added. "He had to find other means."

"I still don't understand." I held up my hand. "But, look, you haven't told me anything. Just let Max and me go, and we'll be on our way."

I sounded just like a captive in every movie I'd ever seen. Desperate. Pleading.

O'Shea laughed. "Right. No. But I will tell you what I did, if you'd like to hear."

He wanted to share. He was pleased with himself, maybe proud.

I nodded and swallowed hard.

"Edwin and his tours. How arrogant of him. Those auctions. Money to burn. Starting a few years ago, about six months before each tour, Edwin takes me out to dinner as a thanks for getting the school opened for him." He shrugged. "This year, we met for dinner at his lady friend's restaurant." O'Shea smiled into the memory a moment.

"Okay?" I said, hoping my voice didn't crack. It did, but only a little.

His eyes snapped back to me. "Of course. Edwin is a lovely man. Polite, always does the right thing. He always paid for those dinners. However, this last time he had to use the loo, so he left the table for a moment." O'Shea remained seated, though he leaned forward as if he was going to tell me a secret. "And he left his wallet right there, on the table."

Edwin had made a deal with his girlfriend, Valerie. When he ate at the restaurant alone, it was on the house, but when he brought people with him, he insisted upon paying for the meals. She'd fought him a little on it, but not much.

"So, you took his wallet?"

"Heavens no, that would have been too risky. No, instead I took pictures of its contents. We were in a corner booth. No one noticed me. I had his credit cards—both sides of them—his driver's license, and, get this . . ." He sat back up and smiled with self-satisfaction. "I also took a picture of this tiny piece of paper that he kept in one of the pockets. It listed his passwords." O'Shea chortled. "Can you even believe it?"

I could and I couldn't. I hadn't known about Edwin's carrying around his password list in his wallet, and, honestly, I was sure he knew it was a terrible idea. I also knew how, like the rest of us, he couldn't ever remember his passwords.

Oh, Edwin.

"How did the hotel get involved?" I asked.

"Oh, they were involved long before all of this. They are one of my partners here in this fair city."

Max snorted. "'Partner.'" He looked at me. "I went to school here. I came back to do some math tutoring, and I got caught up with working with him. Pickpocketing. And he got my dad involved, blackmailed him—O'Shea would turn me in if my family didn't help with his . . . *work*. He's not even an investor in the inn, like he tells everybody."

"Pickpocketing?!" I said to Max.

Max nodded. "I'm good at it."

"What about the room you quit renting out at the hotel? Why?"

"I'm also really good at forging, changing documents."

That would jibe with what Inspector Winters told me about the alcohol and sandpaper.

"Why did Tillie pretend to be Meera—a tour member?"

Max shook his head. "I don't know what you're talking about, but . . ."

"What?" I asked him.

"Tillie has a sister named Meera, lives in Ireland."

Answers were coming, but more layers of mystery were too. I looked at O'Shea. "Did you kill Geoff?"

O'Shea smirked.

"Of course he did. My da was going to turn O'Shea in. He always admired Edwin MacAlister," Max said, seething.

O'Shea had killed Max's father. As my mind tumbled through the mess I was in, I realized that there was a very good chance Max and I could get out of here together, if he was willing to fight O'Shea. Surely, he was willing—but I didn't know how to make that work quite yet.

I looked at O'Shea, who wasn't denying the accusation. He was a big man. He could have feasibly thrown Geoff's body off the roof.

"O'Shea?" I said, hoping I was still somehow appealing to his ego and he'd keep talking.

He sighed. "I'll never admit to murder."

"What about Tillie? The man who hurt her?" I asked.

"He's another partner in my fine city—who has disappeared now, by the way. Thanks a lot for that."

I blinked at his sarcasm. I was sick to my stomach, but I thought he wanted me to smile at him. That wasn't happening.

"Tillie?"

He continued, "I'd been working with just Max and Geoff. Tillie wasn't part of my schemes, but she was getting in my way. I don't know anything about her sister."

"Did you grab her from the old gasworks building?" I asked.

"I'm impressed you figured that out. I texted her that Max was going to meet the same fate as Geoff if she didn't come with me. That's where she was, so I got her and took her home. I was sure she was about to tell you everything."

"Me?"

O'Shea smiled. "Yes, you, Delaney. I think she was trying to get someone to help her."

"Me?" I asked again.

"She wanted Edwin, but he wasn't there."

I couldn't immediately put the pieces together, but what he said made some sense. Maybe that's why she'd impersonated Tillie in the first place, to talk to Edwin.

I looked at Max, who wouldn't look at me. Why weren't we fighting O'Shea together?

"You asked me where the fourth person was. That day we came in here. Why did you ask that?" I said.

O'Shea shrugged again. "Just wanted you to know I was paying attention."

"You wanted me to think you cared."

Again, he shrugged.

I looked at Max. "He got you and Carmel too?"

Max shrugged. "Me, sure, but not Carmel. She refused, though she promised not to tell anyone what was going on. When she got out of the hospital, she took off, afraid of what he"—Max nodded at O'Shea—"would do to her."

"Who hit her over the head?"

"Max always does what I tell him to do," O'Shea said.

Max shook his head. "He had my dad." Tears came to his eyes. "Said he'd kill him if I didn't hurt her. I tried not . . . I had no choice."

O'Shea had killed Geoff anyway.

I looked at O'Shea. He stared back at me but didn't say anything more.

"Why?" I asked, but I was wondering about so many things, not just one specific thing.

O'Shea huffed one laugh. "Money." He held his hand out toward me, displaying a credit card. "I'm going to give this young man, Max here, one hundred pounds for bringing me this card."

"A hundred pounds?" I looked at Max. "You'd do this for that amount?"

"Sure. I'm not proud of it, but it's money I didn't have before. The bank will reimburse the cardholder if it's caught soon enough. It's a victimless crime."

"Well, not really. The bank would be the victim then."

"Who cares about banks?"

He had a point, but I still didn't endorse perpetrating fraud against them.

I looked at Max. He wasn't telling the whole truth. I suspected he'd just gotten in too deep, and there was no way out of this. He was going to have to keep doing O'Shea's bidding forever, or at least until their activities were exposed.

How could Max and I escape?

As that question came to me, I realized, again, that no one knew where I'd gone. No one knew where I was. O'Shea was so much bigger and stronger than me that he could probably hide my body without even breaking a sweat. I told myself to stop thinking like that and come up with a solution.

"Max hit Carmel?" I asked the already answered question, focusing on continuing to talk, to keep myself working on a solution.

O'Shea nodded and looked at Max. "All heartsick over the girl. Sheesh, why he was so head over heels for her, I'll never know."

"You killed his father as Max was hurting Carmel?" I said, anger finally finding its way through the terror and adrenaline. Good, I thought. I could work better with anger than with fear.

"I was up on the roof with Geoff, told Max to keep everyone out of my way. That girl knew something was up. She was trying to figure it out. He had no choice. I was proud of him."

This man had gotten away with the unimaginable. I looked at Max again. There was nothing in his return gaze that instilled me with any confidence that he was on my side, or that he wasn't too scared to help us get out of here. I was on my own.

My phone! I suddenly remembered. My phone was still in my pocket. I just needed a moment without O'Shea watching me. Just a moment.

I put my hand on my stomach. "Could I use the restroom, O'Shea? Please?"

"Sure. This is the teachers' lounge. There's a loo right on the other side of that door—and you can't get out through the small window." He smirked. "Have at it."

"Thank you." I stood on legs that were even shakier than I thought they'd be, and stumbled a little before I could lift one foot.

"Stop," O'Shea said just as I'd managed one tiny step. "Give me your phone."

"I left the bookshop so quickly, I didn't bring it with me."

"Uh-huh."

He lumbered toward me. I knew he was going to pat me down, and I almost caved and just gave him the phone. I didn't want him touching me.

But the phone was in an obvious spot, my front jacket pocket. He barely had to touch me as he grabbed it, held it up, and smirked again.

"Oh. Sorry. I forgot."

"Sure you did. Okay, you may now use the facilities."

I hurried into the bathroom, shutting and locking the door behind me. I noticed the size of the one rolling window in the room. O'Shea was right—I would never fit through.

But I had to do something. I had to think of something.

A latrine behind a privacy wall. A sink. A paper towel dispenser. Was there anything in here I could use?

The mirror, I supposed. If there was a way for me to break it and use a piece of it as a weapon . . . It didn't really make sense, but maybe it would work if I couldn't think of anything else. There wasn't even a garbage can in the room I could use to throw at him.

What else?

The memory of the movement of ghosts coming up through the toilets in Hogwarts made my lips quirk into an involuntary small smile, but it was only temporary. Though I sure could have used a Moaning Myrtle right about then, there was nothing funny about any of this.

I patted my pockets and found two pens that I'd somehow picked up along the way. There was no paper. But there was a paper towel. I reached to the dispenser and pulled out one sheet. It was a thick ply. Quickly, I wrote a note.

"Help, Edwin and Tom. Being held in Heriot school. Deliver to The Cracked Spine, asap."

It was a huge stretch, and I didn't have an owl, but I knew how to make a paper airplane. With shaky hands, I folded the paper towel into a plane and then hurried to climb up on the toilet and reach the window crank. The window was about a foot wide, but only opened about three inches after I turned the crank before it stopped. I would never be able to see where the plane went, or if it even flew anywhere. But I had to count on a little magic, didn't I?

I let go of the plane and then crossed my fingers.

O'Shea pounded on the door. "You should be done. I'm coming in if you don't come out."

"Just a second. My stomach's not doing well."

He didn't respond.

Maybe I should let him try to break down the door, but I didn't know if he had a gun. I needed to do whatever I could to keep that sort of weapon out of the equation.

I looked at the small window again. No, there was no way I was getting through. But as I stepped off the toilet a clinking noise sounded, and I realized my pendant had hit the crank.

I climbed back onto the toilet, took the monocle from around my neck, and held it out the window. I had to stand on my tippy-toes to see it out there, but I was thrilled when I noticed the light from the sun—it was actually out!—glimmer off the glass.

Fast, slow, fast, three times each. I knew that was Morse code for SOS. Could I move the pendant to make such a pattern so someone would see it?

I held it low, beneath the window, and moved it, working with the glare. It took a couple tries, but I was pretty sure I got the "fast, slow, fast, three times each" out there a few times before O'Shea beat on the door again.

"You're done, Delaney. Come out of there, now."

I pulled the pendant inside and lifted it back around my neck. If this was my last day on this planet, at least I'd have Tom's name with me.

I let O'Shea pound as I stepped off the toilet and made my way back toward the door. I was sure no one had seen my call for help, but at least I'd tried. I'd done what I could. I'd done *something*, and knowing that helped me relax some—well, maybe not relax, but maybe not be quite so panicked.

I turned the bolt on the door and opened it wide, a new

calming sensation running through me. But O'Shea wasn't calm at all. His face was red and contorted with anger.

"Out here now!" he commanded.

He didn't touch me, didn't throw me, but he pointed at the couch. I made my way to it and sat again.

"What are you going to do?" I asked him, now just wanting to understand my fate, to not be surprised by it.

"Shut up!" he commanded.

I did as he said and sent another glance at Max, who was still sitting in almost the same exact position as he had been, his arms resting on his knees. He still wasn't on my side.

Now that my brain wasn't firing in a million different directions, I took in my surroundings in a different way. Was there something in here I could use as a weapon? There were two very sturdy lamps. If I could wrangle one of them and then manage to swing it at O'Shea before he could stop me, I might be able to land a blow.

There were windows in this room, too, a long line of them. They also opened and closed with the use of a crank. These were bigger windows. I could feasibly squeeze myself through one of them, but O'Shea would have to be out of the room. Max wouldn't stop me. I wouldn't let him.

If I could just get O'Shea to leave for a minute, I could either get ahold of a lamp or try to escape through a window.

"My blood sugar is low," I said. It was a lie; I didn't know anything about my blood sugar. "Do you have something, maybe a candy bar?" I put my hand to my forehead. "I'll faint if it gets too low."

"Go ahead and faint," O'Shea said. He meant it.

I was going to have to think of something else.

Or maybe not.

A second later, in a flurry of unexpected sights and sounds, something happened, or some *things* happened.

The door burst open, and a person dressed all in black came through.

But she didn't come in by herself. Another woman followed behind, and she held a gun.

The woman in black immediately ran for O'Shea, attempting to tackle him.

"Hey, hey, what the—" O'Shea said as he pushed back. O'Shea was going to win if the battle was between the two of them. He was simply bigger and stronger.

But the woman with the gun was sure to win the day. Meera—the real one—stood at the door and watched as Carmel and O'Shea battled for a moment.

I was trying to take in everything at once. Could I escape out the now open door? Meera had come inside far enough that I could try to run around her. But would she shoot me? I wasn't sure it was something I wanted to risk.

My eyes caught Max, seemingly debating whether or not to join in the fracas. I sent him a stern look, hopefully relaying that he should stay out of it. He did as my eyes commanded.

"Enough!" Meera yelled. "Get off him, Carmel. Stay right where you are, O'Shea. I will shoot you so fast you won't even know what hit you."

I was lucid enough to know that that's exactly what she was intending on doing.

"Meera," I said, a little too loudly.

While keeping the gun aimed at O'Shea, her eyes darted to me. "I'm not going to hurt you. You can just go. Go!"

The out I'd been hoping for had just presented itself.

"Meera, you can't kill him," I said, staying right where I was on the couch. "You can't."

"Yes I can."

"Please!" I stood. "No, don't. Let the law take care of him. They'll lock him away. There's no doubt. We'll all testify against him."

"He killed Geoff! He hurt my sister! Who knows all the damage he's done?"

"I know. I know." I took a deep breath. "But you're not like that. You don't need to be the one paying for all the damage he's done."

Carmel had pulled herself off O'Shea and was moving to stand beside Meera. O'Shea was on the floor, on his back, rubbing his chin. His nose had been bloodied, so Carmel had gotten in a good punch at least. Max stood and moved next to the women. I realized that they'd planned this. They'd worked together to get O'Shea here in this otherwise empty school so they could take care of him—probably get rid of him. I'd been the only fly in the ointment.

"Wait!" I exclaimed, holding my hand up.

Everyone looked at me.

"Look, let's call the police. They'll take care of him."

O'Shea made a move to get up.

"Stop!" I said to both him and Meera as she aimed the gun at him. "No, no. Stop. Here, Max, let's you and me tie him up; we'll use the lamp cords. Seriously, this decision could make or break your lives."

I was pleading with them, but I also knew that if someone had done to the people I most loved what O'Shea had done, I might not be able to be stopped. But I had to try.

"Please!"

Meera took a step closer to O'Shea. "Stay down."

I moved quickly to grab a lamp, pulling the cord from the plug. The lamp was heavy, and I wasn't sure how all of this was going to work, but maybe it would at least give everyone time to cool off.

"Max, grab the other one." I took a step closer to O'Shea.

Max hesitated, but then did as I asked. But as I crouched next to O'Shea and directed Max to do the same on the man's other side, O'Shea proved he had yet another trick up his sleeve, even if it would prove to be his last.

As I crouched next to him, my eyes on Max, O'Shea swung his arm up quickly and hit me on the side of my head. As the world turned black, I heard a gun fire somewhere in the murky distance.

CHAPTER TWENTY-SEVEN

"Lass, can you wake up?"

Was that Tom? Wait, wasn't I just . . .

My eyes popped open.

I struggled to sit up. My head hurt and my vision swam. I lay back down and closed my eyes.

"You're all right," the voice—yes, it was Tom's—said. "You were out a bit, but you're going to be fine."

I opened my eyes again, and without moving my head too much, I looked at Tom. We were in an ambulance. I was on a stretcher, and he was right next to me.

"Did they kill him?" I asked as my eyes began filling with tears. The tears came because I was so happy to see my husband, but I still had to ask the question.

He shook his head. "No one died. Meera shot O'Shea in his arm, but he's going to be okay too."

"Oh, good," I said. But I had another urgent question I needed answered. I'd seen the look on Tom's face—the pain, the anguish. "Carmel and Max?"

"Carmel's fine. Max is going to be okay . . . in time. He's hurting."

"Oh, Tom, what in the world happened?"

Tom sighed. "I'm not sure I understand everything yet, but we'll get the answers."

Tears were still flowing down my cheeks, now because of so many things.

"How did you know? Did anyone get my signal or note?"

He shook his head. "Inspector Winters called me. What signal? A note?"

Inspector Winters appeared at the open end of the ambulance.

"Oh, good, you're awake." He frowned at my tears. "Are you okay?"

"I'm fine." My head did hurt, but I would be okay. "What happened?"

"Carmel called me after you were hurt and O'Shea had been shot."

"What happened? Why . . ."

Inspector Winters sighed. "I don't have the whole story, but I'll get it. I think they were plotting together to get O'Shea here, to kill him. You being here saved at least one murder, maybe more. You did all right, lass. I'm glad you're okay."

I nodded and wiped away some tears.

Inspector Winters turned away, but then back around again. "Oh, we got a call that someone appeared to be sending an SOS from one of the windows. Was that, by any chance, you?"

I smiled. "It was. It would have worked!"

"Well, we just got the call a few minutes ago, so we might not have gotten there in time. But we did. All is well. All right, lass, I've got to go. I'll be in touch. Do what the doctors tell you, aye?"

"Of course."

Tom smiled and reached for the pendant around my neck. "Smart girl."

I smiled back and shook my head. "Just lucky. The luckiest girl ever."

Turns out, I'm not a very good patient. I refused to go to the hospital, telling everyone I was going home with my husband. He agreed to monitor me throughout the night, and we did just fine. There'd been no sign of a concussion and over-the-counter meds took care of the headache.

The next morning, I was excited to get to work, excited to get back to my normal life, anxious to hear the news, see if the pieces of the puzzle had been put together. Tom drove us into town, and we decided I'd check in with him in person at lunchtime.

I hurried into the bookshop and was greeted by not only Hector, but all my coworkers. They'd all called and texted me last night. I'd told them all I was fine. But their warm greetings helped me feel even better.

"There's someone here to see you," Edwin said. "She's in the back."

It could have been so many people, but I was surprised to see Tillie, the woman I'd originally known as "Meera," the person I thought was still in the ICU.

"Delaney," she said as she stood. "I'm so glad you're okay. I'm sorry I . . . pretended to be Meera."

I nodded as I noticed she didn't have anything on her head, neither a hat nor a bandage. "Are you okay?"

She nodded too. "I know you wanted to see me in the hospital, and the doctor told you I was in the ICU. The police did that to protect me, or make sure they could question me without others influencing me, I'm not sure which. Maybe both. Anyway, I recovered quickly, no real concussion either. Thanks to you."

"I'm so glad to hear that."

"I am sorry, though, that I pretended to be Meera. My reasons were . . . well, I thought . . ."

"It's okay," I said. Though I would have liked an explanation, I could see and feel her pain. She would tell me if she wanted to. "I'm glad you're out of the hospital."

She nodded and smiled awkwardly. "I'm glad it's over, but we'll never get Geoff back."

"Yes, I'm sorry about that too."

"Thank you."

"Would the two of ye like some tea, coffee?" Rosie said as she peered around at us.

"I would love some," I said. I looked at Tillie. "You?"

She shook her head. "No, thank you. I just came in to apologize. I've got . . . Max and Meera and my mother all need me right now."

Rosie stepped closer. "Aye, lass, they do. But have a cup of tea first. Life can wait for one cuppa."

She looked at Rosie, and I was sure it was relief that relaxed her features. She sat. "Thank you."

Rosie turned to me. "Sit, lass. I'll get it."

"I'll grab it," Hamlet called. He was already on the stairs, headed over to the dark side.

I sat too. Rosie left us alone, though it was an illusion—the bookshop wasn't big enough for us to really have any privacy. But it was enough.

"You're really okay?" I said.

"I'm fine. I'm . . . Well, it's been rough, but I'm fine."

I hesitated but then forged ahead. "What happened?"

Tillie shook her head. "I guess it all started with Max working for that horrible man. He brought that world to the inn, and Geoff got involved, at first to somehow rescue Max. But then everyone got in too deep." She sighed. "I only learned this later, but Geoff got word that O'Shea had stolen Edwin's information, money, so he was going to put an end to all of it, turn O'Shea, all of them in. O'Shea was very sophisticated, though. Geoff couldn't figure out how to expose him, but he wasn't going to give up." Tillie bit her bottom lip and paused. She continued a moment later. "He really wanted to get Edwin away from any trouble."

I nodded. I had to know. "Why did you pretend to be your sister?"

She swallowed hard and then continued, "When everyone gathered in the lobby for the tour, I thought I would just come along and explain to Edwin that Meera wasn't there. She told me that morning that she forgot to email Edwin. But he wasn't at the bookshop, and I immediately thought his absence had something to do with what O'Shea had done with his money. Everyone thought I was Meera. I thought I'd just see what happened, what I could find out. I felt terrible lying, and then O'Shea texted me about Max. It was too late to explain. . . ."

"You went to hide in the gasworks building?"

"I never went inside that building. I went around it, to the back. O'Shea picked me up, took me home, where a man was there to watch me. When Max told O'Shea that I'd gone with you all as Meera, O'Shea was sure I'd mess up his plans, asked for your help. But I hadn't, and I told him as much so he might leave you alone. The man O'Shea had watch me is the one who ended up hitting me. You and your husband saved me."

"I'm glad we were there."

"I would have surely died." She smiled sadly. "As it was, doctors were able to help me quickly." She paused. "I know you won't believe this, but Max is a great kid. He just made some terrible choices. And Meera really had emailed Edwin to become a part of the literary tour—Geoff told her about it and gave her Edwin's email address. But she did have to take care of our mother. Her money was never stolen; she's never had much anyway. She just came to Edinburgh to try to find Max. When you and the police inspector called her, she could only guess it was me impersonating her, though she didn't want to give me up. She called me, and then I eventually called her from the hospital. I asked her to take care of Max if something more happened to me. She got scared and needed to know what was going on. She disappeared from your house after Max finally texted her his location. They, along with Carmel, put together the plan to get O'Shea alone in the school. Max was hiding, though only by moving around Edinburgh, trying to get away from O'Shea until they could get their plan put together."

"Oh no. Is Meera okay? Is Max? How's your mom?"

"Meera is in trouble with the police—O'Shea is fine, but she did shoot him. The police and an attorney we hired have assured us that she'll be okay soon. Our mother is the same— unwell, but that's just the way it is. We'll care for her the best we can. Max is in some trouble too, but we'll get it sorted."

"I . . . I talked to the bank up there. They said they didn't want to discuss you or Meera ever working there."

"I guess I don't know . . . Well, it *is* banking. Maybe privacy laws prevent them from doing so. Maybe if more banks kept things to themselves, identities, money wouldn't be as easily stolen. I don't know."

I sensed she wasn't telling me the whole truth, but maybe their time at the bank didn't matter. I'd told Inspector Winters about the call I'd made to the bank. He'd have to be the one to determine if any of that was important.

Hamlet set mugs of tea in front of each of us, then stepped away.

"What will you do now?" I asked.

"Go back to Dublin at some point, after we figure out what Max and Meera have to face. I'd like them both to come with me. We'll need to get that figured out, but we will."

"Carmel?"

Tillie laughed once. "I don't know. She took off, and no one's been able to find where she went. She and Max got along well, though. I wouldn't be surprised if she shows up someday. Would you like me to let you know?"

"I would."

"Happy to."

I nodded and repeated what I'd said a couple times already. "I'm so sorry for everything that happened."

Tillie nodded. "Tell me about the bookshop. I'm sorry to say, this is my first time inside."

As we finished the tea, I told her about how I'd come to Scotland, and how fortunate I felt. As I shared my story, she seemed to lighten some—just a little, as if some weight had come off her shoulders. Sometimes you just needed to talk.

Edwin met us as I walked Tillie to the door. He told her to call him if she ever needed anything. He said that Geoff was a lovely man, and he was so sorry for her loss.

She thanked us graciously, then left. Edwin and I stood at the window and watched her make her way toward the inn.

"How is she really?" he asked.

"I think she's gutted. I . . . Well, I don't think she's telling the whole truth, but she doesn't owe me anything."

"No, I suppose not."

The world was happening out there on Grassmarket. People moving here and there, in and out of shops, restaurants, and pubs. We saw Tillie disappear around the corner just as Luka appeared, headed toward the bookshop.

"He's supposed to be leaving today," Edwin said. "I'll miss the lad, but he'll be back."

"Oh, yes, he'll be back." I didn't say it aloud, but the words "If he actually does leave" did run through my mind. Hector whined at my feet. I reached down and picked him up.

Edwin had walked away by the time I looked out the window again. Yes, Luka was still coming this direction, but so was someone else.

Tom had exited the pub and set out this way too. Even from across the market, he saw Hector and me watching him through the window, and smiled and waved.

I suddenly felt sorry for Luka, if he actually was leaving. I'd been lucky to grow up on a farm in Kansas, but this home, my home, was exactly where I wanted to be, for the rest of my forever.

I touched the pendant I'd put on again today, and smiled and waved right back.

ACKNOWLEDGMENTS

Though I've only been to Scotland once, I am so grateful for the chance to write these books and travel there in my imagination. When I'm working on this series, and as I stop writing for the day, I always shake myself a little to bring myself back to my office in Arizona. Don't get me wrong, I love my office in Arizona, but it's wonderful to venture over the sea in my mind and visit with everyone at The Cracked Spine.

The bookshop is fictional, though there really is (or at least there was) a bookshop in the same spot in Grassmarket. When I thought about using an inn for this story, the first one that came to my mind was the one we stayed at while we were there, The Grassmarket Hotel. We had a perfect experience. However, because of the nefarious activities that take place in this story, I made up The Green Inn and everything about it.

I love nothing more than hearing from readers how much they enjoy seeing the real locales and sites I mention in the books. Forgive me for inventing some that aren't really there.

In April of 2022, I was invited to be a part of an authors'

panel at an Anaheim Public Library Foundation event in Anaheim, California. It was truly an incredible time. I am ever grateful to the Library Foundation board members as well as the other writers I got to "panel" with—Matt Coyle, Wendall Thomas, and Mike Befeler—and, most of all, to the enthusiastic readers who were in attendance. Goodness, it was fun!

Each author had a future book character's name auctioned off during the event. A lovely woman named Kevin Moore bid the highest for a Scottish Bookshop character. I'm pretty sure I got the story of her name correct. Apologies if I didn't, and thank you to the real Kevin Moore in Anaheim.

Thank you to my wonderful agent, Jessica Faust, and my amazing editor, Hannah O'Grady. I'm so lucky.

Thanks to everyone at Minotaur who does such amazing work—Sarah Haeckel, Allison Ziegler, Kayla Janas, Tom Cherwin, and Rowen Davis are just some of the talented team I get to work with. I'm double-lucky.

Thanks to Charlie, Tyler, Lauren, and Lil Foot, who, as I turn this in, is about a month away from being born. I can't wait!

Most of all, thank you to my readers. You are the absolute, positive, and unequivocal best!

CHAPTER ONE

"I know of no single formula for success. But over
the years I have observed that some attributes of leadership
are universal and are often about finding ways of encourag-
ing people to combine their efforts, their talents, their in-
sights, their enthusiasm." The familiar voice came through
the taxi's radio speakers.

I sniffed and then grabbed another tissue from my bag.

"Lass, are you all right?" Elias glanced at me as I sat in
the passenger seat.

I smiled sadly and dabbed my eyes. "I'm fine."

Elias and his wife Aggie had shed plenty of tears too.
They'd been at my and Tom's blue house by the sea when
we heard the news of the queen's passing.

Queen Elizabeth II had died, right here in Scotland, in
fact.

Though it hadn't been a surprise, it had most definitely
been a shock. Her death would have made me sad had I

still been in Kansas, but here in my new home in Scotland, I thought it probably hit me even harder. In one way or another, she'd been a part of my everyday life since I'd answered the online ad for my job and traveled across the sea, chasing the promise of an adventure. The promise had been more than fulfilled, and the queen had been a part of it, even so far as surprising us all one day by making an appearance on behalf of my boss, Edwin MacAlister. If she hadn't been endeared in my heart already, she certainly would have been then.

Edwin was more upset than the rest of us, unable to discuss her death without breaking down into sobs. Edwin's sobs were executed in a more sophisticated way than mine would be, but they were sobs nonetheless.

I'd asked him, as well as my coworkers, how well he'd known her, and he said that his sadness was wrapped around what a lovely woman and public servant she'd been. Both Rosie, my grandmotherly coworker, and Hamlet, my other coworker who had become like a younger brother to me, claimed that Edwin had never told them any more about his relationship with any of the royals than that he'd simply had the opportunity to meet the queen a long time ago and had been fiercely loyal to her since.

Rosie did confide in me that the queen was their favorite royal, and she would always be close to the hearts of the people I cared for. I understood completely.

Though she had passed a week ago now, tributes were still resounding from all media outlets. Elias had tuned his taxi's radio to a station that had been playing snippets of her speeches throughout the years, and we had just listened to an inspirational moment.

My bookish inner voices seemed to be on respite, making way in my head for only her voice. I kept hearing her words, via the radio and television, as well as when all else was silent and my mind worked to conjure what I'd heard earlier in the day. In fact, I felt somewhat distracted. We'd all been having trouble focusing.

As if knowing I needed a distraction from all the distraction, Edwin had called me the night before, telling me he had a project specifically for me, something different than I'd ever done.

I'd been excited to hear all about it, a new endeavor to sink my teeth into was exactly what the doctor ordered.

After I'd spoken with Edwin and told Tom about my new assignment, I'd called Elias, asking if he would be willing to drive me to a destination, at least on the first day of my new project. After that, I'd borrow Tom's car and drive myself.

I was a capable driver. At least I had been, back when I'd driven on the right side of the roads and the steering wheels were on the left sides of the cars. The differences in Scotland, along with so many narrow two-lane thoroughfares, had been a dizzying change from Kansas roadways. Wichita had its fair share of heavy traffic, but Edinburgh congestion had been a new and sometimes terrifying experience.

Nevertheless, I'd adjusted—mostly. But this trip was a little south of Edinburgh, in a village called Roslin, known for many wonderful and historic things, not the least of which was its big role in *The Da Vinci Code*, popular back in the early 2000s.

The Rosslyn Cathedral had been a key location for the main characters' hunt in the book as well as the movie.

Another of its claims to fame was the Roslin Institute, where Dolly had become the first cloned sheep. The institute was still there, its mission to make the world a better place for animals and humans.

But my new project had nothing to do with the institute or any sort of treasure hunt—though treasure might be involved.

Roslin was seven miles south of the city, but I'd never been in that direction before. Since it wasn't too far away, Elias would drive me and then pick me up later. He'd been more than happy to do it. In fact, as I'd gauged his excitement, I'd realized that I probably should have been asking him to drive me more often. Today's ride might be melancholy, but we still had a chance to catch up with each other's lives.

We were on our way to an estate that belonged to a woman named Jolie Lannister, a "grand old broad" according to Edwin. I'd been startled by my buttoned-up boss's words. "Broad" wasn't something I thought he'd ever used to describe a woman. He'd chuckled then and said, "Her words, not mine."

I couldn't wait to meet her.

I was excited about the project that I was being sent to explore, retrieve if at all possible, and keep to myself at all costs. At least for now. Edwin had asked me not to give Elias any details. He'd suggested I might not even want to tell Tom quite yet, though he would never ask me to keep any secrets from my husband. I'd gone ahead and told Tom everything, and he'd been mightily intrigued.

Jolie Lannister had found something she was sure was rare and valuable, and had immediately thought of Edwin. She'd called to ask him if he wanted to take a look at it, maybe buy it or sell it in those auctions she knew he was a part of. That was the story he'd given me, though I sensed he'd left out things he didn't want *me* to know yet. I was too intrigued by all of it to push him for more information. I'd learn everything I needed to eventually.

Fleshmarket Batch, the auction group, was, at its most intrinsic level, a group of rich people who got together secretly (mostly) so they could buy and sell thing things for more money than most of us could understand. During his call, Edwin shared with me that a long time ago the group had invited Jolie to join but she'd declined, telling Edwin that she was unable to part with anything, ever. She liked her *things* and wanted to live her life and die with them surrounding her.

Edwin had also told me that in setting up this meeting, Jolie had surprised him by stating that she was now "ready to throw it all in a bin."

But before she did that, though, she wondered if Edwin wanted any of it, particularly the secret item that had recently been found on the grounds of her home. Edwin had told me that he'd been willing to take a look at everything himself but preferred that I do it instead, or at least first. This sort of thing was my job now, or it should be. He hadn't loosened his grip on the reins enough, he claimed, but he wanted to now. This was going to be my project until I thought he should become involved.

And I was grateful to have this new distraction.

Though I felt like I knew him and knew how he would want me to handle most things, I had asked if maybe he should come along on the first visit, and then I could take it from there.

"You will do fine, Delaney," he'd said. "In fact, I would

guess you would do better than I've ever done. You have my blessing to make whatever decisions you deem appropriate." He'd paused. "Honestly, I'm not sure Jolie has what she thinks she has. You and I will discuss later, but, aye, give it a go."

So here I was, giving it a go, and very excited about it too.

The assignment had accomplished one thing already—I hadn't been quite as sad after the call with him as I had been before. Hearing the snippet of the queen's speech on the radio had brought more tears to the surface, but I was able to wipe them away for now so I might focus on the job. I would be sad about the queen's death for a long time, and I was okay with that. She was worth being sad over.

Jolie's estate, named West Rosebud House, was a mansion that had been in her family for a hundred years. According to Edwin, the family had always been populated with "lively characters," though he didn't go into more detail, telling me I'd enjoy learning about them on my own.

"Here we are." Elias nodded to his left.

I leaned forward and looked out the windshield toward the mansion. "Oh."

"Not what you expected?"

"Not even a little bit. It's . . . it looks like it could fall down any minute."

"Aye. It does."

The house belonged in a horror film. The wide, dark-brick structure was two gothically tall stories in height. Windows that were probably a normal size reminded me of castle windows that always seemed too narrow for the building, made more for shooting arrows out through than letting in the light. The tall façade overpowered the windows.

Nothing appeared plumb. None of the edges were without imperfection. A cobblestone circular drive appeared neither welcoming nor all that utilitarian—potholes throughout, even though two vehicles—a bright yellow van with illegible and faded red letters and a boring blue car—had already parked on it, one directly behind the next. A partially broken cherub sculpture sat atop a fountain in the middle of driveway, but no water ran through.

"More cars? Did you expect anyone other than Ms. Lannister?" Elias asked.

"I didn't know what to expect."

"Aye, and maybe they belong to her."

Elias pulled the taxi to the available spot behind the second vehicle.

"I'll be coming in with you," he said.

"Elias, I'll be fine."

"Aye, I'm sure. But I willnae drive away from here without checking things out inside. I'm sorry if that makes you uncomfortable or breaks Edwin's rules." He slipped the taxi into park.

I nodded. Edwin would never send me someplace unsafe, but he might not have known about possible other visitors or the state of the house and the impression of danger that it presented.

Tom and I had visited my family in Chicago a few months ago. It had been a wonderful trip, and moments with my own father had reminded me again how alike Elias was to him. He'd been the one I'd gravitated to that day I'd arrived in Edinburgh, stepping out of the airport in search of a ride.

I'd been lucky to have so many good men in my life, even when I'd just been looking for a taxi.

Carefully, Elias drove over the cobblestones, or what was left of them, and toward the three stairs that led up to the front stoop.

As we stepped out of the taxi, a man came around the side of the house. His head was down, and he appeared to be deep in thought.

"Aye?" Elias said as he cocked his head and looked hard at the man. "Homer, is that you, auldjin?"

The man stutter-stopped and looked up. He squinted one eye as he looked at Elias. Another moment later, a smile, with one missing front tooth, lit up his wrinkled and age-spotted face.

"Elias?"

"Aye!"

The two men came together and hugged and patted each other's back heartily, lifting a cloud of dust from Homer's jacket.

"'Tis so good to see you," Homer said as they pulled away. His accent was just as strong, if not even stronger, than Elias's. "I'd've ken you anywhere."

"Same." Elias laughed. "I ken you by yer walk, lad."

I thought I saw tears in their eyes. It took another beat for Elias to remember I was there.

"Och, apologies. Lass, this is an old friend from a long time ago, Homer Vanton. We worked the docks together a hundred years ago. Homer, this is Delaney, a lass I've come to think of as my own kin."

Homer extended his hand. "A pleasure."

We shook. "Nice to meet you."

"Are you on here?" Elias asked.

"Aye. I've been the groundskeeper for nigh on thirty years now. Ms. Lannister's parents hired me, and here I've been."

I hadn't taken the time to look at the grounds, but I did now, at least the parts I could see—the front and a downward slope on the side. They were green and well-groomed, in far better shape than the house. I knew the main item I'd come to investigate had been found somewhere on the grounds—had Homer been the one to find it? I didn't ask that question. "How much land do you care for?"

"Near a hundred Cunninghams," Homer said.

Elias, catching the question in my eyes, clarified. "A Cunningham is a wee bit more than your American acre."

"Wow, that's a lot of land," I said.

"Aye. Much of it is untended woods, but I'm still able to manage the parts that arenae."

Elias was still strong—he was the type of man I thought had probably always looked that way, with wide shoulders and a barrel chest, not sunken yet with age. I could tell Homer's arms were thin, though, underneath the worn jacket.

"Of course you are," Elias said as he patted his friend on the shoulder again.

"Are you here to visit the miss?" Homer asked.

Elias looked at me. "Yes. Delaney has an appointment with Ms. Lannister. I came along for the ride."

I nodded at the other vehicles. "It appears we aren't the only ones."

"Aye. She rarely welcomes guests, and it's been a busy day." Homer frowned.

A beat later, Elias asked, "Everything okay in there?"

Homer shook his head. "I'm sure everything is fine. I'm

protective is all, and . . . well, none of us are getting younger."
He smiled. "My heart is glad you are one of her visitors. She
will be fine with you."

"Aye. Of course." Elias rubbed his chin. "Homer, you must
come for dinner some night soon."

"Aye? Please tell me you are still with the most beautiful
lass of all time."

Elias laughed. "Aye. Aggie's still keeping me in line. Join
us this week. Let's exchange mobiles."

I stepped away as they exchanged numbers and hugged
again.

"Nice to meet you, lass," Homer said as he continued on
his way around to the other side of the house.

"A pleasure, Homer. See you again, I hope."

"Aye."

"That had to be a surprise," I said as Elias came up next
to me.

"A pleasant one. We have a history together made of hard
work followed by tired nights in pubs."

"Sounds like a good history."

"Aye." Elias smiled into the past a moment. He looked at
me. "Come along, lass. Now I'm even more curious to see
what's going on in there."

It had been a pleasant reunion, no doubt. But I could see
in his eyes the melancholy that comes with running into an
old friend. It would give us something to talk about on the
trip home.

"Let's do this." I led the way to the door.

CHAPTER TWO

The peaked and ornately arched, though dilapidated, entryway led to two front doors, both made of wood and chipped varnish. I was now even more aware of the stark differences between the conditions of the house and the grounds. That said, there was a lot of land we hadn't seen yet. I wondered how much we might get to explore.

As we stepped closer to the doors, the distinct sound of raised voices came from inside. It wasn't easy to discern if we were hearing anger or excitement.

I looked around for a bell, but had to settle for a large, tarnished knocker in the shape of a dragon's head, a fabulous piece of art that we didn't have time to contemplate. I lifted by the beast's tongue and let it drop. The voices inside stopped with the first heavy blow.

Elias and I shared raised eyebrows as we waited.

Just as I was about to try again, the door opened slowly with a lingering squeak. A small woman with a crown of gray hair peered through the opening.

"Jolie?" I said. "I'm Delaney from The Cracked Spine."

"You're who?"

I cleared my throat. "I work with Edwin MacAlister."

"Och, Edwin. Aye. One moment please." The door closed.

Elias and I shared another look, and just when I was about to try again, the door pulled wide.

Another gray-haired woman greeted us, but this one was tall, with wide shoulders. She was dressed in a long, purple velvet gown.

"Greetings, Delaney. I'm Jolie. Welcome to my home."

"Thank you."

She didn't move or extend her hand for a shake but stood there a long minute, looking over both Elias and me.

"This is my friend—and Edwin's too—Elias," I said.

Elias stepped up and extended his hand as he smiled in his sweet way. "Nice to meet you."

Elias was always charming. Jolie's tall stature had been stiff, but it softened as she smiled and shook his hand.

"A pleasure to meet you both. Please come inside. Forgive the mess as well as all the people. I've been trying to get rid of them, but they don't seem to want to leave. Well, the mess can stay. I'd like the other people to leave though."

We stepped into the capacious entryway. It wasn't exactly like the castle great halls I'd seen, but it wasn't too far off. On the second-story roof was a stained-glass skylight. Though it was mostly cloudy outside, different colored rays came through the glass. The kaleidoscope effect only added to what felt like confusion inside.

There were other people, but it was mostly the stuff everywhere that made the space, which should have felt voluminous, give me a sensation of claustrophobia.

The entry extended all the way to the back wall, which was made of paned floor-to-ceiling windows—much larger than the home's front windows. The ceiling topped off at the first level back there, under a second-level balcony that could be reached by two curving stairways on each side.

There were so many things stacked everywhere that I couldn't digest them quickly, though it was easy to tell that we'd walked into the home of a hoarder. If there were degrees of that affliction, I would immediately guess that Jolie's would be somewhere in the middle of the spectrum. I neither smelled nor saw any garbage, and there was still space to walk up the stairs and across all the floors, if you stayed in what seemed like designated paths.

I counted five people other than Elias and myself. They were spread throughout the great room, all of them in a pose that indicated irritation. And their attention was currently directed toward Elias and me.

I wondered if we'd come at the wrong time, but I'd confirmed the meeting time with Edwin more than once.

I felt the need to apologize for the intrusion, but Jolie beat me to the punch with a heavy sigh.

"Well, as you can see, our tête-à-tête has been invaded by opposing forces," she said to me as she waved an arm toward the others.

"Jolie," a woman in a suit began. Her arms were crossed in front of herself as she leaned against the right stairway railing. "We aren't invading, and we are far from opposing forces."

"I don't know what else to call all of this then," Jolie said.

The suited woman frowned. "We are here to help. That is all."

Suddenly, everyone looked right at me.

"I . . . uh." I was speechless.

I turned to Elias, thinking he might just want us to get out of there, but he was making no move to leave. Instead, he stuck his hands in his pockets and sent me some raised eyebrows. He was more curious than anxious that we might have come at a bad time.

"I know why you're here, Delaney," Jolie said. "You've come to look at the books. I've been expecting you and I look forward to taking you through the library . . ."

The suited woman bounced herself off the railing but didn't try to walk around the stacks of newspapers near her feet.

"Bowie Berry." She waved in my direction. "I'm Ms. Lannister's legal counsel."

"Bowie is an attorney I hired a number of years ago. However, she is currently overstepping her bounds," Jolie said.

Bowie cringed. "Not at all, Jolie. I just want to make sure the best thing is done for you, my client."

"Oh, pishposh." Jolie's hands went to her hips. She frowned at the other two men in the room, who stood next to each other, close to the front wall, appearing to me as if they'd been trapped there. "The men are people from an auction house Bowie hired to take away all my things."

"I didn't hire them to take anything away. I hired them to take an inventory." Bowie looked at me. "Gilles Haig is the best in the business. His assistant, Alban Dunning, joined him today." She gestured toward them with her arm.

The two men smiled awkwardly, the younger one wearing the brightest orange sweater I'd ever seen—though he'd call it a "jumper." Whatever this confab was, it wasn't what they'd signed up for, I could tell that much.

"Mr. Haig," I said. "I spoke with you," I nodded at the younger man next to him, "My name is Delaney Nichols. I was inquiring about a carriage that has been kept in my boss's old stables. His name is Edwin MacAlister."

"Aye. I remember. Did it get sorted?" Haig asked.

"Edwin is still considering what to do. Thank you for your patience," I said.

"Aye, and we're Gilles and Alban. No mister needed," Gilles said.

Before I'd spoken to him, I'd heard of Gilles Haig. Considering the circumstances of Edwin's business, the warehouse in the back of the bookshop, and the auctions, Haig's name had come up many times over the last few years, and always with a positive endorsement. I'd only spoken briefly with him and remembered nothing but a good experience.

"Aye, he's a fine reputation. But I do not want him here," Jolie said, as she looked directly at Haig, "Not yet."

Bowie bit her top lip. "Okay, Jolie. Okay. One more day wouldn't hurt. We'll give you today to talk to . . . Delaney Nichols and her associate, but we'll be back tomorrow." Bowie stepped around the newspapers and toward me. "I am Jolie's legal counsel," she repeated with vigor, "and I have a right to know what's going on here."

"Oh." I looked at Elias who was frowning at Bowie. I looked at Jolie, who sent me a quick, almost imperceptible nod. "I am here to look through Jolie's library as a representative for Mr. Edwin MacAlister."

That was kind of the truth, but I figured that Jolie had set the lie in motion when she'd mentioned the library. I'd just hitched a ride upon it. I wasn't exactly here to look at her library, at least not solely. I wasn't about to spill the beans on the real deal though, legal counsel or not.

"Fine. That's fine, but you will not take anything out of this house without my approval," Bowie said.

I smiled wearily. "Ms. Berry, you might work for Jolie, but I work for Edwin, and no one has served me with any sort of cease and desist here. I will work with Jolie to her satisfaction. If you know anything at all about Edwin MacAlister, it is that he is a fair man, one who only does business on the up and up." I held my chin firm.

"I will be back tomorrow with the proper paperwork, Ms. Nichols, but I would highly recommend that you do as I ask and not take a thing."

"I will take your instructions under advisement," I said.

The withering look she directed my way caused Elias to chuckle once.

"Sorry," he said when Bowie glared at him, though he wasn't.

Bowie looked at Gilles and Alban. "Let's go. For now."

Bowie, Gilles, and Alban filed out, Bowie the last one through the doorway. She closed it lightly, as if she was forcing herself to not to slam it but wanted everyone to know that she could have very well made another choice. Elias, Jolie— the older woman who'd first answered the door—and I were left in the wake.

Jolie sighed again. "I'm so glad they're gone. Come along. We have work to do."

Jolie's gown swished as she made her way around stacks of things and then past the older woman who'd found a perch on the second step up the left stairway, before disappearing down a hallway.

"I'm Trudie," the older woman said. "I work for Jolie. Have no doubt, she is the force of nature she appears to be."

"I believe it," I said.

"I do too," Elias agreed.

He still made no move to leave me there, and I didn't push him to go. I decided it would still be good to have him with me. It had been so far.

"G'on into the library. I'll gather refreshments and meet you there," Trudie said.

Briefly, I wondered if we should leave a trail of breadcrumbs as Elias and I set off to follow Jolie into the depths of her messy home.